WALK-IN

T.L. Hart

BELLA
BOOKS

2016

Bella Books, Inc.
P.O. Box 10543
Tallahassee, FL 32302

Printed in the United States of America on acid-free paper.

First Bella Books Edition 2016

Editor: Medora MacDougall
Cover Illustration by Jared Primm
Cover Designer: Judith Fellows

ISBN: 978-1-59493-521-3

Dedication

This is for all of you who have believed in me:

My friends and family, too many to list, who always had faith in me.

Jodi, who made me send my work out into the big, scary publishing world.

Jack and Jean, for my wonderful OED full of all the words I love so much.

My DFW Writers Workshop family, who pushed me and made me a better writer.

My person, Susan, who has loved and been there for me through good and hard times.

Conan and Jared, who always accepted their crazy mom was a writer and loved me anyway.

And to the Universe for whatever combination of providence and dumb luck that makes me have the compulsion to tell stories about my invisible worlds.

CHAPTER ONE

I think the peaches were the first thing I noticed that were wrong. They were in a bag in the refrigerator, a plain plastic produce bag, tied in a knot at the top just like all the others in the crisper. Peaches. Not nectarines, smooth and shiny, but three definitely fuzzy peaches.

I don't like peaches.

It seemed a small thing at first, but it niggled at my mind. Why would I have peaches in my fridge? I moved things around, looking for any other strange vegetable kingdom materializations, but that was it. At first.

Gregory—that's my husband—said not to worry. The doctors told us it would be some time before my brain was working normally. Closed head trauma, they call it—severe closed head trauma with concussion. Very scientific words to explain why my thoughts and memories are scrambled like eggs.

I like eggs.

God, I've been obsessed with food. I think it's because it is such a simple, available clue to who and what I was. Am. What I am.

There is a method to my thinking. I call it Jennifer's Scale of Order. Food is simpler than clothes. Clothes are simpler than work. Work is simpler than friends. I am simpler than I used to be.

I figured the scale out last week, scribbled it in my notebook in big, unfamiliar letters that crawled off the lines and up the page. Gregory frowned and said my penmanship would probably improve along with my memory. He was right; it's a lot more even now, yet still not much like my old handwriting.

I don't show my notebook to Gregory anymore. I'm beginning to think I don't like him any better than I like the peaches.

It isn't just the strange foods or the unfamiliar man in this house that make me realize how dense I've become. I remember things sometimes and am beginning to recognize people, but it's sort of like an old movie I saw years ago: the plot is familiar and the actors have faces I know and names I almost recall, but the details are hazy and I'd really just as soon watch the commercials.

Doctor Carey, my psychiatrist, says, "Episodes of disorientation and emotional detachment aren't rare with injuries like yours. It will take time for everything to resolve." She really does sound that way. She says the fog will clear. Probably. "Ninety-five percent of head injuries like yours are back to normal within a year."

That's great. In the meantime, all I have to do is figure out how to fake everything until I get back to normal. Whatever that means. How will I know I'm back to normal if I can't remember what normal feels like?

Is it normal to look at a man I've been married to for four years and wonder how the two of us managed to stay together for so long? I may still be a little dysfunctional a year from now, but I'm pretty sure Gregory will be as pompous and overbearing as he is now.

Did I always cringe every time he so much as touched me in passing? Lord, I hope not. That would mean I'm either an idiot or a masochist. On the other hand, it's more frightening to imagine making love to him and actually enjoying it. I think

I'd rather be one of the walking wounded than get naked with that man. Wanting to be normal again is one thing, but there are limits.

A hunger pang gnawing its way from my stomach to my backbone provides perspective. I'm hungry, and I have no intention of eating fuzzy fruit. I shut the refrigerator and decide to explore the pantry. Popcorn—a huge box of extra buttery.

This is more like it! I throw a bag in the microwave—this side up—and punch five minutes. I do remember how to cook popcorn. What more could a woman ask? A Diet Coke and popcorn. Breakfast of…breakfast of…something. I know I should know how that saying goes, but no matter.

Life is good. Wait for the beep.

Beep. Beeeeeep. Beeeeeeeeeeeeeeep.

"We're losing her!"

"She almost bled out before they got her here. Hang two more units!"

Beeeeeeeeeeeeeeeeeeeeeeeeeeeeeeep.

"Call a code. Get a crash cart in here. Stat!"

Beeeeeeeeeeeeeeeeeeeeeeeeeeeeeeeeep.

The long, flat sound of the monitor muffles the voices of the doctors and nurses. The fog blurs the sight of them bending over the still, blood-drenched woman lying on the narrow bed, erases their frantic efforts as I watch from some uncertain vantage point.

Fog rising like magician's smoke, filling the room, wrapping me in a blanket and carrying me away. No more headache. No more pain. No more day after day of day after day. Freedom after a long time of doing time. Just rising with the fog.

Not a cold lonely fog, but a warm living mist. Filled with comings and goings. Busy ones, going back. Tired ones, in for a rest. Communication without conversation.

I'm ready to rest now, for a while, ready to break the faint, silvery thread still connected to that body back somewhere in a frantic, crowded hospital room.

"Wait." A voice from somewhere, someone. "Wait for me."

Someone going, wanting to follow the thread back. Secrets told. Bargains made. Presto chango! The thread passes and I settle into the enveloping fog.

Beeeeeeeeeeeeeeeeeeeeeeeeeeeeeeeeeeep. Beeeeeep. Beep. Beep.
"We've got her! We've got sinus rhythm. Good work! She's back."
Beep. Beep. Beep.

The persistent timer signals the job is done. The microwave stops and the smell of popcorn fills my nose. I rip open the bag and rescue a hot kernel from the steaming interior and pop it into my mouth. Salt and warm butter melt into my taste buds.

Aah, yes. This I remember. This is living.

CHAPTER TWO

Gregory went back to work today, thank God. He's in the market—make that The Market—stocks, not groceries. He's been at my side since the accident, him and his laptop and cell phone. He has been considerate, though, I'll give him that. The phone is on vibrate, not ring. And he moves a few feet away and speaks very softly so as not to disturb me.

It's all right with me. I've learned to block out all the low, urgent talk of buy and sell and margins to the point that it has become background noise. Sort of a rumbling, high-tech, semi-human Muzak—familiar, bland and vaguely annoying. His return to the safety of his steel and glass safe room in downtown Dallas has turned the volume to "off" for a few hours.

The silence is blissful. I revel in the lack of noise. It gives me time to wander barefoot over cool Saltillo tiles and try to find anything of myself in these impeccably decorated rooms. I must have had some say in choosing this furniture, must have agreed to so much leather and wood and beige. I swear I don't see myself as a beige person, but this house makes it hard to argue the point.

My closet is full of clothes in colors that run the gamut from basic black through a range of screaming neutrals—ivory in shades from eggshell to candlelight, a riot of taupe, and whites so pure they could star in laundry soap commercials. I wonder what would happen if a red T-shirt made an appearance here? Would there be chaos? An alarm summoning the fashion police? What is the penalty for standing out from the antique white walls? I shudder to think.

Even my underwear drawer has neatly arranged rows of pristine white bras and matching panties, discreet nude satin sets for a bit of variety. And for those nights of wild abandon, a champagne and cognac-colored lace teddy and robe. For once, I'm glad my memory fails me.

This memory thing is a lot more complicated than I realized at first. From the way Dr. Carey explained it, things will come back bit by bit, with pieces missing for a while or maybe forever. She didn't mention that things would come back that didn't seem to fit anywhere—certainly not in this elegant test tube of a house. Things are coming back, popping into my head like disjointed flashes from God knows where.

I remember blue jeans. I remember plaid shirts with a Gap label. I remember a woman with black hair and piercing eyes and a fireplace with ashes left over from an actual log. There are smells I knew that I've never known here. Spice and incense, like a church, but without the holy feel; some kind of cedar, old and a little damp; the odor of animals—a dog, a cat? Hell, it could be a muskrat for all I know.

But the strangely familiar, totally out of place flash fades and here I am in my perfectly perfect home, lost as a loon. What is a loon, exactly? I certainly don't remember loons.

I don't know how long I can keep on fooling everyone. Every day I meet people who ask how I am, how I'm feeling, can they do anything to help? They seem to be truly concerned, nice folks. I nod and smile and make remarks I hope are appropriate to whatever relationship we shared in my distant and dim-witted past, the life I must have had before the crash with the big red thing.

That's all I can find of anything before the accident. Not my life. Not my friends. Most assuredly not my husband. Just a flash of something big and red and fast heading straight for me—then the hospital.

They said it was a truck. I believe it. I was sore enough to have been hit by a truck. My ribs still ache and my head is numb when I scratch the skin underneath my hair. Everyone says it's for the best that I can't recall the accident or all the pain I was in, but they're wrong. I'd take all the pain for one clear day of my past.

Weren't there memories strong enough to penetrate this dullness? Didn't I have a day so glorious that it refuses to be stifled? My wedding? Falling in love with the stranger I live with? I'd like to remember a dark and rainy day when my dog got run over if it would come in clear-edged and certain.

I think I had a dog once. Sometime—I'm pretty sure I had a dog.

Looking around me, Rover or Spot must have come before Gregory. I can't imagine any self-respecting dog living in this house.

What I need is someone to talk to. Someone real. Someone not Gregory. Not my shrink. Just somebody besides myself. There have been calls from friends who offer to do anything to help. I think I'll just call and ask for help. Not that I can phrase it that way, can I? That would sound lonely and desperate and a little crazy, right?

Lunch would be a better idea. I'll just look in my handy, well-organized desktop file and ask...Let's see—Joanie, Kelli, Marybeth? Oh, I remember Marybeth. She came to the hospital and brought balloons and brushed my hair. Yes, I'll do lunch with Marybeth, if she can make it.

Less than an hour later Marybeth picked me up in her pewter Jaguar convertible.

"I'm so glad you called me today," she assured me. "My bridge group is on a break right now and I was really in no mood to stay and watch the maid cleaning the windows."

"Wow, I really rate. More fun than watching the maid," I said. And there I sat, feeling unimportant.

"Now, Jennifer. You know I didn't mean it that way." Marybeth pulled her gaze from the flow of traffic and looked at me as if she had farted in public. "I've been dying for us to get together. It's just that I didn't know if you were up for it yet."

"A joke, Marybeth. I was making a joke."

"Of course you were." She smiled politely in my direction. "You were never much of a joker before...Before, you know. It took me kind of by surprise."

"I'm more clever now that my brain is rearranged?"

"It's not that you weren't smart—just not the joking type. Know what I mean?" She checked the rearview mirror as she changed lanes, then looked again, pressing her lips together in a tiny, satisfied moue. "Do you like this lipstick? It's called Poppy Kiss. The girl at Neiman's said it was perfect for my skin."

"It is perfect." No way I'd question the Neiman's girl. Right now, trying to figure out the intricacies of cosmetics was as out of reach as quantum physics. "Very, uh, floral," I improvised.

"Exactly." Marybeth breathed a contented sigh. "You always were so perceptive. Not everyone realizes that floral has completely replaced berries. I can't wait 'til you get well enough to shop again. I sure have missed your advice."

"I gave *you* advice? On shopping?" This was one of those moments when my head injury made me aware I'd lost more than my mind. I'd lost my fashion sense, which I was beginning to learn was a crucial part of my erstwhile charm. "I'm a good shopper?"

"World class! The stores in the Galleria have noticed that you've been out of commission." She giggled, a witchy peal one note shy of fingernails on a chalkboard. "Their commissions are tied to yours. Get it?"

"Uh-huh." My stomach was starting to hurt. "It seems I'm not the only witty one today."

Marybeth looked pleased by the compliment and said, as if bestowing a reward, "After lunch, if you feel up to it, we could go by the mall for a little while and pick up a few things. Maybe just run into Nordstrom."

"Maybe. Could we go to the Gap? I think I need some new jeans."

"Oh, Jennifer, you are funny today." The tinkling laugh rankled my nerves again as she turned into the restaurant parking lot. "The thought of you in the Gap. It's great to have you back."

I followed docilely in her expensively scented wake as she swept into the restaurant. As the fawning waiter showed us to our "usual" table, I began planning an imminent relapse. Lunch, a drink or two, then back to the beige cocoon with a sudden, splitting headache. Marybeth would have to take her chances without my legendary fashion expertise.

Maybe the girl at Nordstrom could call the girl at Neiman's in case of an emergency.

CHAPTER THREE

I've marked six months off the calendar. Everyone expects things to be settling in and back to the good old days by now. Don't I wish! I sympathize with Dorothy—I'm sure I'm not in Kansas anymore either. The tornado blew over, but there's no sign of Toto or the Tin Man and the only ruby slippers I've seen have been in evening shoes at Willowbend Mall.

My concentration is much better and I've been watching television and movies. A lot of movies. It's the strangest thing—I know these stories better than I know my own life B.C.—before the crash. Rhett and Scarlett are old friends. Likewise Thelma and Louise—love 'em.

Who I don't love is Gregory. In fact, he gives me the heebie-jeebies. The man makes me feel like I've wandered into the Twilight Zone, a place where I'd feel more comfortable than this pretty mausoleum I live in now. If I walked into the living room and found a quartet of redheaded Martians playing bridge, they wouldn't be more alien to me than Gregory is.

Dr. Carey finds the subject endlessly fascinating. Our last session started where they all seem to start lately.

"I hate my husband."

"And why is that today? What did Gregory do to upset you?"

Dr. Carey uncrossed her legs and made a note on the newest of the yellow legal pads that chronicle my life. I watched as she repositioned her legs, noticing that her calves didn't squish flat even crossed. Good muscle tone for someone over fifty—a runner, maybe. She was looking at me looking at her legs. Another squiggle on the pad. Uh-oh. "Can you tell me why you're so angry at Gregory?"

"I'm not angry at him. I said I hate him. Okay, that may be too strong a word—hate. I dislike him. A lot. Whatever he does annoys me. I loathe him."

I paused, warming up, getting into my rhythm. Dr. Carey nodded, waiting without helping fill in the silent spot, waiting for more fodder to fatten her legal pad.

"Well okay." I wanted to be fair. "It's not what he does. He just gets on my nerves. He has a perfect job, a perfect car, eats at the best restaurants. For God's sake, he's a Stepford husband, executive model. Makes me seem like an idiot for complaining. The only thing wrong with him is me."

"That's an interesting observation."

"I hate it when you do that shrink thing. If you want to ask me something, just do it. Don't give me that Jungian-Freudian-Dr. Phil coy 'isn't that interesting' bullshit."

She smiled, a real-person smile, flashing even white teeth and revealing a killer set of dimples. Who'd have figured the cool Dr. Carey for dimples?

"Fair enough," she said. "I'll just ask. What makes you think the problem is with you?"

"Have you been listening to anything at all for the last few months? Read your notes. Head injury. Lala-land. Didn't even know my hair isn't naturally blonde until the goddamn roots started showing. Now that was a shock."

"I'll bet." Dimples again. "But, Jennifer, having a head injury and memory impairment doesn't make everything your problem. Did you ever consider the possibility that you and your husband were having adjustment issues before the accident?"

"Before?" The thought set off a mind explosion. "Before the accident? You mean I didn't like him then either? That's too weird; it's ridiculous. It's...it couldn't be. I wouldn't be living with him if I hadn't liked him before. Why would anyone live like that?"

"You'd be surprised what people will live with and for what reasons." Dr. Carey returned to the inquisition. "There are a few things that make me curious." She looked right into my eyes. "For example, you have made a point of avoiding any questions about your intimate marital relationship."

"Sex?" My voice squeaked, sliding up half an octave in the one word. "You want to talk about my sex life?"

"Is that a problem for you? Are you uncomfortable discussing sex?" I swear behind her professional exterior, she was enjoying watching me squirm. "Tell me about your feelings," she pried. "Are you embarrassed because you and Gregory are incompatible in bed? That may be part of your hostility toward—"

"As a matter of fact, we don't have problems in bed. He sleeps in his and I sleep in mine." Her pen flew over the notebook, but her eyes were still on me. Oh well, might as well make the rest of the session a triumph for her. "It was a convenience after the accident and it sort of just stayed that way."

"So you don't have sex at all?"

"I have great sex sometimes. Gregory just isn't there when I do it."

"Oh I see. And Gregory hasn't complained?" I shrugged, and she pressed on. "What does he do for his needs?"

"Sweet God, I try not to think about Gregory and sex." I suppressed a shudder. "For all I know, his laptop probably has a special port for sex—he uses it for everything else."

The choking sound she made might have been a cough.

"And you're satisfied with things the way they are? You don't want to reconnect with your husband sexually?"

"Not unless it's a choice between that and being shot with a small-bore weapon at close range." I stretched a smile over my face, but it may have still sounded a little hostile. "Look, I hate the man and if I hated him a year ago, you should have been treating me for a long time." I fidgeted on the sofa. "I'm really bored with this subject. If it has to be discussed at all, I think another time would be better."

"As you wish, but I think this is a sign of progress. Are you sure?"

"Right. Like I'm sure of anything. I mean, it's like the dreams. The fog. How many people do you know who have dreams about total strangers? *Only* about total strangers."

"Are you still having the same dream?"

"Sort of, but it's getting more detailed, more real feeling. Pieces here and there are new."

"Tell me what's new."

"It starts in the usual way. I'm walking down a street, talking to the dark-haired woman. We're laughing, our arms linked. Celebrating our success. Celebrating—I still can't remember what it is or why we're so excited."

"And that's bothering you?"

"I need to know what's going on. Who is she? Not one of the people who'd ever fit with Gregory, that's for sure. It makes me crazy trying to make it fit. Why can't I remember?"

"What happens next?"

"The fog starts to come in. Sudden. Thick rolling fog. Jo's afraid."

"Jo? Is that the dark-haired woman's name?"

"I...I think...yes. Jo. Jo's afraid. I try to calm her, but the hair on the back of my neck starts to prickle." I glance around Dr. Carey's familiar office, reminding myself of where I am, but I still feel the threat. "Now I'm afraid too. Someone's in the fog, just behind us, but I can't see who it is. The fog is heavier, so thick now you can't see the lights of the bar or the lights on the street.

"Someone's near. You can hear footsteps now. Jo is there with me one second, then there's a yank and her hand is gone from mine. She's gone. No scream, just a muffled gasp of surprise.

"I turn, spin around in the fog. Call her name. Nothing. Then a flash of light. A streak of red, something fast and red heading straight for me. Then nothing. No fog. No Jo. Nothing."

Dr. Carey stopped writing, her pen hanging in the air above the page. She was watching my face. Without saying a word, she got up and brought me a bottle of cold mineral water from a small refrigerator built into the wall.

"Here, sip on this and take a few deep breaths. You're very pale. Are you all right?"

I nodded, but my hand was trembling and my voice wouldn't work at all. She stood beside me, close enough that the faintest hint of her perfume wafted around me. Something soft and flowery and spicy. I closed my eyes for a second and gave in to the small womanly comfort.

Her fingers were firm and warm against my clammy wrist as she checked my pulse. She gave a slight squeeze before returning to her usual chair. Notebook back in hand, she wrote for a couple of minutes while I sipped my water and tried to hold onto the dream. No use—it was fading, slipping away the more I tried to pin it down.

"This dream is important," I said, surprised at the solid certainty in my voice. "I don't know why, but I have to find out. You've got to help me."

"Have you talked to Gregory about the dream?"

"It doesn't have anything to do with him."

"Perhaps he could tell you who Jo is. Some old friend you can't recall yet? Family?"

"This isn't about Gregory. I'm certain of that in my gut. He and Jo have nothing to do with each other." Hope flickered in my stomach, a tiny flutter of bright butterfly wings. "Dr. Carey, I don't have much in life I'm sure of right now, but this is clear beyond all else. Gregory doesn't know Jo, but I do. I know it. You've got to help me get to the bottom of this. You just have to."

She stared at me, not like I was a bug under a microscope, but as if she were looking inside my muddled head, seeing part of the real me for the first time, knowing how desperate I was.

"I have a suggestion, but you must let me know if the idea frightens you or makes you uncomfortable." She put down her pen and pad and leaned closer. "There is one possibility I think we should try. Hypnosis."

CHAPTER FOUR

"The whole thing strikes me as pretty extreme." My husband was his usual charming self this morning, reading the *Wall Street Journal* as he checked the latest listings on his laptop and drank his second cup of decaf, no sugar, no cream. "What's the point in rushing into some faddish treatment when all the doctors have said time will probably do as well?"

Gregory was a very busy man, but generous enough of spirit to offer support, between turning pages and clicking down screen, and always willing to share his opinions.

"You'd be better off to let yourself relax and not overthink for the time being. Go to the gym. Shop with your friends. Get a pedicure. You know, just get into your usual routine and let nature take its course."

"Dr. Carey is hopeful that the hypnosis sessions might speed the process."

"Dr. Carey this and Dr. Carey that," he said in a singsong voice. "If I'd known you were going to quote her every other breath, I think I'd have found a therapist for you who was a little less aggressive in her treatments."

"I think she's very kind." I liked Dr. Carey and didn't want to hear his criticism. "And this is a creative approach, don't you think?"

"Oh, she's very creative. I read an article in *People* magazine last month. She's written a thriller about urban violence that they reviewed very favorably. Watch out or you might be the subject of her next one."

"She's a very good doctor." I had no idea if that was true or not, but she was the only hope I had. "You did a great job in finding her."

"She was very highly recommended," he said as if he had created her expressly for me. "One of my clients had a problem she helped him with. He said she was a miracle worker."

"I could use a miracle. I think I'm going to give the hypnosis a try." I hated the defensive tone in my voice, so I said more firmly, "I've made up my mind."

"Whatever you think, but it's not as if you have anything that urgent to get back to, is it?"

"Excuse me for wanting my fucking life back, pitiful as it obviously seems to you." It was a good thing that at the moment I was holding a cereal spoon in my hand instead of a knife. "Can you imagine for even a second that I might have something better to do than shop with my boring friends or work the cellulite off my ass?"

The insufferable idiot was looking at me, wrinkling his nose as if he had sniffed a bad bottle of wine and the offensive odor was directly my fault.

"Really, Jennifer. I can't believe the way you curse lately. What's come over you? Maybe you've had more brain damage than we know."

He slammed the lid on his computer and then patted it as if in apology. More affection than he'd shown me, not that the sight of those manicured fingers with black hair on the knuckles didn't make my skin crawl.

"Why ask my opinion if you've already made up your mind? Do whatever you want," he said, heading for the door. "I'm late for a meeting."

"Gregory?"

He turned and looked back at me with hostility or, to give him the benefit of the doubt, maybe it was only indifference.

"Gregory, did we always dislike each other this much?"

He didn't pretend to not understand me; I'll give him credit for being honest in his own casually callous way.

"Not always." He sounded regretful, but his eyes were icy blue and empty of any sorrow, stonily set on a horizon miles away from here. "Just for a very long time."

He left and I sat at the table for a couple of minutes, stirring my cereal into a high-carb goo, thanking all the gods and goddesses whose names I couldn't summon that I didn't have to feel bad anymore for hating the cold bastard's guts. I left the dishes on the table for the maid and went to get dressed for my appointment with Dr. Carey.

* * *

"Are you comfortable?"

"I guess so." I wiggled my toes, aware that they weren't pedicured to the proper degree for North Dallas standards, glad they were covered by the lightweight afghan Dr. Carey had provided. I felt strangely naked and ill at ease taking off my shoes in her office. "I am kind of nervous."

"Don't be."

Dr. Carey could have a second career as a marine drill sergeant. She didn't quite snap at me, but I recognized her air of authority as she picked up the yellow pad and dimmed the lights.

"Relax." It was a direct order and I obeyed like a well-trained soldier, giving up my fear to her command. "That's the point of hypnotism. It's a simple technique, a deep state of relaxation."

"What if I can't be hypnotized? They say some people can't. What if I'm one of those?" I was stalling and she wasn't having any of it.

"Not likely. It's not as if I'll be putting you into a coma. I'll count backward from ten to one, then we'll wake you up by counting up to three. You'll feel refreshed afterward and remember what happened during the session. I'll also run a tape recorder as well so there's a durable record."

"Aren't there some people it doesn't work on?" Nothing else was working properly in my head these days. It would be embarrassing to be a failure at relaxing. I sat up, intent on calling the whole thing off. "Maybe Gregory was right and I should wait for this to—"

"Hold on Jennifer. You're quoting your husband?" Dr. Carey stopped my flight before I got airborne on the winds of doubt. "Since when has Gregory done one thing you thought was right?" There was that dimpled smile again, although it seemed to appear against her will. "The worst thing that can happen is that nothing will happen. If you don't remember, you just don't."

"I'm sort of an expert at not remembering, so what's to lose?" I sank back into the deep leather cushions and flexed my toes for emphasis. "Let's just do it."

* * *

"Five…Four…You are very relaxed. Very safe."
I feel very safe. It's nice here.
"Three…We're going back to the time when you are six years old…"
Six is good. I liked being six.
"Two…Almost there. When I say one, you will keep your eyes closed and be able to remember and to talk. You can see the world around you. Like watching yourself in a movie. You feel very safe."
Nice and safe. And movies. I like it.
"One."
The woman's voice is low and rumbly. Not fast and funny, like mama's. Nice though. Real safe.
"You are very comfortable, and you remember this time very well."
"I have a 'markable memory. Daddy says it all the time."
"And a very good vocabulary, it seems."

"Yes, it's 'markable too."

"Indeed."

"I can read *The Pokey Little Puppy* all by myself."

"That's wonderful," the lady with the nice voice said. "But let me ask you a few questions. Can you tell me where you are?"

"Uh-uh. I'm hiding."

"You don't have to hide from me. You're safe here."

"Course I'm safe here. That's why I'm hiding."

"Who are you hiding from?"

"Nana Jean."

"Nana Jean? Why do you need to hide from Nana Jean? Does she hurt you?"

"Course not. She's my Nana. I'm hiding 'cause I'm not gonna wear that dress."

"Nana Jean is making you wear a dress?"

"Uh-huh. Mamma says it's polite to wear it 'cause it's a present, but I'm not gonna wear a dress."

"I see. It's all right. You don't have to wear it right now. Let's just talk a little. Is that okay?"

"Okay."

"Where do you live? Do you know?"

"I live in Dallas, 'cause Daddy works at the school, and Mamma has to be at the jail all the time."

"Your mother is in jail?"

"Uh-huh. All the time."

"And does that make you afraid or sad?"

"Uh-uh. Mamma helps the 'pressed people at the jail."

"Oh, she's a lawyer then?"

"Uh-huh. Lots of people are poor and get 'pressed by a system. Mamma helps them go home. She—"

"Jennifer. Slow down."

"Cotton."

"Excuse me? What about cotton?"

"Cotton Annie."

"Your mother is named Cotton Annie?"

"No." I laughed. "I'm Cotton. Daddy calls me it 'cause my hair is white like cotton. Get it?"

"But your real name is Jennifer Ann?"

"Uh-uh."

"Ann Jennifer?"

"There's no Jennifer at all. My whole real name is Bailey Ann Claymore, but you can call me Cotton 'cause you're nice."

"Cotton?" She clearly hadn't been expecting that name. "All right. Cotton, I want you to listen to me. One."

"I can count to a thousand, if I wanted to. Daddy says—"

"I'm sure you can. Two. You're coming up now. You are safe, Jennifer."

"My name's not Jennifer."

"You're almost awake now."

"My name's Cotton."

"Three. Wide-awake now. Back in my office. Open your eyes, Jennifer."

"My name's Cotton."

I heard the words from my own lips, and they felt like the truth.

"Holy shit, Dr. Carey. I know you're going to think I've gone crazy, but my name is Cotton Claymore." I swallowed hard, trying to clear the choking lump at the back of my throat. "I don't know this Jennifer Strickland."

"Just take a few deep breaths and try to give yourself a little while to relax." Dr. Carey sat staring at me as if I were a total stranger, and God knows this *is* getting pretty strange. "You *are* Jennifer Strickland. I'm not sure what just happened, but you can't be Cotton Claymore."

"Maybe I am. Maybe there was a mix-up at the hospital when I was hurt...Maybe I have amnesia or something weird like that."

"There is something strange going on, but it isn't amnesia. And you are *not* Cotton."

"How can you be so sure? You've only been treating me for a few months. You only think I'm Jennifer Strickland because that's who I told you I am. Maybe—"

"Because I knew Cotton Claymore very well. She's been dead for more than six months. She was murdered."

CHAPTER FIVE

"Not dead," I whispered. Shifting walls, sliding certainties. "Not dead. I'm here."

"Yes, Jennifer. You're here. You're safe Jennifer." Dr. Carey kept repeating the name like a talisman.

"I'm not Jennifer." Things in my head weren't as sure as my words. Bottom's falling away like an elevator dropping out of control. "Who is Jennifer?" I asked, begging for reassurance, not knowing quite what I wanted the answer to be.

"Jennifer Strickland," comes the quiet, certain reply. "That's you."

"I don't think so." Elevator falls and I want to hold on to something and scream for help. "I think...I..." I don't scream, though; just wait to hit the bottom floor, bracing myself for the inevitable. "Then who is Cotton? How is she here?"

I waited, clenching my fists as the ground rushes upward. A lurch, a grab low in my gut—ground floor, solid landing. Still breathing.

I looked around the room, silent except for the echo of my question. Dr. Carey is sitting in her chair, pen in hand, a very strange look on her face. Checking me out. Okay this is familiar. I remember this.

"Tell me please," I begged. "Who is Cotton Claymore?"

"She was a friend, a colleague of mine," she said. "A psychologist."

"Was?"

"She was killed."

"Murdered? You said murdered."

She nodded. I closed my eyes, hoping the darkness would blot out the confusion scrambling my brain. For a few seconds the loss and disorientation that has made up my life had lifted and there was a person I thought was me. "Dead? I can't be dead. I'd know."

"You aren't dead Jennifer." Smooth, silky shrink tones, reassuring as hell usually, I'd bet. "Jennifer, I want you to breathe and relax for a couple of minutes. Reorient yourself. See where you are right now. Feel where you are."

"Okay. While I'm orienting, you be thinking up an explanation for what happened here." I shut my eyes and counted slowly to ten before speaking again. "Ready, set, go. Why am I remembering a dead woman's childhood? A dead woman you know and I've never heard of?"

"I'm not sure what happened. I don't intend to lie to you about that." Dr. Carey tapped her pen on the edge of the legal pad and fidgeted slightly in her chair, the first sign of uncertainty I'd ever seen her display. "Perhaps you knew Cotton Claymore too. Isn't it possible that she's someone you've forgotten since your accident?"

"No."

"Don't you think you should consider the possibility, Jennifer? She was a very well-known figure in this city. There were articles about her in the papers; she was on the news from time to time. It makes more sense that you've forgotten her than…" She stalled, shaking her head. "I don't know what to call this episode. I've never come up against this kind of experience before."

"I think it's fair for me to second that, but for all I know, maybe Jennifer Strickland made a habit of thinking she was dead people before the accident. Maybe we should do it over and see who else is hiding out in my crowded little skull."

"I can safely assure you that no one is hiding in your brain. There is a reasonable explanation for this aberration."

"And that would be found on what page of *The Bedside Hypnotist?*"

"It's a good sign that you're able to joke about this," Dr. Carey said, having regained her composure enough to scribble on the notepad. "I know it was confusing and upsetting, but—"

"Confusing, yes, but it gives me hope that I'm going to be all right."

"I don't quite understand your thought process. Can you explain how this makes you feel more hopeful?"

"It probably won't make sense to anyone but me."

"Don't try to defend or analyze it. Just go on."

"For months now, I've only had memories other people gave me. An identity someone said was me. Jennifer Strickland's memory was from Gregory, from friends, from clues around my house. There was nothing I had in my own right, nothing except a fragment of crazy dreams."

Dr. Carey was listening, but how could she really understand? I didn't really understand it myself.

"I know it's weird." I struggled to find the words that could make us both understand. "It's strange, but when I was Cotton I felt real. I remembered a mother and a father. I had a past that was in my head without any help. Things are fuzzy again right now, but for the first time I can recall, I know who I am. I don't know how to explain it, but I think Cotton Claymore has a lot more to do with me than Jennifer."

"I'm going to be honest with you, Jennifer." Dr. Carey wasn't going to let go of Jennifer that easily. "I'm not going to pretend to have a scientific answer, but there has to be a rational way to explain what happened today."

The good doctor believed in her science. I, myself, was having a few problems making the theories fit the potsherds we'd unearthed in my brain sediment. Maybe I'm sort of a psychiatric Missing Link.

"I think we need to stop for today. Are you comfortable with that?" I nodded and she continued. "I have a couple of people I'd like to consult with about our session. Can you meet with me again tomorrow?"

"Double sessions now? I guess since you've had two of me today, you ought to charge both of us." Reality was in serious flux and I was crazy for sure, because I was finding this funny. "I think now is the time you start earning your fee, Doc. I'll see you—we'll see you—tomorrow."

On the way home from Dr. Carey's office, I was so excited by the plan forming in my head that I forgot to be nervous driving myself around town. My neurologist had given me clearance to drive the car and on the way over, I had felt like the Beamer was a tank that I was maneuvering through a sea of land mines. Now I was on automatic pilot, slipping in and out of traffic with the unthinking skill of a race car driver, my mind on only one thing—this living ghost, this familiar stranger, Cotton Claymore.

The house was empty when I got home, pristine and chilled to a perfect seventy-two degrees against the humid June day of early Dallas summer. Gregory was still at his office, I presumed.

I dumped my bag on the kitchen table and grabbed a soda from the refrigerator, then headed directly for the home office/ library tucked behind the den. I had a mission and a few precious private hours in which to accomplish it. There was no way I was going to try to explain this to Gregory.

The desktop computer sat like a high-tech oracle, enshrined in a wooden-shelved grotto, waiting for the touch of a high priestess to perform the mystical rites. I approached it with uncertainty, a novice daring to summon the knowledge of the gods. I, who barely know how to work the gadgets in the kitchen, was more than a little intimidated.

"Think of it as a space-age toaster," I mumbled, punching the power setting to "on." It hummed instantly to life, presenting me with a display of options, neatly laid out in invitingly simple little pictures. I touched the mouse and watched as a blinking arrow skittered around the brightly lit screen, then stopped and clicked with false confidence.

"Okay Magic Genie. Let's get cooking."

Either I have forgotten my abilities as a computer whiz—which is always a possibility—or Gregory had installed some pretty foolproof shortcuts on the road to the Internet. Whichever, in an amazingly short half hour, I managed to access the back files of the *Dallas Morning News*.

I triumphantly typed in Claymore, Bailey Ann. Then my courage failed completely, and I sat with my finger poised, unable to carry out the simple double click that would achieve my goal. Cotton Claymore, whoever and whatever she was to me, beckoned, and I sat frozen, scared to even breathe too hard, desperate to know, terrified to find out.

What if...?

I tapped the mouse one click.

What if...I didn't even know what question followed what if. What if I read everything and none of it makes any more sense than it does now? What if I read it and something makes sense? What if I'm just plain crazy and either answer leaves me someplace lost and as confused as I have been for months? What if...?

"What the hell! I can't be any worse off than I am right now."

Click double click, and the headline screams in heavy black type: PROMINENT PSYCHOLOGIST MURDERED—DR. BAILEY "COTTON" CLAYMORE BLUDGEONED TO DEATH.

I jerked my finger from the mouse and scrambled out of my chair as if distance would protect me from the unexpected jolt of terror. I was gulping ragged splinters of air into my lungs, trying to stop the knot of panic in my chest from erupting in a scream. This is what I was searching for. It's not as if it was a revelation.

"Don't be such an idiot. Stop it." I ordered myself to calm down. "You knew she was dead. Read the damn story."

I glanced back at the screen, seeing the article in smaller type below the banner headline. Seeing it, but maintaining a distance that safely blurred the type until I could stop trembling enough to read it. A few deep breaths, I thought, and everything would be all right.

I forgot about nerves, forgot about breathing completely when I saw the photograph at the bottom of the page. Even in the grainy black and white newspaper reproduction on the screen, I recognized that face.

No matter how different it was from the one I saw in the bathroom mirror this morning, I knew that was my face under the name Cotton Claymore. *My face.*

CHAPTER SIX

I floated up from a deep sleep, anticipating the day as if it were Christmas morning without quite knowing why. It was early enough that the room was dark as a cave and I was the proverbial bat, scoping out my surroundings with senses sharpened by limited sight. Sliding one bare leg out from under the cover, I used my body radar to check things out. I stretched; I sniffed the cool air; I waited for an answering vibration.

This is a stranger's room, not my own. Sheets too silky, mattress too firm. No lingering scent of spicy sandalwood or earthy hint of sage. No soft and warm body tangled in the covers on my right. Whose room am I in? Whose room am I missing? Who am I in which room? I ask as I stumble toward being fully awake.

Under the sheets my hands touch skin, skimming breasts and flat stomach, moving lower to stroke curly silky hair. This body is mine, whoever I am. It feels touch and tenderness and responds without needing facts or memories. My thighs close around my hand and with a shudder of self-love, sleep reclaims the darkness. I dream of muskrat love and sandalwood.

The sun wakes me, lighting a room unlike the dream room, beige and modern as a spread in *Architectural Digest*. Sleepy satisfaction morphs into wide-awake anxiety.

Something has changed, is changing, in my mind. Today is different in some way than in the weeks before. I have a restlessness, a furtive gnawing as real as pain, but more diffuse. It curls in my stomach, just under my breastbone and low in my pelvis, tension so acute it is almost excitement. I feel it in my head, too, a cousin of the memory loss from the accident, but a superior relative, mocking me with hidden knowledge. There are secrets I know that I can't tell myself. Or that I won't.

Then I remember all the hours yesterday spent browsing the newspaper files. Haunting and oddly familiar stories about Cotton Claymore, her life and death. The unsolved murder left me shaken and confused. I ran hard copies of all the articles and sealed them in a large brown envelope, trying to stuff all the questions I had inside until I could dump my literal and figurative load on Dr. Carey's solid and sensible shoulders.

That still sounded workable today, so I took a shower, pulled my wet hair back in a ponytail, then rummaged through my drawers looking for running shorts and a plain T-shirt. All I could find was a khaki pair, starched to cardboard, but the white tee was passably soft. I have to admit to a small thrill of pleasure at leaving the neatly folded rows in purposeful chaos.

There were several pairs of sneakers, all so white they could have been new, lined up on the closet floor. I picked a pair at random, hoping to get out of the house before Gregory was up. No such luck.

He was standing just inside the front doorway, a cup of coffee in one hand and the newspaper still in its plastic bag in the other. He looked startled to see me.

"I haven't seen you up this early since…" He made a show of looking at his watch. "Now that I think about it, I've never seen you up this early." The top-to-toe appraisal he gave me was clinical, and the expression on his face made me feel I had failed whatever test he had administered. "Where are you going?"

"Out for a run."

"Excuse me?" He smiled, I swear to God. "In case you've forgotten—"

I was wrong. It wasn't a smile, but an oily smirk. "You don't run."

"What do I do for exercise?"

"You don't play golf," he continued in a professorial singsong. "You don't play tennis. You don't—"

"What *do* I do?" I interrupted his litany of my inadequacies. "For exercise. There are five pairs of sneakers in my closet. I must do something."

"You do Pilates. The shoes go with your leotards for that. Oh—you do yoga."

"Not anymore," I snapped, embarrassed at the very idea of having to ask him. "Starting today I run."

I left him standing there and tore off down the block at a full lope, head held high, ponytail whacking damply between my shoulder blades. Pilates my ass.

Two blocks later I was clinging to a street sign, gasping for breath, a tearing pain in my left side. Obviously I was going to have to build up to running. What made me think this was a good idea? After a couple of minutes sucking in air, the pain abated and I started walking—slowly, but away from the house. The damned shoes pinched every step.

I was limping by the time I got back to the house. Limping and proud of myself and thinking of nothing more than a second shower. I guess that's why I didn't pay much attention to the old car pulled up to the curb in front except to notice that the faded blue paint would look better with a wash and wax.

I was a few steps away, about to make the turn up the walkway when the driver's door swung open, effectively blocking my path. Instead of stopping, I sidestepped onto the lawn, not comfortable with getting too close to the strange blond-haired man who unfolded his lanky frame from the open door and stood staring expectantly in my direction.

"Hey, Jennifer. Wait up."

I hesitated, sizing up the situation as quickly as my brain could work, scanning through my memory banks for a glimpse of this face, a hint as to who this affable stranger was and how he might fit in my world. No clue. He was new to me.

"Sorry it took me so long to get to Dallas," he said, tucking the tail of his T-shirt into the waistband of his jeans as he walked closer. "You're looking good, honey. From what I heard you were next door to dead."

Well, at least he had his facts straight, although who he was and how he knew were still a mystery. I didn't want to come across as a dim bulb, but he opened his arms, obviously intent on hugging me, and I wasn't quite ready to go blindly into his embrace. Being polite was one thing, but still.

"Do I know you?"

"Know me?" He laughed, showing gorgeous teeth and crinkles at the corners of his very blue eyes. "Don't tell me a knock on the noggin has made you forget your favorite cousin."

Before I could protest, he grabbed me and twirled me around a couple of times and gave me a kiss right on the lips. Nothing too fresh, but not something that made me want to repeat the experience either.

"Your kissing cousin." He put me down and I backed far enough away to reestablish my comfort zone, then one more step backward to make it clear. "Your favorite cousin. Actually your only cousin."

"Sorry." I shook my head and tapped a finger against my temple. "I'm still having gaps in here since the accident. Could you tell me exactly who you are? Are we close?"

"You aren't kidding, are you, Jenny?" There was a skeptical half-shrug, followed by a grin that could only be described as devilishly charming. "Not even a tiny memory?" When I shook my head, he reached out and gave me another big hug, not seeming to notice he was the only one participating. "Let's go inside for a cup of coffee and I'll remind you how wonderful I am. Remind you of our plans."

"Plans?"

I wasn't up to plans. I dug my heels in, slowing his progress toward the front door. No way I was going to invite a total stranger, cousin or not, into the house alone.

"I don't mean to be rude." I paused, realizing he'd never even told me his name. "What did you say your name was?"

"Right. It's Dewayne. Your daddy was my daddy's uncle. We're second cousins or once removed or some such nonsense."

"Dewayne what?" All this cousin stuff was beyond Greek to me.

"Winters, of course. Just like your name before you married that Gregory guy." He curled his lip. "Is he still pretending he didn't marry you to get Uncle Jack's money?"

"I beg your pardon?" This guy might be rude and pushy as hell, but the fact that he didn't like Gregory made him go up a step in my opinion. "You don't think Greg and I are a good pair?"

"Didn't mean to hurt your feelings, Jenny, but this guy isn't hard to read. Greedy, self-centered. Thought you'd come to your senses and divorce him long before now." He glanced at the door. "He's not here now, is he? I don't want to waste our time if he's still home."

"No, but he will be any second." I lied too easily, grabbing the excuse to get rid of him. Jennifer might love this guy, but I wasn't feeling it. "Maybe you should call me later."

"Yeah good idea. I'd rather have you all to myself," he said. "Just like the old days when—"

"Sorry, Dewayne. The good old days are a lot of work for me right now and I have a doctor's appointment soon. Gotta shower." He looked ready to hug me again, so I moved out of his reach and cracked the front door, just enough to make it clear I was going inside. "Call me and we'll find a time. Do you have my number?"

"Cousin Jennifer, what a question." He grinned and gave me a little salute. "No way I'd lose your number, honey. We've got lots to talk over."

As he drove away, I hoped Jennifer didn't have any more long-lost relatives that were going to show up. I also wondered how long it took to have a phone number changed.

* * *

My appointment with Dr. Carey wasn't until two, so I filled the morning doing something everyone expected of me. I shopped. After my second shower, I dressed, grabbed my keys, the brown envelope, and a purse crammed with cash and a platinum American Express card and headed to the mall. I bypassed the Galleria and ended up at Northpark, a few blocks from the doctor's office.

I won't say my legendary love of shopping flamed back to life, but it did feel great to indulge in impulse buying on an epic level. The plastic was smoking by the time I finished. It took three trips to the car to stash huge bags in the trunk before the lust was slaked. Blue jeans—from the Gap, thank you—shirts, ten pairs of running shorts, sweats, sandals, Coach shoulder bags in three colors, a diving watch, half a dozen silver rings. Oh, the goodies were endless.

At noon, I took a break and ate lunch at a little French place where the tables were right out in the wide hall beside a fountain. I drank a double espresso and wondered if I used to smoke, because the thought of a cigarette with the strong, bitter coffee sounded perfect. I people-watched and, for the first time I could remember, I felt totally at peace.

Tired by the day's frenetic binge, but revved up by the caffeine, I was fried when I arrived at Dr. Carey's. Her inner door was closed, so I nodded at Donna, the receptionist for the three doctors who shared the office, and took a seat in the waiting area.

I amused myself by looking at all the expensively framed degrees and certificates hanging discreetly on the wall. Dr. Carey had her SMU pedigree prominently displayed—in Dallas going to Southern Methodist University was practically expected of a girl from Highland Park. Summa cum laude, no less. Rah. Rah.

There was a man sitting in another chair, leafing through a sheaf of papers. He had on those little wire reading half-glasses that perched on the end of his nose. He looked up at me and nodded before returning his attention to his reading. Something about him was intriguing, and I studied him when he wasn't looking.

He was in his late fifties or so and had a full head of longish salt-and-pepper hair and a short, but rather bushy beard. A kind person would say he was plump, but even his expensively tailored business suit couldn't quite disguise the round belly and broad butt that scarcely fit in the chair. I suppressed a smile when I realized who he reminded me of.

Make the hair and beard all white, give him a pipe and a bright red suit, and I swear he could have fooled Mrs. Claus. I was still amusing myself by imagining what kind of lurid neuroses Santa would have to confess in therapy when Donna said the doctor was ready for me.

"How are you feeling today, Jennifer? Yesterday was pretty rough on you."

Dr. Carey motioned for me to take my usual place on the sofa. She had added a second chair to the room, next to where she always sat.

"Actually, I'm having a really good day. I slept all night without the dreams. I went shopping this morning. Bought tons of things I don't need and had a fattening lunch. All in all, better than I could have hoped for."

"That's good," she said, but she didn't seem all that interested in girl talk. "Jennifer, yesterday's session was quite unusual. I took the liberty of calling an old friend, Andrew Waters. He is not only one of the most gifted psychiatrists I know, but he has some special interest and experience in these matters."

"These matters? You mean there are actually specialists for my kind of head case?" I was amazed. "How do you look them up? Yellow pages under Missing Minds? Or Multiple Occipital Occupations?"

"Jennifer," she admonished gently. "This isn't about labels. Just talk to Dr. Waters. I think he may have ideas that will help you." She leaned over to press the intercom button. "Are you willing to talk with him? It's up to you." I nodded and she asked Donna to send the doctor in.

I should have been expecting it in my strange little world, but I was surprised nonetheless when an Armani-clad Dr. Santa entered the room.

CHAPTER SEVEN

"Hello, Ms. Strickland," the fat man said in response to Dr. Carey's introduction. "Thank you for allowing me to sit in on your session. I know it's difficult to throw a new factor into the mix at this stage, but I'll try not to be too obtrusive."

Santa—I mean Dr. Waters—had a voice like distant thunder—low, resonant and vaguely ominous. Not scary ominous, but portentous, promising knowledge and with the faintest edge of a first-rate showman. I was prepared to be dazzled, drawn in by his voice and imposing physical presence. He watched me with—what else?—twinkling blue eyes as he settled his considerable girth in the wing chair next to Dr. Carey.

"Hello," I said, nodding in his direction, uncertain of proper protocol when your shrink had to call in a backup. Was I supposed to start over and go through all the basics again? Was Dr. Carey going to hypnotize me and let him see the dog and pony show firsthand?

"Jennifer, I've explained your background—the accident, memory loss, dreams—so that we would all be on the same page today."

Crisp and efficient as usual, Dr. Carey took over. Why did I waste time worrying with her around? If the people at NASA had a handful of staff as capable, there would be a McDonald's serving cheeseburgers on the moon by now.

"If you don't mind," she continued, "I'll let Dr. Waters take the lead for now. He has some very interesting theories that may shed light on your hypnosis and the...uh..." She stuttered, showing uncertainty for the first time since I'd known her. "The situation with Cotton Claymore."

At last, here was my chance to do more than sit like a lump on a log. I fished the manila envelope from my bag and held it in the air. They both watched, saying nothing until the moment stretched uncomfortably long. Feeling like an over-the-top drama queen, I lowered the envelope to my lap.

"It's research material," I said in my own defense. "I have printouts of all the information I could find on Cotton. And even if you both think I'm crazy, the more I find out, the more I remember about her. I do remember."

"Do you think you're crazy?" Dr. Waters asked in a quiet tone.

"We don't do those shrinky questions around here, Dr. Waters," I answered with bravado. "House rules. Just talk to me like I'm a regular person."

"Fair enough." He smiled. "Then let's drop this Dr. Waters and Ms. Strickland business. Please call me Andrew."

I shot a surprised glance in Dr. Carey's direction. She was scribbling, as usual, but her mouth turned up as she wrote.

"You don't need my permission," she said. "I should have told you Andrew prefers a more casual approach than I."

"Okay, then. Andrew. You can call me—"

I stopped, baffled by my own uncertainty. This was going to look bad, but damned if I knew what to do. I felt less like Jennifer every day, but asking to be called by a dead woman's name would probably be pushing me into being measured for a straitjacket in the end.

"Maybe you shouldn't call me anything," I murmured. "Just yell, 'Hey, you!' if I start to head off into the deep end."

"You aren't going to drift off anywhere. Let's not worry about what to call you for now, shall we? Just humor me and answer the question. Are you crazy?"

"I think we have to consider the possibility."

"All right, we'll put that on our list. But just to eliminate a few other choices, can you tell me what makes you think you might be crazy? Do you see visions, for example?"

"No."

"Good. Do you hear voices when no one is around?"

"No."

"Any overwhelming urge to harm yourself or anyone else?"

"No, not if you don't count the fleeting fantasy of putting rat poison in my husband's Sumatran roast." I grinned. "Just kidding."

"I think that falls well within the norm." He smiled in return.

Andrew stroked his beard and sat for a few seconds, looking at me. Looking at me, not watching me, a distinction that made me feel like a person instead of a case.

"This problem with your head injury complicates things because you can't tell me much about what you knew before the accident. But if you'll indulge me and answer a few marginally shrinky questions, I may have a possible explanation for a few of your concerns."

"Ask away."

"Tell me what you remember of life before the accident."

"I've tried to come up with a clear memory, but it's like a blank wall. I have a lot of information from Gregory, from friends, photographs with me in them, stuff like that, but I don't know if I really remember them or just remember people telling me I know about them."

"What about your parents? Your childhood?"

"That bothers me a lot. I've stared at old pictures of them. Of all of us from the time I was a baby. I look like my father." I closed my eyes, trying to conjure up feelings of love or hate or sadness. Nothing. Nothing except vague flashes of carefully pasted snapshots.

"They died in a plane crash five years ago. My father was in the oil business and they were on a business trip. Their plane went down over the ocean. I inherited a lot of money and property, according to Gregory, but I truly don't have any feeling that I knew them at all. Isn't that strange?"

"You had a very bad injury. Things get rattled."

"Things don't usually stay this rattled this long though. Right?"

"Not usually, no. But not unheard of either." He shifted his bulky body. "So you have no clear memory of anything before the car wreck?" I shook my head, and he continued. "Including your husband or friends?"

"Nothing. Except for waking up in the hospital, and a lot of that has been blurry until the last few weeks."

"While you were in the hospital, do you know if there was a time when you stopped breathing or had to be resuscitated?"

"Yes. Gregory said I went into some sort of cardiac arrest right after they brought me in. Had to shock my heart back into beating. I don't recall it though."

"What hospital were you taken to?"

"I was driving down Inwood, about six blocks from Parkland Hospital, so they took me there. If I hadn't been so close to their trauma unit, my doctor says I probably wouldn't have made it because of the amount of blood I'd lost."

"And this was in January."

"January eleventh."

"What time of the day?"

"Around ten that evening. They said I was coming home from a dinner party with friends in the West End."

"Interesting." He leaned over and tapped a pudgy finger on the envelope still clutched in my fingers. "May I?"

I let him take it. Dr. Carey and I looked at each other, then watched silently as he opened the flap and pulled out the sheaf of pages I had compiled. He read and shuffled through them, pulling out two pages and putting them on top of the others. He nodded and turned his attention back to me.

"Did you notice the date Cotton Claymore was killed?"

"Not precisely," I said. "Is it important?"

"I think it is."

Andrew lowered his chin and crossed his hands over the expanse of his stomach, studying the papers as if they were the Rosetta Stone.

"You see, Cotton Claymore was taken to Parkland Emergency on January eleventh too. Her injuries were so extensive, it was a wonder she was still alive when they got her to the hospital." He leaned forward and placed a warm hand on my arm. "Cotton was pronounced dead at the very time you were being shocked back to life."

CHAPTER EIGHT

Fog. Coming and going. Secrets told. Presto chango!

"Wait! I remember something." My voice was a scratchy whisper, pulled from a mouth suddenly bone dry. "Something... Strange. Somewhere foggy with lots of people—well, not exactly people I could see—but they were there, I know. In the fog."

"Good. Good," Andrew soothed, still patting my arm. "Don't try to make it make sense. Tell us what you remember."

"I don't remember, exactly. But I was lost, gone, gone... somewhere. Then something changed and I came back. I came back and Jennifer didn't."

The silence in the room must have lasted for only a few seconds, but it seemed to go on for ages. I watched the two people sitting across from me, seeing the expressions on their faces flicker and change as they watched what I supposed were similar reactions on my own. Dr. Carey went from shocked disbelief to shocked possibility to logical scientific disbelief. Consistent even in chaos.

Andrew was harder to read. He managed to avoid the stunned denial I saw in Dr. Carey, looking more like a long-hoped-for gift had been laid in his lap and he didn't know quite what to do with the bounty.

I was more surprised and confused than the two of them put together and doubled again for good measure. At least they had the vantage point of being outsiders, uncertain of whether this was some magical occurrence or an intriguing, detailed delusion. Unless I had lost my mind—a possibility that was becoming more likely with each passing moment—I *was* Cotton Claymore, in spirit, if not in body.

How this sea change came about and what it meant, I had no idea. The knowledge of who I was didn't suddenly open the hidden floodgates of my brain. Cotton's life wasn't any clearer to me than Jennifer's had been. The past was fuzzier than ever, a mishmash of the woman I and everyone else had believed me to be and foggy wisps of an entirely different life.

"Let me ask you something, Andrew." When I found I could speak again, my voice had lost the parched croak of initial shock. "Now are you ready to reconsider the possibility that I am crazy? Maybe there are no cars between my engine and my caboose."

He grinned. Giving my hand a squeeze, he withdrew his comforting touch and retrieved the stack of printouts I had given him.

"You have plenty of cars, I'd bet. They've only been temporarily derailed by your head injury."

"You really think so?" I asked, relieved to hear him so positive. "Got any clues as to who's running the train?"

"Engineer Claymore, it seems, for the moment."

"Excuse me." Dr. Carey spoke for the first time in a while. "I think I'm the only one here who still has a foot in reality. All this talk of trains is clever, but I think we should try to find some rational explanation for Jennifer's persistent dissociative state without jumping to conclusions that are essentially unsupported psychobabble."

"I resent the labeling, Ronnie." Andrew never raised his voice, but the force of conviction behind it was evident. "If you don't have any faith in my research or methodology, why did you ask me to sit in?"

"To tell the truth, because I felt I had no other option," she said bluntly. "But right now, I'm not sure that I can let Jennifer proceed in what may be a very dangerous and ethically unreliable direction without some empirical data to rely on. I don't want to trigger a deeper level of delusion and have her end up in a hospital for God knows how long."

"There is research supporting this possibility," he replied. "If this were the first case on record, I'd be skeptical myself. However, I've spent the past ten years traveling the world and studying too many cases to dismiss the unusual as impossible."

For once all my attention was focused on something besides my problems. It was fascinating to listen to the Titans challenging each other. Strangely, I—who had only weeks before been confused by anything more complicated than brushing my teeth—had no trouble at all following the disagreement between the two of them. In fact, I found the discussion of dissociative states and empirical evidence easier to follow than directions for applying makeup.

"Excuse me Dr. Carey. Andrew?" They turned at my interruption. "I think I'm understanding way too much of this argument to be Jennifer. So why don't we go on the assumption that somehow Cotton Claymore is running my train—my brain, that is. How the hell is that possible?"

"It isn't possible," Dr. Carey said flatly. "Jennifer, I think this whole session was a huge mistake on my part. I think it would benefit us more to go back to solid principles and try to establish the roots of this delusion. Cotton Claymore is dead."

"Come on, Dr. Carey," I said. "Do you really think we can just ignore my new imaginary friend and find a reasonable explanation for all of this?"

"I think we have no rational alternative. This is a potentially dangerous experiment. I think you need to know that."

"Consider me warned. I'll take full responsibility. Do you want me to sign a release or something?"

"Of course not," she said, sharply. "I just don't want to base your treatment on an untried experiment. Anything could happen."

Andrew sat silently, listening to the two of us. He wasn't going to interfere with Dr. Carey's treatment plan. Old school protocol. But he didn't agree with her; I could see it in his eyes.

Well, I wasn't about to sit here and be a passive spectator while Dr. Carey made me over in Jennifer Strickland's oh-so-boring image. I'd rather take a leap of faith into the unknown. Ending up in the straitjacket life I'd been leading was far worse than anything else I could imagine. Of course, there was always the danger that I could end up in a literal straitjacket and it wouldn't be Prada.

"Andrew, will you help me? I don't know how this is happening, but I think you can tell me."

"There is an explanation, but without Ronnie's consent and cooperation, it wouldn't be proper for me to go any further."

"I don't give a good damn about what's proper!" I raised my voice to one decibel below hysteria, rather liking the effect it had on them—complete silent attention. "Dr. Carey, you started my therapy, but if you force me into it, I'll get Andrew or someone else, if I must, to take over from here. Please don't make me do that. I trust you. I need you."

"This could be a serious mistake. One with consequences we can't even start to fathom." She was a bit less emphatic than before. "Won't you give it a little more time to—"

"Time to what?" I interrupted. "Time to pretend I'm going to wake up tomorrow and be good little Jennifer Strickland? Time to waste trying to get back a life that may have some meaning to me? My God, I can't keep treading water forever. I'm drowning here and you don't seem to care."

"I care," she said softly. "More than I should, probably. I care about you enough to let Andrew at least explain his theory. Then, if you decide to continue, I'll be here for you."

"Fair enough." I turned to Andrew. "Will you help me?"

He studied my face for a long moment before turning to Dr. Carey. She didn't look overjoyed, but nodded her consent. Andrew took his glasses from the end of his nose, folded them neatly and put them in the inside pocket of his jacket. Only then did he say, with conviction, "Yes, my dear. I will help you."

CHAPTER NINE

"I'll give it my best shot," Andrew said. "However…"

He smoothed his gray-streaked beard and contemplated heaven knows what inner muse. He was quiet for so long it made me nervous, but I wasn't going to say anything to break his concentration.

At last he began in a tone straight out of that old television show where the announcer warns you not to change the channel, they have now taken control of your set. You know, the one that scares the bejesus out of you. Yes, he had that part down to an art.

"Sometimes things happen that don't fit any of the rules of science most people consider to be normal." He paused, not helping my goose bumps. "Have you ever heard the term 'walk-in'?"

"Walk-in?" I pondered the word. No bells, no whistles, no clue. "Not other than trying to get a haircut from the best stylist in town without an appointment," I said. "And I'll bet that's not even warm."

"Equally improbable," he allowed with a twitch of a smile, "but in the same virtual range of possibility. Tell me. Do you believe in reincarnation?"

"I don't know if I'd say I believe in it. As a theory I like the idea of recycling souls, but I'm not sure I have a really strong spiritual opinion, either way."

"Well, for the time being, let's assume reincarnation is a given. Most of us understand the concept on some level. After one dies, the soul reenters the corporeal world in the form of a newborn, ready to begin another turn of the wheel." He lifted an eyebrow quizzically. "With me so far? Yes?"

Dr. Carey and I nodded impatiently. This was hardly breaking news.

"There is a second method of reincarnating. Sometimes if a person dies suddenly or is violently taken out of an emotional or spiritual situation, they need to return right away—in adult form—to complete a cycle."

"So they just hijack some other poor soul's body and move right in?" I interrupted, torn between indignation and laughter at the notion. "Wouldn't that run up some serious cosmic debt on their karmic credit card? It would take a few turns of the wheel as a tree frog to pay that off."

"Karmic credit card?" He laughed and his stomach did shake like a bowl full of jelly. "No my dear. The deal is made between the soul leaving one body and the person who needs the body to come back. More of a loaner vehicle than a carjacking, if you see the difference."

"I do see." This was an exciting possibility, one that stirred some vague memory of comings and goings in a misty otherworldly place. "I see, but why can't I remember, if it was such a peaceful transfer? Why don't I know what I came back for?"

"First of all," he said patiently, "not everyone is consciously aware of his or her change of soul location. Maybe due to cell memory interference, maybe as a result of divine purpose. However, those who do so usually recognize their new selves rather gradually and often reject the truth or are talked into rejecting the truth by some of my more traditional colleagues."

"I can hear you, Andrew," Dr. Carey said. "I may be traditional, but I'm not unable to listen to new theories, no matter how outrageous I personally find them." She snorted, rather inelegantly for her normal demeanor. "Please try not to dismiss my concerns as if they were petty. You know very well this is hardly blessed by the American Board of Psychiatry. She could decompensate and end up—"

"At the risk of seeming like this is about me, could the two of you discuss this over drinks and dinner later? I want to know more." Petulance is not a fabulous character trait, but sometimes you have to go with what works. "So what next? Can we just keep doing hypnosis until we get caught up?"

Their stunned silence was pretty easy to interpret as a double no. Next question.

"Why not?"

"Jennifer—"

"I can't keep answering to that name, especially with the two of you."

"Well, you surely don't think you can start using the name Cotton Claymore, do you?" Dr. Carey was not above sarcasm herself. "If we went along with that, we'd be writing letters to you in your nice room at the mental hospital. If they let us send mail from wherever they lock up doctors who are crazier than their patients."

"Too true." Andrew laughed, but it wasn't a totally carefree sound. "You are going to have to take things slowly if we proceed down this path. You are never going to be able to *be* Cotton Claymore, even if that turns out to be what you believe."

"Isn't that what you believe?"

"I think it's a little early in the game to be a believer just yet. Tonight is a start, a first baby step in our investigation. We have to move slowly, let your brain heal inside and your memory fill in missing pieces." Andrew pointed to Dr. Carey. "Ronnie is right to be cautious. It would be easy to convince you of this as the truth, when we have to make sure not to influence you or indulge a mistaken identity. We don't know anything yet—we only surmise."

"So what do I do now?"

"You do nothing," he said, folding his hands over his belly and smiling serenely, like Santa doing an impression of the Laughing Buddha.

"But—" This was not what I wanted to hear. "But shouldn't I—"

"You do nothing." He grinned at my impatience. "You go home. You eat. You sleep. You wait."

"But..."

"Things will begin to come back to you, probably more quickly now that it has begun. Keep a journal and next week we'll go over it with you and talk about what discoveries you've made."

"Next week? I'm supposed to keep all this to myself all week?"

"Jenni—" Dr. Carey caught herself, mid-name. "What are we going to do about this name? It's even beginning to make me uncomfortable."

"It will work itself out," Andrew soothed. "The right name and the right time to know it will happen. Don't force it."

"Okay. But there is something very important for you both to keep in mind." Dr. Carey sounded ominous. "I don't want a word of this outside of the three of us. Not a whisper."

"I wasn't planning on a rebirth announcement in the country club newsletter, if that's what you're afraid of." It felt good to laugh at our seriousness. "And I certainly wasn't going to discuss it over coffee with Gregory."

"I want you to listen to me. I want both of you to remember one thing." She paused, waiting for us to stop smiling. "If you are, somehow, Cotton Claymore, don't forget this fact for one second. Cotton was murdered once. If her killer gets the tiniest hint of this possibility, it could happen again."

CHAPTER TEN

I spent the whole week thinking about Dr. Carey's warning.

In all my confusion and delight at finding an identity in Cotton, I had kind of overlooked the nasty fact that she/I had been killed. Not just killed, that sounded too neutral. Brutally murdered. Violently beaten to death with a blunt instrument.

That kind of up-close-and-personal, hands-on murder spoke volumes. Someone hated Cotton. Personally wanted her dead, wanted to see her smashed and bleeding, wanted to watch her die.

That person was still out there. According to the newspaper reports, the police had never made an arrest, although there were rumors that a jealous ex-husband or lover of one of the women she helped had been responsible. Cotton had founded Outreach Oaklawn, a shelter and haven for abused women and children. Her outspoken advocacy and public fundraising as the face for the Outreach made her a target for vilification and a thick stack of death threats—so many threats the police hadn't been able to narrow it down to one person they could link the murder to.

There was also a hint, veiled and not quite overt, that one of the other women in Cotton's life could have led to her death. In addition to being a social activist in a very conservative city and a vigorous defender of women against poverty and abuse, she was identified with the modern-day scarlet letter—a capital L. The letter didn't stand for Liberal or Left-wing, which would have been scandalous enough. Oh no—it was far worse. Cotton Claymore, for all her good works, was a Lesbian.

And horrifying as that was, the situation was more dire. She was *out*. Proudly out, marching in the Razzle-Dazzle-Dallas-parade out, pink-triangle out. Unrepentant and without a scrap of shame.

In a city with more Hard Shell Baptists than hard-core feminists, it was an ugly issue. For the first couple of her years in the public spotlight, it was a slur that made her a social pariah, but after all the civic awards and the interview on *60 Minutes*, it became more of an honorary title. Her Lesbian Activist, her Royal Gay Psychologist, and finally Our Local Protector and Defender of Gay Rights, Cotton Claymore.

It didn't hurt that she was photogenic, tomboyishly gorgeous, and sported a tough-cookie charm that worked on anyone who talked to her for more than two minutes—at least according to *Inside Edition*. Photos of her grinning into the cameras like a modern version of Kate Hepburn made me wish I had that easy bravado instead of Jennifer Strickland's pale and ordinary demeanor. But people in Dallas loved a winner more than they hated a queer, so she had gained grudging tolerance, if not outright acceptance in Big D.

But there were *those* rumors, whispered, insinuated. Cotton had lady friends, many of whom had ex-husbands or boyfriends who weren't big fans of the whole Lesbian Chic movement. One of these jealous men allegedly played a key role in the team of detectives working the murder case. No one came out and said that was a factor in the case being unsolved, but the idea crawled around town, nonetheless.

Finding out I am a lesbian was a mixed blessing. While it made me giddy to know there was a reason Gregory gave me the creeps and that I never had to worry about sleeping with him, it was also daunting. I don't remember being a lesbian, especially a lesbian with a reputation for being a great womanizer. How am I supposed to work that into my list of things to relearn? Let's see now: take makeup lessons, reestablish my counseling career without any credentials (Jennifer's art history degree didn't count), avoid lurking killer, learn how to pick up chicks. And do that with a head injury so bad I still am not sure I'm crazy or just a lost reincarnated walk-in looking for a few clues to find my way back to some semblance of my old life.

* * *

When I went to my next therapy meeting, Andrew was pleased with my progress. If he had been making a list and checking it twice, I had no doubt I'd have been on the nice side of the page.

"You have no idea how much confidence you've gained since the last time we met. And judging from the entries in your diary, I think you are making huge strides in regaining your memory."

"Either I'm beginning to recall my world as Cotton Claymore, or I may have to take up writing fictional resumes for brain-impaired patients. It seems more and more real to me. More memories every day."

"That's pretty much what happens. A trickle of memories at first, then a whole ocean." He was thumbing through my journal. "Some of this is pretty detailed—foods you like, favorite restaurants, perfume...Interesting."

"Yeah, but I do have a question."

Andrew and Dr. Carey both looked at me and nodded. I almost laughed aloud because they were both doing the therapist head-bob, as if synchronized. Maybe it was a required skill in the profession, something one had to master before moving on to saying, 'And how does that make you feel?'

"What if none of these memories are real? I mean, they feel genuine to me, but what if I am just thinking things at random and writing them down? It's not like there's anyone around to prove I'm wrong."

"That's true," Andrew said reasonably.

"And I've spent a lot of time online, reading old news clippings, studying Cotton's life. That could account for some of the information I think I recall."

"An absolute possibility," he admitted.

"It would make more scientific sense than this metaphysical supposition." Dr. Carey had to get in her incisive skepticism. "Cotton's life had an amazing amount of press coverage. It would be easy to speculate."

"So how do I know if these are real or only an active imagination processing information and writing a script?"

"You don't," Andrew said. "At least not yet. I think it might be helpful to get out into the neighborhood where Cotton Claymore lived and see if you get any flashes," he said. "Visit the shops and stroll around. Often sights and smells trigger spontaneous memory."

"Oh, Andrew. I'm not sure she's ready for that." Dr. Carey sounded very doubtful. "And, if—I'm saying *if*—any of this walk-in theory is true, I'm not sure she should be all alone and have a rush of memories. I don't want her alone if she recalls something confusing. She could misinterpret it without one of us to guide her."

"I don't think that's likely, Ronnie," Andrew said, giving her a puzzled look. "She seems to be handling this situation better than I'd actually expected."

"She's had too many changes in a very short time." Dr. Carey was unyielding. "Being alone could be overwhelming. That's a good way to trigger a full-blown panic attack."

"I think it's a great idea," I said. "I want to go down to the area anyhow. That's where Outreach Oaklawn is. I've been feeling like I want to see it." Watching Dr. Carey's expressive face, I could see she was about to expand on her objections, so I hurried on. "I'm prone to memory lapses, not panic attacks. Besides, I've got both your numbers on speed dial, so if I start panting or going gaga I'll call right away."

Andrew laughed, but Dr. Carey just shook her head and made notes on her yellow pad.

"Don't encourage her, Andrew. I think she should be far less impulsive and a good deal more cautious."

"I'm not suggesting rash or dangerous behavior, Ronnie. But I don't think a couple of hours downtown is likely to send her over the edge." He turned to me. "Would you like me to go with you? If you have worries about being by yourself I don't want to minimize Ronnie's concerns."

"Thanks, but no. I need to do this on my own. I'll be fine." I was beginning to feel like a teenager negotiating curfew. "I'm ready to start getting back into the world. And, speaking of that, I've made a decision I think you need to know about."

They looked at me with polite interest.

"I'm thinking about finding my own place." A leap to listening intently. "And I'm leaving Gregory."

Speechless shock from a duo of shrinks. Now that's what I call bringing down the house.

CHAPTER ELEVEN

Gregory wasn't the soul of understanding when I told him I wanted a divorce, although the horrified expression on his face eased considerably when I told him I was the one who would be moving out. In all fairness, he turned his laptop off and took several minutes of his valuable time to discuss things with me.

"Jennifer, I'm afraid you've lost your mind."

"That's a hard point to argue."

I knew better than to talk to him about my sessions with Dr. Carey and Andrew. He'd have Jennifer locked up in a very expensive, very lovely loony bin if he caught a hint that we thought Cotton Claymore had moved inside her head. Thank God and doctor-client confidentiality protocols that my therapists would never be talking to Gregory. What a mess that could stir up.

"However," I continued, "losing some of my memory is hardly the same thing as being crazy."

"It's not just that." He glanced at me, then away, barely making eye contact. "After the accident, the doctors all said it would take time, but you can't expect to get back to your old self by running away from home, from reality." He sighed. "I've been patient with you and, quite truthfully, it hasn't been a picnic for me. I haven't had any kind of normal life these past few months. The visits to the hospital and that rehab place were a nightmare. No companionship; no social life. I'm not complaining, but you have no idea how hard it's been waiting for you to get it together. My whole routine has been shot to hell and now you're going to complicate things more by threatening me with a divorce."

"Forgive me if I can't feel your pain, Gregory." This guy was such a prince. "You missed a few hours at the office and had to reschedule a couple of golf games before you found out I wasn't going to die. Maybe someone will nominate you for sainthood."

"When did you get to be such a bitch, Jennifer? You were always so sweet and loyal." He looked like a seal pup waiting to be clubbed. "I don't think I should be punished for your condition. It's not my fault."

I almost felt sorry for him. I suspected I'd always been a bitch, considered it one of my better qualities, actually. A smart mouth and a smile on the side worked miracles if you knew when to use them. *I* did, but obviously little Jennifer had better manners. Gregory probably did feel like a bloodied martyr now that I was getting my feet back under me. Maybe Jennifer's way would work better since he was more accustomed to kid gloves than a buzz saw.

"I'm sorry, Gregory." The lie sounded almost sincere. Like his ego would care about truth as long as it got stroked. "I know this has been hard on both of us. I know I've changed. That's why I'm suggesting a divorce. It's not your fault." That at least was true. "We can't help what's happened, but we also can't pretend things could ever be the same again."

"But you still might get better, in time. You could get back to being yourself." He didn't sound hopeful—or particularly saddened by the possibility that I might not. "There are other considerations, as well. Financial ramifications, property—the sort of things I've always handled for you…for us. A divorce will play havoc with our tax situation. I'll have to call Dick Williams at the CPA firm and get him started on a game plan."

He was beginning to sweat, a few beads popping out on his forehead, just between his eyes. I wasn't in any shape for a lecture on marriage and the intricacies of joint filing with the IRS, so in the hopes of distracting him, I tossed out an alternate plan, a meaty bone for him to worry instead of me.

"How about a legal separation—just to give us time to see how things shake out?" He still looked inclined to argue, so I added hurriedly, "You could still handle all our assets, keep track of the financial things until we come to a final decision."

He went for it like the greedy dog he couldn't help but be.

"That could be a workable idea."

I could almost see him dancing in his blackhearted fantasies, though he tried to keep the enthusiasm from bursting out. Poor Jennifer, I thought. Hopefully, wherever she had gone, she hadn't had good enough sense to know what a piece of work she'd been married to. No wonder she'd taken the chance to get out when the big red thing mowed her down.

"Yes," Gregory went on in a more sepulchral tone. "We could try that." He absently wiped the sweat bullets from his forehead and lowered his shoulders from up around his ears. It was as though the weight of the world had eased by a cosmic ton. "Maybe we do need a little space. Take some time to consider where we're going."

He sounded as if this were a new concept instead of the oldest cliché in the breakup book. I gladly nodded my assent. Whatever it would take to get out of this tomb was good enough for me.

"Thanks for being so understanding," I said sweetly, squelching my delight with how easy he was making things. "I'll start looking for a place tomorrow."

"There's no rush, Jennifer. Take all the time you need," he said grandly. "This separation wasn't my idea in the first place." A sudden expression of horror washed across his face, draining it of color. "My God! You don't think anyone will think this is my idea, do you?"

"Excuse me?"

"Our friends. The people at the office." He reached out and touched his laptop, lightly brushing his fingers across the cold plastic security blanket. "It wouldn't be fair if they think I did this to you. After the accident and all."

"Maybe we could put a statement in the paper, explaining it for them, sort of an official separation-Gregory absolution announcement."

"Don't be flippant. You may not care, but I have a career, a reputation in the community to consider."

"Oh, I doubt if our living in separate houses is going to lead to the downfall of modern civilization." Lord, what a drama queen he was turning out to be. "The Dow probably won't crash down around your ears over this. Even with Alan Greenspan gone, I think the economy will survive our little trauma."

"People will talk though," he said importantly. "There will be gossip."

"If Brad and Jen and Angelina lived through it, so can we."

"I just want things to be handled the best way."

"Whatever Gregory." My patience was wearing transparently thin. "Do we have to keep talking? We're giving me a headache."

"There's no need to keep sniping at each other," he said, flipping open his faithful computer and punching the power button, signaling the end of the discussion. "I'll take care of the financial things on my end and you can send me the bills."

"I want to handle my own bills, thanks. I'll need some money to get started."

"Have it your own way, then." His attention was already back on the screen. "You have the passbook to your trust fund and your checking account in your desk. What else do you need for now?"

"Nothing. Nothing at all."

I didn't look back to see if he was listening. Instead I walked slowly out of the room and headed for my desk, a desk I had never bothered to explore further than the Rolodex and address book. Don't run, I ordered myself. Don't look too eager.

I may have speeded up a bit when I was sure I was out of his sight, but it wasn't exercise that made my heart beat so hard when I had the bankbooks in my fingers and skimmed the paperwork. All in my name—well, all in Jennifer Strickland's name—numbers with lots of zeros following them, even by Dallas standards, lots of zeros.

"Thank you, Jennifer, honey, wherever you are," I whispered. "We can kiss that bozo goodbye. We're rich!"

CHAPTER TWELVE

Being rich makes coming back from the dead so much easier. I don't remember what Cotton Claymore was worth, and I doubt I was poor, even then, but for sure I wasn't this kind of go-for-a-Big-Mac-in-Paris-if-the-mood-strikes-me rich. A talk with my banker—I have my own banker—cleared up a lot of questions about all those zeros in Jennifer's passbooks.

John Allen White was born to be a banker. Really. His father and grandfather were bankers and had established an empire for him to run. There was probably a genetic predisposition to understanding spreadsheets and interest rates. One of those genes that have a linkage to thinning hair and the ability to wear a two thousand-dollar suit without looking self-conscious.

John seemed to find it odd at first that I needed him to explain everything about my accounts, but a fragile blonde with a story about a dreadful car accident and an imminent divorce made him very chatty and very eager to keep me happy. He was the modern incarnation of chivalry, patiently giving financial advice, offering to take me to lunch if I had further questions and promising his help in any way short of detailing my car. I'm sure the possibility of me moving all those zeros out of his vault never crossed his mind, but I think I could have gotten a toaster out of the conversation if I'd asked for one.

* * *

The next few days were a whirlwind of shopping that would have made Jennifer and all her old North Dallas shopping buddies proud. Clothes, dishes, furniture—all bought in a frenzy that left me exhausted and had American Express calling to make sure I was the one authorizing the purchases. The amount didn't faze them; the stores weren't the kind of places they were used to seeing, I guess. Jennifer had been more of a designer-driven buyer than I was now, but I had a lot of fun.

Moving back into an old life isn't quite as easy as moving into a new home, but there are similarities. I didn't know where all the pieces in my head fit together or if they would ever really fit together any more than I knew how the furniture I ordered would work in my new apartment. Oh well, sometimes you have to jump in and let all the details take care of themselves.

I did love the new place though. It was big and airy, faintly industrial in design with exposed venting pipes in the kitchen and tall windows that looked down from the second-floor balcony onto the green trees of Lee Park. The furniture I found was funky and mostly modern Italian—curvy sofas and tables chosen as much for the fun of the shapes and colors as their function. Not a speck of beige in the place.

I loaded up on plants too. Palms for the balcony and inside, a virtual garden of green and flowering baskets. The house in North Dallas didn't harbor so much as a silk philodendron. Maybe plants required some sort of commitment to nurture that the marriage couldn't support. Maybe Gregory had allergies. Who knew? Tending the plants made me feel alive as I watered and touched them. Good enough reason for me.

Gregory would absolutely hate this apartment, would look down his aristocratic nose at the lack of elegance. I glanced around and smiled. Yes, it was perfect.

And wouldn't Gregory have a fit if any of his friends found out his soon-to-be-ex-wife, no matter how crazy I am, lived in such a neighborhood? Though it was in an expensive complex on Turtle Creek, the building itself was a little seedy, a few blocks from the newer and trendier high-rises that were becoming the rage. It was a stone's throw from all the gay bars and eclectic stores and strip shopping center restaurants.

It was perfectly acceptable for North Dallasites to come downtown to eat at the famous Mansion on Turtle Creek or to have drinks and a night of fun at one of the hot restaurants strung up and down McKinney Avenue, but when the news got out that I was living in a rented apartment in Oak Lawn, Gregory would die of embarrassment.

His pride had taken a hit with the separation, and he was playing wounded husband to the hilt. I don't think he had been invited out for drinks and golf so much in years. I'm sure there was lots of male bonding and shrewd advice on the best divorce lawyers and suggestions for second-wife choices. Most of his pals had plenty of experience in that area.

It was important for me not to take anything from the house I had shared with him—nothing that ended up in my new apartment, that is. I had no intention of leaving it or throwing it all away though. The movers must have thought I was crazy, but they didn't say a word—just loaded all the stuff into the truck and delivered it directly to the warehouse for Outreach Oaklawn's donation center. It offered me a backdoor entry into Cotton's old world, coming in as a wealthy benefactor, wanting to give items for redressing, reselling, restoring.

A short, square woman with short-cut silver hair and a no-nonsense attitude met us at the ramp to the back door, clipboard in hand.

"Hold on a minute before you guys start unloading all this stuff." She motioned for the workmen to stand back and looked at me, astute enough to have picked the person in charge to interrogate. "Looks like you hijacked half of Highland Park here. Sure you got the right address?" I got the once-over, ending with a growl of grudging acceptance. "So's this your loot?"

"Mine to dispose of, let's say."

"Let's keep it simple and just say it's yours. Okay lady?"

"Okay. I'd like to donate everything here to the Outreach. And I would like to volunteer to work a few days a week as well."

"Doin' what?"

"Whatever needs doing."

"Uh-huh." Another sharp-eyed head-to-toe before looking me straight in the eyes. "And I'm betting you have a lot of on-the-job experience?"

"Just because I'm rich doesn't mean I'm helpless," I said, not letting her buffalo me with the sarcasm. "Or stupid."

"Never thought you looked stupid. We don't get too many volunteers from your part of town. At least not without a charity ball and press coverage."

"I live four blocks from here, and all my ball gowns seem to be in this truck." I stuck my hands in the pockets of my too-new jeans and gave her my best bluff of street-tough. "Sorry the press isn't following me today, but unless I need a note from the society page editor to file or clean, I'm still here to help."

"No," she said, only the dull red on her cheekbones acknowledging her rudeness. "Okay." She wiped her hand on the rear of her pants before sticking it out to me. "We always need free help around here. I'm Molly Rayner." Her hand was as square as the rest of her and callused, but her grip was surprisingly gentle. "They keep me out here because my manners are a little unpolished." A lopsided smile transformed her from gruff to halfway charming. "Maybe more than a little today."

"Jennifer Strickland."

"Nice to meet you, Ms. Strickland."

"No," I responded too quickly. "Strickland is about to be out of date, so just call me…my name…"

While Molly stood looking at me, a polite social nod caught in expectant waiting mode, I was at a total loss as to what to say. I had a new chance at life—a new identity—and damned if I wanted to spend the rest of it as Jennifer Strickland or Jennifer Anything for that matter. Jennifer was a name for a social type, a country clubber, Gregory's wife.

"Not Ms. Strickland. You can call me J.C." It was a spur-of-the-minute decision—J.C. for Jennifer Catherine. "J.C. Winters." Winters for Jennifer's late parents. A little bow for all those zeros in the bankbook. And C. for Cotton, for me.

"J.C. it is then." Molly christened me, giving my new name a solid welcome into the world as she printed it on her clipboard. It was official now. "You'll need to check in at the front office and let them assign you wherever they need help most. Ask for Aggie Burke." She turned back to the guys loitering by the truck and motioned for them to start unloading. "See you around, J.C.," she said without another look in my direction. "Thanks for all the loot."

I turned to go, smart enough to know when I was dismissed. It stung a little, being casually brushed off from the place I'd spent so many years in as Cotton, but I welcomed the discomfort. It meant I was remembering some of the feelings of my old life. Every day a bit more.

Even if I didn't remember Molly, I had no doubt her reactions would have been different if I were in my old body. Yes, I thought smugly. I would bet big money Molly wouldn't have been so cocky if her old boss had been standing nearby.

"C'mon, fellas, let's get cranking." Molly's voice was loud enough I knew she meant it to carry. "Move these boxes inside. I want to get first pick of the ball gowns. I really hope there's something with bugle beads."

That's a bet I would have lost.

CHAPTER THIRTEEN

When I met Aggie Burke for the first time, I felt as if we had been friends for years—which as it turns out, we had. This time around, she was the first person I actually remembered on sight since my accident.

First of all, it was weird walking into Outreach Oaklawn. I felt I should know what to expect, but there was no rush of fond memories washing over me as I pulled open the front door. There were so many interviews and articles about my determination to get funds and get it opened, how it was my creation, that I fully believed it would feel familiar. No such luck.

The huge old building had been a warehouse at one time and still had that kind of urban sprawl ambiance. The bottom story of floor space was divided roughly into an unsymmetrical four areas. At the front entrance were office cubicles with the requisite chairs, desks and computers where three women were working, talking on the phones and typing. A couple of rambunctious little boys were playing tag around the desks, having a grand old time.

To the left of the offices was a storeroom, outfitted like a small general mercantile, rows of canned goods, diapers and formula prominently displayed. A few people were choosing items and pushing shopping carts. And, in a surreal touch, a wizened old lady in overalls was standing atop a ladder swabbing the things on a top shelf with a giant pink feather duster. She was singing at the top of her lungs, a really not-bad rendition of "Chain of Fools." It echoed through the air, bouncing off the walls before being absorbed in the vast main building.

Right in the center of the Outreach was the largest part of the ground floor area, a kitchen and dining area with several long rows of tables. To one side was a long row of countertop filled with bins of silverware, trays of plastic drinking glasses, paper napkins and big metal bowls piled high with apples, oranges and bananas. Two large glass-front coolers held cans of juices and bottles of milk and water. No one was in the cafeteria's eating area, but I could see people working in the kitchen, and an aroma of what smelled like beef stew permeated the air.

The section farthest to my right was a colorfully painted and brightly lit expanse filled with game tables and sports equipment. A jungle gym, a tent with mesh sides filled with multicolored plastic balls, a couple of pool tables, an air hockey table and one lonely old Foosball table. Along one side was a row of slightly out of vogue arcade games. *Ms. Pacman! Centipede!* Okay, I'll admit it; I think I could live here.

The showpiece of the whole place was in the far back corner—a full-court basketball gym with high gloss wooden floors! And in midair doing a layup was Aggie Burke. My heart lurched so hard it hurt. Aggie my God. Aggie.

Pride of the Texas Tech Lady Red Raiders. Six feet of brawny, black woman, built like you carved her out of ebony wood and strong as four cups of espresso. And—may I mention it again? —that fabulous layup.

"Sister shoots—sister scores!" I shouted.

The words were out before I knew I was going to yell them. Aggie Burke spun around, sending the ball banging off the rim. Her eyes scanned the room, paused briefly on me, then moved on, looking for someone else, someone who always yelled those words, looking but not finding. Then back at me. Her black eyes weren't friendly as she covered the distance between us in impossibly long strides.

"Who are you calling sister?" she growled.

I knew there was no way I should say it, but I couldn't stop myself. The answer came of its own volition.

"Did I say 'sister?' I meant sissy." That was the drill between us—between Cotton and Aggie. I knew better than to say it, but it was automatic. "Or something like that." No backing out of it; she made a noise in the back of her throat that had me taking a backward step.

"Wrong answer." Aggie towered above me, her face a mixture of emotions. Shock. Disbelief. A touch of fear. Dismissal of possibility. "Where did you hear that? Why are you here? And who the hell are you?"

"A basketball game a long time ago. Molly Rayner sent me." I took a deep breath and stuck out my hand. "And my name is J.C. Winters."

She glared at me, ignoring my outstretched hand.

"Never heard of you. What are you doing here?"

"Volunteering. Reporting to you."

"Volunteering for what?"

"Whatever you need me for."

"You might want to rephrase that." She stepped back and circled around me, checking me from all angles. "I might want something not on the menu."

"Oh, for God's sake, this isn't a pickup joint. I'm here to work." I rolled my eyes at her and shook my head. "Besides, I'm not your type. I have you more pegged as liking something a little more voluptuous and a lot more kinky."

"And how do you know my type any better than you knew that sister-sissy shit?" She was nervous again; her eyes went all narrow and suspicious. "There is some very spooky stuff going down here. Have we met before?"

"Possibly. A long time ago."

"Nah. I'd remember anyone as mouthy as you." She shook her head, puzzling the connection over in her mind. "I don't know what it is, but I can almost swear I know you."

"*Déjà vu* maybe."

"Too much like voodoo for my liking," she said. "Still…"

"Yes still." I smiled and held out my hand again. "You might as well shake it and get used to it. Aggie, you and I are going to be good friends and there is nothing on earth you can do about it."

"That so?" she asked. "I lost a friend a while ago who told me the same thing when we first met. You ain't a bug on her ass, but there's something about you makes me think you might be right." She took my hand in hers, enveloping it. "So you're here to work?"

"I am."

"Can you type?"

"Only if speed and accuracy aren't important."

"File?"

"I know the alphabet."

"So what's your specialty? You cook?"

"No. Not if you want people to actually eat it."

"You clean?"

"If that's my only choice."

"Lord woman. What are you trained to do?"

"My degree says art history." I grinned. "And if you need someone to shop, I have very good references."

"I'll check and see if we have an opening in that department." She scoffed, but she was thawing out a little. "Okay. I'll give you a tour and then we'll talk hours and pay."

"Just about any hours. No pay."

"What's with that? Are you one of those rich uptown white chicks down here to do good?"

"That's my story." I was smiling as I followed her out of the gym. "You have something against rich uptown white chicks?"

"Don't go messing with me, Ms. J.C. Winters," she warned. "You have no idea who you're dealing with."

"I think I do, for a change, Aggie." My heart was banging inside my chest. "It may be a one-time thing, but I think I do."

CHAPTER FOURTEEN

My first week at the Outreach was like coming home late at night and finding someone has moved your furniture around and unscrewed all the lightbulbs. You know it's your place, but you keep knocking things over and running face first into walls.

I no longer wondered if I was Cotton Claymore. I just wasn't sure how it happened that I now lived in Jennifer Strickland's body. Not that all my memories were back—far from it. Details were a blur of maybe and maybe not, and the big picture was so out of focus I sometimes doubted my sanity.

My sanity! What a joke. Most people in my shape were in locked wards or had so many happy pills on board, they might as well be locked up. My therapists would be kicked out of the club if their colleagues had any idea they were going along with my delusions.

And yet, all that said, I'm a happy camper. Every day I wake up in my happy space—surrounded by color and a closet full of blue jeans. Yesterday, I walked into a tiny hair salon and came out with outsides that matched my insides. After two grueling hours of burning peroxide hell and flying shears, my hair is as blond as Cotton Annie's was at six years of age, cut in a short tousled mop that requires several different types of what my stylist kept calling "product."

"I bet I can't get it to look like this tomorrow."

"Sure you can, sweetie. Just layer in enough product and it will practically do itself."

And it almost does. I like it. And I got my ears pierced—twice. No metal bars or skull and crossbones, just a little row of silver rings above my North Dallas diamond studs. Aggie says nothing and shakes her head at me, but she grins. Of course, Aggie grins a lot anyway.

I have to fight the urge to follow her like a homeless baby duck. I can't help it if she's the first thing I imprinted on. She makes me feel safe. And tired. I am her personal gofer. She took me to heart when I told her what a great shopper I am. She had no way of knowing I was totally bluffing. Nor is she ever going to know.

I've put more miles on the Beamer in a week than since I got it new three months ago. I'm thinking of trading it in on something more practical. And I've decided to buy a couple of pickups or vans for the Outreach if I can figure out a way to do it without leaving any of my fingerprints on the deal. It's bad enough being seen as a rich dilettante. It would be worse if I actually started throwing money around.

The navigation system in my car is so simple that even with my battered brain I can find my way around. Trust me, Aggie has sent me all the way to and from anywhere and back. I've picked up donations and delivered mystery bags to some areas of town I never knew existed. Well, maybe I used to know, but that's part of the blurry stuff.

I've been asked to pick up people a couple of times. Once it was a terrified middle-aged woman who met me on a street corner with only her purse and the clothes on her back. That and an angry welt darkening her cheekbone. I didn't know what to say. She didn't talk much either, but I felt good when we got back to the Outreach and she had a safe bed to sleep in for a while.

The second floor of the Outreach is residential, small and clean bedrooms and bathrooms like a big nice health club. Not the Ritz, but no one has to feel like they are in a flophouse or smelly charity ward. Security is unobtrusive, but omnipresent. Aggie isn't the only strong-arm in the place, and not to my surprise, martial arts classes are always cram-packed full.

I go home most nights so tired I actually hurt. This is the kind of exercise Marybeth pays a personal trainer to inflict. I've found a great little Thai restaurant off Lemmon Avenue that I get takeout from half the week. Luckily there's an equally good Mexican food place across the street for the other nights. As far as I can figure, neither of my alter egos can cook worth a damn.

Neither can Jennifer's cousin. At least that was his excuse for meeting me in a restaurant, if the little diner we ended up in qualified for the title. Red plastic booths, paper napkins— sounds a lot more charming than it turned out to be.

After at least ten messages left on my answering machine, I finally decided to agree to lunch, if only to keep him from turning up on my doorstep. Over a plate of rather nasty pasta, Dewayne got right to the point. I knew there had to be some reason for his persistence; there turned out to be about two hundred and fifty thousand reasons.

"Two hundred fifty *thousand* dollars? Let me get this straight." I wished he would stop staring at me although I didn't expect my little makeover to go unnoticed. Other than a theatrical wolf whistle, he'd had no reaction other than the inability to stop looking at my hair every few minutes. "I promised to give you this money for what reason?"

"You just wanted to give me a little start-up capital. You've always been a very generous person, Jenny." He was oilier and more obsequious than I remembered the other day, not so much oozing charm as leaving a slime trail. "Don't you remember telling me since Uncle Jack and Aunt Belle died, you wanted to help me since I was your only family?"

"Sorry I don't."

"Yeah, you and I were hanging out and right out of the blue, you told me you'd decided to reach out to your family. You know—since you and Gregory didn't have any kids or anything. You could have knocked me over with a feather. You always were so sweet to me, ever since we were kids, but this was too much. That's what I said. And you said 'I want you to have it, Dewayne. We're family.' I couldn't believe it!"

"I know the feeling." This guy was too much. "When exactly was this, Dewayne? I'm having trouble recalling—head injury, you know."

He toyed with the paper napkin, rolling it into a cylinder then flattening it out again. Too nervous.

"Oh wait," I said. "Was it last Christmas? At the club? I have a vague recollection…"

"That's right, Jenny. Now that you mention it, I believe it was then."

"And I just wanted to give you this money, no strings attached?" The bastard was a liar. I could have made up any time and he'd have agreed. I had a hard time believing Jennifer had been softheaded about this con of a cousin. Or that Gregory had agreed to it. For sure any cash giveaway over a buck had to go through him.

"Out of the kindness of my heart?" I knew Jennifer was loaded, but a quarter of a mill was a very generous gesture. "That was right before my accident. Gregory must have forgotten to take care of it with all the chaos."

"Well, this was just between you and me. Gregory and I never exactly hit it off, you know. You said it was none of his business."

"Strange, I don't recall that part." Because it never happened, I'd be willing to bet. My brain was banged up, but my instincts still caught a whiff of rat. "I'll give him a call and see what the holdup is."

"I thought you two had split," he said quickly. "I heard you weren't even living together anymore."

"We've separated, but you know he's still counting the pennies." I didn't know what his game was, but Cousin Dewayne was pulling Jennifer's leg. "How did you know I've moved? Matter of fact, how did you get my new number? It's unlisted."

"Some woman at the old number gave it to me when I called there. I think it was the maid."

The problem was, the maid couldn't have given him my number. Even Gregory didn't have it.

"Mmm." I was ready to get away from here. They say we all have a funny uncle or two, but I was starting to think my cousin was more than a little bit on the shady side—he was a liar for sure. "I'll check into things and get back to you. Where are you staying?"

"Here and there."

"Excuse me?"

"Traveling," he said. "I'm kinda on the move and in and out, you know. It'll be easier if I call you. Or I can drop by for the check and you can show me your new place."

You bet—when my friend Marybeth shops at Walmart. Jennifer may have truly loved Dewayne, but he was beginning to make the hairs on my neck prickle.

"I'm on the move and in and out a lot myself lately." I slid out of the plastic-covered booth and edged my way toward the door before he could get up. "Just leave a message and I'll get back to you. Thanks for lunch."

* * *

As a result of my horrible lunch, I was starving by the time I met Aggie at Uncle Julio's for dinner. In the few minutes she took to wash up, I emptied half a basket of tortilla chips and most of the salsa. The waiter swooped by and refilled them with a smile. I was glad to look like less of a pig with the refill. I picked up a chip and nibbled on it delicately as I waited for Aggie.

The woman is definitely a player. Basketball? Bona fide champion. Pool? Did you ever see Paul Newman in *The Hustler?* Poker? Just go ahead and give her your paycheck. In every sense of the word, Aggie knew how to play. I watched her work the room, stopping to talk to half a dozen women as she made her way back from the bathroom. She left them all smiling. Player.

"You amaze me, Aggie."

"How's that?" She handed me a frosted mug filled with the house specialty—a frozen margarita swirled with sangria.

"How do you make it to work every morning when you play so hard every night? I can barely move after staying out so late."

"That's because you've been stuck playing housekeeper for some old dude and I've been in training escorting fine, feisty women to dinner."

"You don't know what you're talking about. I'm nobody's housekeeper. Besides, I don't play for that team anymore."

"Ho-ho!" Aggie burst out laughing. "Since when? And how do you know anyway? What secrets are you holding out on me?"

Good grief, I didn't want to have this conversation. There was no way I could begin to explain to Aggie how a person like Jennifer became J.C. No way I could explain I was her old friend Cotton stuck in the body of a known heterosexual. My only option was to change the subject.

"We all have our secrets, Aggie," I said, arching a brow in faux intrigue. "I'll tell you when I've had more to drink. A lot more." I took the world's tiniest sip. "How many of those women are you stringing along at the same time?"

"No strings J.C. I love them all a little. That's the problem." She laughed. "I just don't love any of them a lot."

"Oh, come on now. You aren't nearly the hard-ass you want everyone to think you are. Haven't you ever seen true love?"

"I've seen it, but not up close and personal." She looked across the room and returned the wave of a red-haired admirer.

"Don't you want to find true love someday?" I teased.

"No way." Her face was still and all the laughter went away. "The last time I saw true love, it got my best friend murdered."

CHAPTER FIFTEEN

Whoosh! My hearing vaporized. I could still see people in the room, moving their lips, smiles stretched silently over pearly white teeth. I could feel the planet spinning like my head was spinning. Aggie was looking into the past, so lost in memory that I don't think she noticed the world pulse out of sync then jarringly slam back into balance. Whoosh! A chaotic din of noise and the sound was back on.

"Who was killed?" I reached across and grabbed her arm hard enough to make her flinch. "Who was killed and what does love have to do with it?" I started to laugh, a little hysteria kicking in. "Forget how I said that. I know that's a Tina Turner song."

"You're white as a sheet." Aggie pried my fingers off her arm and held them in hers. "Your hands are like ice. Don't you go fainting on me."

My laughter stopped in a strangled hiccup.

"I'm all right. Tell me. Who died?"

"We can talk about that later." She got to her feet and threw a couple of large bills on the table. "Let me get you out of here."

"I want you to tell me what you were talking about. I want to know—"

"Not until we get somewhere quiet and you settle down." Aggie's voice was implacable. "Come on."

Aggie half-led, half-dragged me from the restaurant. From the looks we were getting, I'm sure everyone thought I had been overserved. I couldn't have cared less what they thought.

It was like being smothered under a steamy, wet blanket when we stepped out of the cool central air conditioning into the Texas heat. A hundred degrees at midnight still. I was hardly able to catch my breath from shock, and the thick air wasn't helping.

"Aggie please tell me."

"This is hardly the place for a conversation like this," Aggie muttered, glancing around to see if we had an audience.

"The short version," I begged. "Please."

"Short and simple then. My best friend Cotton met the love of her life. Jo was married to a man who wasn't impressed by true love—"

"Jo? You know Jo?" Whoosh-whoosh. Reverberation. "You know who Jo is!" That's when the lights went out.

I am enveloped in the blanket. Not hot and suffocating anymore. Glistening and glowing and safe. The fog is back...lovely, lovely mystery mist.

Here—in this nowhere place—I am safe, no echoing chaos, no confusion. I am home, and I think I'll stay. Voices without words, without the need for words, whisper encouragement.

I am surrounded. I am embraced. I am welcomed without condition. As I immerse myself in the bliss and prepare to let go of it all, a tiny sliver of reservation insinuates itself into my consciousness.

To my surprise, even here, wherever and whenever here is, there are decisions to be made. Not everyone wants me to stay.

Voices whisper encouragement, promise absolution, grant permission. Yes I'm staying here. Safe here. I'm tired of all the confusion. I don't want it anymore.

Out of the sibilant yeses, one voice says, "Wait."

I recognize that voice. Secrets told. Bargains made. Jennifer.

"I waited for you when you called," she said in a voice that was a wordless sigh. "I gave you what I no longer required. You owe me."

"Jennifer? Jennifer Strickland from Dallas?"

"I was."

"How did I get here?"

"We have a link, you and I. Your connection to your new body is still fragile. You come in dreams too sometimes." The chorus of others was like white noise when we spoke—vibrating and ebbing and flowing around us like a current. "We are connected by a promise."

"What promise? I don't know what you want."

"You will in time. Earth time is a blink here; when the time is right you will give me what I need. Now or later, no matter."

"And then?"

"Then I can finish what I need to do to be free again. I will wait for our bargain to be fulfilled. Then we won't be connected any longer."

"Isn't heaven beyond deals?"

"It may be. I'll know for sure when I get there."

"This isn't heaven? Where am I?"

The fog grew a little colder at my confusion, not quite so filled with nurture. The voices without voices receded a bit, their messages less distinct.

"There's no name or map for this place. It is a layover. A place where all souls wait for…whatever comes next."

"I don't remember the bargain. Your brain was injured."

"You needed to be alive, so you needed a body. To find Jo. To find your killer."

"I get that part." There was a faint pulling sensation, as if a drain had opened and I was water being sucked into a whirlpool. "I don't know what you wanted from me."

"I was crippled there. Tied to a situation I didn't have the courage to leave."

"Gregory?"

"I loved him, I'm sorry to say. He took my resolve. I was trying to leave him before the accident—I was trying because of all I discovered."

"Why didn't you? He's no prize."

"No, he was a traitor. And I did leave him. That's why I'm here." The fog sighed sadly at her answer. "I was not a strong person. I had a lesson to learn. It was an expensive lesson."

"If you died to get away from him, what am I supposed to do?"

"Help me make it right."

"I can't even remember my own life. How can I help you?"

"It will happen when time is finished. You'll find what you need to know. I can see more from where I am than you can from where you are."

"But we're in the same place." And as I said it, I knew it wasn't so. "I can't stay, can I?"

"You aren't ready to be here, yet. You aren't through." Gentle and with a smile that was everywhere. "You can't take back all you learned here. Just enough." The voices were fading as I fell. "You're passing through—you aren't here now."

"J.C. wake up! What the hell are you tryin' to do here, girl?"

There were a million stars sparkling in the hot, black sky, still spinning ever so slightly as I looked up at them from the steps of the restaurant. The concrete was burning through the back of my shirt, and the air was greasy with the odor of fried tortillas. My head was woozy, but evidently my hearing was fine.

Aggie Burke was bellowing at me as she knelt beside me, supporting my head in the cradle of one of her big hands, holding it as easily as a basketball. With her other hand she was trying to dial her cell phone, not very successfully.

"God damnit, if you don't wake up, I'm going to dial 911."

She cursed again, then switched to thanking God I was alive when I opened my eyes and tried to sit up. The thankfulness was a short-lived phase.

"What kind of shit is this, J.C.?"

"Sorry."

"Sorry is not enough, not by a long damn shot."

"It's not like I fainted on purpose, is it? I didn't mea—" The memory hit me square between the eyes, with enough force to rock the world again.

"You were talking about Jo." Joy and fear fought for ownership of my voice. "Is she okay?"

"Yeah I guess." Aggie didn't look too friendly in the glare of the pink neon sign illuminating the outer steps into the restaurant. "The question is, how do you know Jo? And why did talking about Cotton and Jo make you turn into mush?"

"I'll try to explain later," I swore, not meaning it for even a second. "Tell me about Jo and I'll explain everything." The promise was a lie, point blank. I didn't know the truth, myself. No way I could make this make sense to anyone. "Where is Jo?"

"I don't think you are in any position—literally—to be having this conversation."

She had a point, I had to admit, as I lay on the steps. My head wasn't clear yet either. I was having little flashes of something downright strange; whispery little voices in the back of my mind—or what was left of the back of my mind.

"Let me get you home," Aggie said. "I'll drive you and we can pick up your car tomorrow."

"And you'll tell me about Jo."

"We'll talk about Jo and Cotton," she promised, not too kindly. "Yes indeed. We are so going to have that conversation."

CHAPTER SIXTEEN

It was a rocky night. Some people pass out from too much alcohol. I think I went down from too much reality in too short a time. All the pain of a bad drunk without any of the fun.

Aggie hadn't spared time on the niceties of admiring my apartment.

"You feeling all right now? Need a glass of water or anything?" she asked in a tone that suggested she didn't really want to know either answer. She settled me on the biggest, cushiest chair in the room. "J.C., I have a simple question: What in all hell is going on with you?"

"I don't know what you mean exactly." I was stalling, hoping for a minor miracle. All I wanted was for her to answer all my questions about Jo and not make me come up with an explanation she wouldn't believe in the first, second or third place. "Just too much alcohol, too much heat. I can't imagine why I fainted."

"Cut the crap." Looking up at her standing over me—way over me—made me glad I remembered she was my friend.

Saying she was "intimidating" at the moment was a polite way of saying she was scary as all get-out. "My momma may have raised an idiot, but it wasn't me. Why did mentioning Cotton and Jo have you fallin' out on me?"

"Will you sit, for God's sake? I'm not quaking in my shoes because of your towering presence. This isn't going to be an easy thing to explain." And man, did I not want to try. "It would make matters so much easier if you would tell me about Jo and let it go at that."

"You think that's likely to happen?"

"I'm thinking no."

"Smart for a blonde. What color are you under all that bleach?" Aggie massaged the back of her neck and stretched it as if it hurt a lot. "You've been riddling me since the day you strolled into the Outreach. Acting like we were old pals. Talkin' like you knew me. Sayin' things you shouldn't know to say."

She plopped down on the ottoman at my feet and laced her fingers together, pointing at me with her forefingers extended like a kid with a pretend cowboy gun.

"You don't know me from Adam."

"I don't know how to explain this so it makes any sense, Ag. Your Baptist upbringing doesn't have any room for what I'm going through."

"My Granny is a Baptist, J.C. I've backslid, as she would put it. Since I figured out I was gay in college, I've accepted the possibility everything might not be covered in the old family Bible." She dropped her still-clasped hands to her lap. "Are you a medium or some such shit? Channeling? I read about that."

"Close enough for now." Why hadn't I thought of that? Psychic abilities are a hot commodity right now. People got to guest star on Montel by being psychics and no one—well, at least not everyone—thought they were crazy. "I have had contact with the other side, now that you mention it."

"Contact with Cotton?" I didn't like the glint in her eyes.

"Among others," I hedged. "You wouldn't know them."

"So it's like that movie with the kid and Bruce Willis? You see dead people too?"

"No, of course not." I understood her sarcasm. "I just kind of hear them or know things they know. Not all of it, just a little sometimes."

"This is nuts," Aggie snorted her disbelief. "If you can talk to Cotton, why are you asking me about Jo? Ask her; she was the expert."

"It's not like that. I can't just ask questions and get a direct reply."

"Tried a Ouija board?"

"Please Aggie. Just tell me about Jo. I need to know. Who is she? Why did Cotton die and not Jo? What's the big secret?"

"Cotton was murdered."

"Yeah, I know about that." I tried to rush her to tell me what I wanted to hear. "I read all that in the paper. I never saw a word about Jo."

"It's funny what the cops do or don't release to the press when famous people want things hushed up."

"Jo's famous?"

"Her husband. Ex-husband now. Max Sealy." She waited for the lightbulb to brighten over my head without reward. "Max Sealy, Baseball Hall of Fame, MVP of the American League three years running?"

"I'm dense, but I don't get the connection."

"Okay. Let me take you through it, really slow."

I nodded, encouraging her to go on, although my stomach was twisting and churning like a television commercial for industrial strength acid reliever. All in all, I decided I much preferred the fainting approach to stressful news.

"Cotton and Jo Sealy were in the middle of a hot affair. Jo was married to former Mr. Baseball, who retired and made a ga-gillion dollars selling cars." She pushed a handful of long, narrow braids back behind her ear. "See how this is not a good idea already?"

Not only could I see it abstractly, a little buzz of Cotton's consciousness was humming back to wakeful mode. A face, not quite recognizable, but dark-haired, materialized in my mind's eye for a split second before blinking out.

"Jo was planning to divorce him so she and Cotton could move in together, but she was scared. He hated queers more than he hated Democrats. She said he'd never let them be together. She was determined not to let Max find out about them before the divorce."

"But then, Jo decided she was being followed, got real paranoid about it." Aggie stood and then sat down again. "Cotton laughed and said it was just a guilty conscience from her sinful ways. Jo said she was sure that she was being followed and insisted someone was watching her. None of us paid her any attention." She paused. "We should have."

"Cotton and Jo were together at the clubs the night of the murder, planning their future together…"

Walking together, hand in hand, laughing. Fog swirling around us. My God, it's us in the dream. It was me and Jo! Then, someone in the fog. A yank and Jo's gone. It was me and Jo.

"He killed Cotton? You think Jo's husband killed Cotton?"

"She was beaten, smashed in the head with a blunt instrument." Aggie looked hollowed out. "He *is* in the Hall of Fame for how well he could swing a bat."

"But what about Jo?"

"I'm not really sure. Her story was that she was zapped with a stun gun and left in the alley."

"You don't sound as if you buy her story."

"Never made that much sense to me. Cotton was real crazy over her, but I had a few doubts myself."

"What kind of doubts?" I didn't like the way this was headed. "I thought Jo was the love of Cotton's life."

"Oh, no doubt about that. Cotton was a goner for real." Aggie shook her head. "Just was never as certain that Jo was totally motivated by true love. I kinda had the idea she liked the parties and the idea of hanging out with the cool kids as much as anything. Sorta strange to make the leap from sports wife groupie to lez chic groupie. 'Course old Max was on the long slide down, if you know what I mean."

"Not really."

"Until he retired, Max Sealy was on every A-list invitation, at every party that counted. Wined and dined and fawned over. But in this town, you get older, retired, a new guy comes along and you start getting moved down the pecking order. You and your pretty little wife. Quite a blow to the ego, don't you think?"

"I bet you didn't share your suspicions with Cotton, did you?" If I was this pissed with half a memory, I'd hate to think about my reaction in the full blush of new infatuation. "You wouldn't have dared."

"You're right about that. I was a coward." She hung her head like a beaten bloodhound. "If I hadn't been such a chickenshit, Cotton might still be alive."

"It wasn't your fault." I felt compelled to comfort her. After all, her guilt would have to be a little less since I wasn't quite as dead as she thought I was. "You knew better than to throw rocks at her girlfriend. It wouldn't have done anything but come between you."

"Yeah, that makes me feel a whole lot better."

"And why didn't this Max kill Jo too? You'd think he would have especially wanted to whack her."

"You've watched enough *Law and Order*," Aggie said. "Who's the usual suspect when a cheating wife is killed?"

"But why wasn't any of this in the paper? Why was there no mention of Jo's attack?" I was outraged. "Why wasn't he arrested?"

"Great questions. Unfortunately, depending on your bias, it was about a couple of lesbians, and no matter how famous you are, priorities aren't the same all over town." Aggie was matter of fact.

"Secondly, it was an open secret in this community that another of Cotton's former girlfriends used to be involved with the lead detective on the case. He never did find any reason to have to tarnish Max's reputation by putting Jo's name in the paper and linking her to such a scandal. Officially, her identity was withheld to insure her safety."

"And is she safe?" My heart was thumping. "Where is she now?"

"We didn't exactly keep in touch. She dropped out of sight." Aggie shrugged. "I guess you could ask Max Sealy. If he was jealous enough to kill someone because of his possessiveness, I'd bet he didn't stop watching her because of a little thing like a divorce."

CHAPTER SEVENTEEN

By the time I made it to Dr. Carey's office at ten, Dallas was shimmering in the heat like a mirage. We were all excited that the weatherman was calling for rain for the next three days, even if it was likely to be accompanied by severe thunderstorms. Tornado watches were so frequent this summer that unless a funnel cloud was closer than five miles away, no one paid too much attention to it. I had an umbrella stashed in the backseat, but so far not a drop of anything except sweat had been seen.

Andrew was a vision in tennis whites, from shirt to shoes, all seemingly chosen as if to accent his beard. I gave him a thumbs-up as I walked in.

"Looking good, Andrew. Nice legs." They were nice for a big man—tanned and surprisingly hard-muscled. "Are you playing in leagues this year?"

"Only as a fill-in," he said ruefully. "My knees are getting bad."

"I'd love to go play at the country club. Nice courts, but since Jennifer never lifted a racquet, it might raise a few eyebrows—if any of them can move an eyebrow with all that Botox."

We were laughing and joking with each other until Dr. Carey put us back in our respective places. Nicely, but with a touch of authority.

"Talk about the inmates running the asylum. The two of you might as well cancel today's session and let me talk to myself." Then she smiled, taking the sting out of the words. "J.C.... it's still hard not to call you Jennifer, sometimes, just out of habit. Although as much as it pains me to admit it, you are becoming more like the Cotton I knew than I can believe. It's really a bit eerie."

"I was wondering about that the other day," I said, reminded of my fleeting thoughts, thoughts that skittered around in my brain only to be forgotten until something triggered them again. "How well did you know Cotton, Dr. Carey?"

"I don't think my relationship with her is important right now." Her face and body language were colder than the air blowing out the central cooling vents. "My concern is with your treatment and well-being."

"Neatly sidestepped," I said. "If you have information you are keeping from me, I think it would help my well-being."

"I'm not going to reinforce the possibility that you are Cotton by filling in the gaps in your memory with my own."

"I'm not asking that. All I want is to know who I am. If you can help me with a few details, is that really asking you to betray your precious code of ethics? Is this code my problem?"

"That is very much the attitude Cotton Claymore would have," Dr. Carey snapped, forgetting her stoic principles in a rare fit of temper. "She had a way of bending the rules to justify anything she wanted, personally or professionally."

"Sounds like you had more than a passing acquaintance with her." I could see it in her eyes, a glimmer of anger that went beyond a casual association. "You knew Cotton pretty well, sounds to me. Why won't you tell me?"

"My relationships aren't part of your therapy," she said, chilling the temperature in the room by ten degrees. "My personal life isn't on the table for discussion."

"When it concerns me, they are. What are you going to say when I remember? Are you going to tell me it's none of my business then?"

"I'm far from convinced that situation is going to happen." She stared at me intently, as if trying to see right into my brain. "Let's just say no matter what the setting, situational ethics are not something I find particularly admirable. But I can understand that sometimes a person has to do whatever is necessary to protect their own interests, even if they have to bend the rules somewhat."

"So I'm an opportunist, a cheat?" I couldn't believe what I was hearing. "You always acted as if it was so important to keep your opinions out of our sessions. Aren't you being a hypocrite to blast me this way?"

"You aren't Cotton!" Dr. Carey was adamant. "I can't continue to foster this delusion."

"And how do you explain this, Dr. Carey? I'm not making up these memories. No one, not even you, could make that make sense."

"I am sorry." She looked truly miserable. "I have no answers and it's difficult for me to keep a clear and unbiased distance. Maybe you should consider another therapist."

"Right," I said, not hiding my disdain. "You know what would happen if I tried telling this to anyone else. Like it or not, the three of us are too involved to consider such an idiotic idea as a new shrink. You guys are all I have."

"That being said, let's stop all this and get back to the business at hand." After sitting and listening in silence, Andrew pulled the plug on the little tempest by acting as if it were totally irrelevant. "Any new memory breakthroughs?" Andrew studied me as he spoke. "Something's changed since we saw you last. I can see it in your face and in the way you move."

"I've had a few breakthroughs this week. I got a job. I met an old friend I recognized. I found who Jo is. And..." I paused for effect; I admit it. "I think I found who murdered me."

The next hour was a blur of who and why and when, followed by gentle admonishments and dire warnings of danger. When

I told them of my plan to meet Max Sealy, they both lost their professional cool and started lecturing me like I was their not-too-bright teenage daughter who was dating the neighborhood sex offender. I felt lucky when I got out of there without being grounded for the whole week.

* * *

Max Sealy Motors was visible for a mile as drivers approached it on LBJ Freeway. An American flag half the size of a football field whipped in the stiffening breeze. Hundreds of luxury cars filled the lot, waxed until they gleamed and lined up like a phalanx of parade tanks in Red Square.

As soon as I pulled up to the showroom/sales office, I was welcomed by a salesman who opened my door the instant I turned off the engine. He appeared so quickly it was like having your own magic genie materialize to be at your service. Like that, except you needed to buy a car to keep the genie happy.

"Where would I find Max Sealy? Is he here today?"

"Why don't you and I look around and see if we can make you a deal?" The car genie wore a plastic badge identifying him as Tony. "Mr. Sealy doesn't handle direct sales on the lot."

"Good, because I'm not interested in buying a car off the lot."

"You don't want to buy a car?" The light in Tony's eyes went to power-saver mode. I could see I had lost him. "Check with the receptionist. She'll know if he's here or not." And the genie melted away into the multicolored maze of cars—poof—without giving me even one wish.

The receptionist was more helpful. Nelda—this according to the name tag on her more-than-ample, impossibly round left breast—was obviously a member of the Big Hair faith. Former Governor Ann Richards had summed it up saying in Texas we believed the bigger the hair, the closer to God. Nelda was knocking on heaven's door. She paged Mr. Sealy and announced that he had a guest waiting for him at the front desk.

Two minutes passed. I spent the time watching two cars spinning on giant lazy Susans. How did they get them in here?

I wondered. I looked around, but didn't see a doorway large enough to get a car through. Maybe they had the cars first and built the showroom around them. Before I could decipher the secrets of the automotive universe, I saw someone who could only be Max Sealy striding toward me.

He was handsome or had been forty pounds and ten years ago. He had that athlete gone to fat look that came from too many rib eye dinners at Del Frisco's and too few days in the gym. Blond hair, now shot through with gray, was offset by a tan that was an announcement of hours spent on the golf course.

He didn't look like a killer. He looked like someone's favorite rich, middle-aged uncle. It was hard to imagine jovial Uncle Max in the kind of bloody rage it would have taken to beat an unarmed woman to death.

"Max Sealy. Just call me Max." All run together and obviously practiced. "And you are?" His hand was outstretched ten seconds before he got close enough to shake mine.

"Jennifer Strickland." I shook hands and gave him the name that would have the most clout in his world. It was convenient to have the use of the name to grease the wheels of commerce.

"Any relation to Gregory Strickland?" Max was a schmoozer, expert at filing away names and making connections. Any good salesman likes to make his patsy feel a sense of connection— harder to say no that way. "Played golf with Gregory at the club a few weeks ago. Nice guy."

"My soon-to-be-ex-husband," I said pleasantly. "Not that nice."

"Might not have been the same fellow," he covered. "Now that I think about it, I think this guy's name was Reggie, not Gregory. Kind of a strange coincidence, thinking it was Gregory and that's your ex's name."

"Yeah isn't it strange?"

"Right. Now what kind of car can we help you with?"

"I don't know much about cars." I said, not needing to play dumb. Either I really don't know much about cars or that memory hadn't resurfaced yet.

"Well, lucky day for you." He laughed, sounding amused even if he was buttering up a potential client. "I know almost everything about cars. How can I help you?"

"I need to buy two pickups and two vans. Top of the line. Could you have them ready to deliver by this afternoon?"

"No problem, Ms. Strickland. Let's go into my office and we'll get the financing paperwork out of the way."

"I don't want to finance them. I'll have my banker call and set up the funds transfer."

He was more than surprised. He was openly delighted. No bargain hunting, no haggling. I could imagine him in his weekly staff meeting, explaining that this was why he owned the dealership instead of working for commission like the rest of them.

Now it was time to find out what I came here for.

"It's been so easy working with you, Max." I made a show of finding my banker's business card in my wallet. "By the way, speaking of strange coincidences, how is your lovely wife, Jo?" The lie flowed easily from my lips. I think I have a real knack for deception.

"We worked together on a volunteer project last year to raise money for the pediatric wing at the hospital," I continued. "She was fabulous to deal with. I have another fundraiser coming up next spring. I'd love to have her help us out again this year."

"We're divorced," he said bluntly, then put his anything-for-a-four-car-sale face back on. "But Jo loves to be of help as long as the project ends up getting her picture in the society pages. Just kidding." He obviously wasn't. "She's always willing to help if the price is right. She lives in Las Colinas now." He didn't look happy chatting with a stranger about his estranged wife, but cash sales softened the pain. "Keesling Consulting. She went back to her old name. She's listed in the Yellow Pages."

"Thank you. Maybe I'll give her a call."

I was ready to get out of his little world. The longer I was around him, the more I had a vague sense of foreboding or perhaps a flashback of a night not that long ago when I was powerless against his rage. I had no memory of it, but Aggie was convinced. Whatever it was, there was something about him that made me sure we had met before. Of course, he was a celebrity who had been on television all the time. Maybe I was projecting my fear onto his famous face.

"I would like these cars delivered anonymously, with the title made out to the recipient. I don't want my identity revealed under any circumstances. Is that clear and acceptable?"

"Absolutely."

"Please have them delivered to Outreach Oaklawn." He didn't make a sound, but there was a change in him, maybe only in the rhythm of his breathing. "Is that a problem?"

"No problem."

I smiled at him, imagining how it would make him feel to see his automobiles given to a place founded by someone he hated so much.

"No problem at all."

I liked seeing him lying through his teeth. Lying and murder and greed, oh my. He was racking up hard time in the world of what goes around comes around.

No matter how much I wanted him to get what he deserved, I felt a little dishonest. Ultimately, I decided to enjoy the situation. After all, Max's bad karma was not my fault. At least not directly. At least I don't think it was.

CHAPTER EIGHTEEN

"Gregory Strickland is waiting for me to join him."

The young waiter checked his seating chart and asked me to follow him. We threaded our way through the crowded restaurant, past the fake Italian frescos and stenciled exposed brick to a linen-draped table in a corner that didn't require outright screaming to be heard.

It was the first time I'd seen Gregory since I moved out of the house in North Dallas, and I found myself looking forward to it in a strange and perverse sort of way. He had always been so smug and superior while I was scarcely able to feed myself. The mental battle now was a bit more evenly matched than he was expecting. This was going to be a lot more fun for me than it was for him.

Gregory was dressed in a pearl-gray summer-weight suit, hair freshly barbered, shoes polished to a gloss. His grooming was as impeccable as that of a model in an ad in *GQ*. He was studying the lunch menu when I walked up, giving me a perfect chance to see his face when he got a look at the new, radically improved Jennifer.

His patronizing expression became one of abject horror as he gave me the once-over, starting at my messy platinum hair and dropping to my Rolling Stones T-shirt, tight jeans and pointy-toed leather boots. In my defense, I did know how to dress—I was wearing a nice, appropriate jacket in spite of the heat. Its taxicab yellow color was a bonus.

I know the term "apoplexy" is somewhat old-fashioned, but it did come to mind.

"Hello Greg." He hated to be called Greg. "Did you order me a glass of wine?" He was still not able to form words, so I looked up at the waiter as he pulled out my chair and said, "I'll have whatever he's having."

I knew whatever Gregory was drinking would be good. Despite his shortcomings, he was an excellent judge of wine. If the Market ever tanked again, with his refined palate and good looks he could work as a sommelier at any number of great restaurants. The job required a certain degree of supercilious snobbery. He also had his own tux.

"My God, Jennifer. What in the world have you done?" I don't think he meant it as a compliment. "You look absolutely… you look nothing like yourself." No, definitely not meant as flattery. "My God," he repeated. "What have you done to yourself?"

"My hair cutter, my colorist and my makeup artist would be horrified to hear that question." I laughed, loving this moment more than anything in recent memory, although that didn't cover a very long time. "It takes nearly a whole village to do a makeover like this."

I stood and did a pirouette, arms on my hips to conserve space in the narrow aisle between the tables. Gregory scarcely glanced at me. He was much more interested in how the other diners were handling my little modeling turn.

"What do you think?" I asked.

"Please sit down," he hissed. "People are watching you."

"Sort of the point of dressing up and going out."

"You're making a spectacle of us both."

"Oh, I am sorry." I gave my observers a jaunty wave as I sat. "I really only intended to make a spectacle of myself."

"This is more than an image change. This is a travesty. You look…" He was obviously at a loss for a word bad enough to describe my new look. "This is loud and obvious. You don't look elegant anymore."

"I'm sorry, but I recently found out I'm allergic to beige. And taupe. And cream too. Had to get a whole new wardrobe."

"I'm worried about you. You move out, you do something outlandish to your hair and—"

He stopped suddenly as he caught sight of my newly pierced earlobes. I swear he did a double take just like people do in B movies, dropping his jaw in open-mouthed surprise.

"Your ears. Jesus Christ." His voice was a hoarse whisper. "The next thing I know, you'll be getting a tattoo."

"It's very small," I said with a smile. "And it's not where many people will ever see it." I *had* been considering a tattoo. Now it seemed like a necessity.

"I think we need more wine."

He caught the waiter's eye and tapped the wine bottle with one finger. Miraculously a second bottle appeared almost instantly. We sat in silence for a couple of minutes, guzzling the expensive red like a couple of sidewalk winos with a bottle of Boone's Farm.

"I have an idea, Gregory. I don't think either of us is really in the mood to have a polite meal together. Let's skip the food and settle what we came here for and get us both back home."

"I couldn't agree more." He nodded his agreement. "You called the meeting. What is it you want from me?"

"I need some information about my cousin, Dewayne."

"Good God, has that loser turned up again?"

"Do you know anything about him and money?"

"I know he's a deadbeat and the only money he has is whatever he's managed to scam. He's not known for working for his living."

"He's been calling me for weeks now, claiming to be concerned about me—"

"That'll be one for the record books. Dewayne Winters caring for anyone except himself." Gregory rolled his eyes. "My advice is stop returning his calls. He's cooking up another of his illegal schemes. Probably end up back in jail."

"Jail? As in really in jail?"

"Oh yes," Gregory sneered. "For the past couple of years. His petty crimes get more serious each time. Probably end up killing someone one of these days."

"Were we close enough that I might have promised him a large—" I hated to ask Gregory, but there was no other option. "Before the accident, did I mention giving him a very large chunk of money? Would I have wanted to do that?"

"Of course not." He was emphatic. "Your cousin has been in prison three times in the past fifteen years, mostly for kiting checks, but this last spell involved attempted extortion, with an assault charge to boot. I didn't even know he had been released."

"I see." So my instincts were better than Jennifer's or else dear Dewayne was fabricating the whole story. "That makes my decision clearer."

"You weren't thinking of giving him money, I hope." Gregory acted as if it were coming out of his own pocket. "I'd think you might consider a restraining order if he keeps bothering you. As a matter of fact, in the state your memory is in, perhaps I need to handle this for you."

"I can handle my own affairs. Thanks all the same." It stung to know he might have a point about my memory getting me in trouble. Even if I started handing out money on the street corner, he was the last person I'd want to handle things. "I can take care of this. It was only a question."

"Now I have a question for you. Have you come to your senses about a divorce? Are you ready to come back home and stop all this nonsense?"

"I think we can safely check 'no' on both counts."

"I don't know how to put this nicely, so I'm going to be brutally honest," he said.

"Why would you change now?"

"Jennifer, please listen to me." He went on as if I hadn't spoken. "You are in danger of making a laughingstock of yourself."

"In what respect?" I was cautiously polite, thinking perhaps I'd committed some grievous social *faux pas* due to my still unreliable brain. "Did I forget to write a thank you note or cancel my Pilates classes before I left?"

"This isn't a joking matter."

"I'm not laughing," I snapped. "Okay, what have I done to bring you out of the house without your laptop?"

"You've been seen in some very questionable company and in some rather awkward situations lately." He cleared his throat uncomfortably. "You were seen out at dinner the other night by Jerry and Fay Hanson. I don't think you are aware that some of your new...*friends* are causing some concern and speculative talk in our circle of acquaintances."

"What is it you're trying to slither around saying? I want you to be very clear." What a snake! What an underhanded, mealy-mouthed snake. "Exactly what's being said about my friends?"

"You've been hanging out with those bleeding hearts at that women's shelter. It's one thing to raise money and help a charitable cause, but there is a point where you have to draw the line."

"And people like us don't socialize with the needy?" I wanted to smack him, but that would have involved having to actually physically touch him. I wasn't prepared to do that without a ten-foot pole and there wasn't one within arms' reach. "Or with the hired help, is that what you're trying to get at?"

"It's not that simple. Even before your accident, you've always been so naïve." He swirled his wine and took a sip before continuing. "According to my investigator, there is a certain element—"

"Investigator? You've had me investigated?" Irritation flamed to outrage. "You have no right—"

"I have every right. I'm your husband. You haven't been well. I've been worried about you, and with very good reason, as it turns out."

He snapped at me as if I should jump to attention. Maybe Jennifer did that in the past, but boy, was he in for a surprise from here on out.

"What exactly are you trying to say? Just skip the sugarcoating and put it in little words, so I can understand you."

"Okay, little words. Half the people you are working with are gay. You've been sheltered, but these people running that Outreach Oaklawn place where you volunteer are known homosexuals."

"I'm hanging out with gay people. That's what's got you in an uproar?" I was nearing the boiling point.

"And psychopaths. You were talking to Max Sealy for over an hour yesterday."

"I had a business matter to discuss with Max Sealy, not that it's any of your concern." I was curious why Gregory considered Sealy to be a nut job. Maybe birds of a feather or it takes one to know one or something like that. "Why is he a psychopath? Is he gay too?"

"Of course he's not gay," Gregory said, obviously horrified. "He was one of the top athletes in the country."

"How stupid of me." I popped myself in the forehead with my open palm. "What was I thinking? I hope no one told Billy Bean or Martina Navratilova about this."

"You can be sarcastic, but you should listen to me. There was talk at the club that Sealy was involved in a bad situation a few months ago. They were vague on the details, but one of the guys from Sealy's attorney's office said he was guilty as sin." Gregory lived and died by the tidbits he gleaned at the club. "I can't let you get tangled up with dangerous types without having you looked after."

"By *looked after*, you mean having me followed."

"I decided it was necessary."

"You bastard, you no longer get to decide what's necessary for my life. How long has this been going on?"

"I've had someone watching over you since the day you moved out." He didn't even have the decency to look ashamed. "Jennifer, I'm worried about your mental and physical well-being. You are still my wife and—"

"And that's about to change."

I pushed my chair back so hard it crashed over on the floor, making a loud enough noise that the room fell into an expectant hush. This wasn't the kind of restaurant where one got to see a rumble very often. Although I was tempted to pitch a fit, I thought it wiser to get out quickly than provide the day's entertainment.

A sea of curious diners watched me make my dramatic exit. I thought I heard a couple of spontaneous claps from somewhere, but it may have been my imagination.

CHAPTER NINETEEN

Gregory caught up with me in the parking lot.

"Jennifer wait." He was out of breath from running, something he hated to do. "Don't make a public spectacle of us both."

"That's so *you*." He reached out to take my arm but drew back after one look at my snarling face. "Smart man. It's fine to stalk people—"

"I'm not stalking you." His smile was pure mockery. "I haven't been within miles of you until today."

"I stand corrected. It's okay to hire someone to stalk me, but don't make a scene in public? Fine sense of ethics you've got."

"Be reasonable. I'm trying to look out for you. You obviously aren't in any state of mind to look after yourself right now."

"If this is your idea of an apology, you're making a bad start."

"You aren't well. You haven't been since the accident. I'm afraid I can't allow you to continue living like you have been. I don't think you are able to make good decisions for yourself."

"I sure hope you aren't threatening me, Gregory."

"Of course not. When your parents died so tragically, I made a vow to look after you. I'm trying to make sure you're safe—physically, mentally and financially."

"And how do you propose to do that?"

"Maybe instead of living alone in that apartment, you might need to have some company for a while. An assistant of sorts, a nurse perhaps, someone who could make sure your head injury isn't causing you to do anything rash."

"Anything rash, like divorcing you, perhaps?"

"I'm only looking out for your best interests."

"And my finances? You looking after my money too?" The plan was beginning to make sense. The stupid shit was going to try to screw his rich little wife to the floor. "Is that what this is all about? My money?"

"You're being paranoid, Jennifer."

"Stop calling me that." I wanted to spit on him, but that would make me look like a crazy person. "Get away from me. And stop calling me that."

"Stop calling you by your name, Jennifer?" He was taunting me, trying to make me lose it. "I think you may need someone to oversee your legal affairs until you are able to think better."

"I'm thinking much better, you ass. I got smart enough to leave you, didn't I?"

"I'm not sure your actions and associations since you moved out don't make you look a little, shall we say, unstable?" He looked around the parking lot to make sure no one was close enough to hear him.

"I have no intention of being made a fool of. I haven't seen them yet, but there are pictures of you arm in arm with that big jock basketball player, so drunk you had to be halfway carried out of Uncle Julio's."

"You have pictures?" I never liked having my picture taken when I didn't know it, but this was ridiculous. "Of me and Aggie? What are you accusing me of? Not that it's any of your business anymore."

"She didn't leave your apartment for hours. Doesn't look good, Jennifer." He licked his lips, as bad a Freudian slip as words ever were. "You get falling down drunk in public, then end up being carried out into the night by that dyke? Doesn't look good at all."

"If it doesn't look good, why are you practically drooling at the thought, you sick shit?"

"I'm not the one providing erotic fantasies for the public." His mouth twisted, but not in a smile. "I have enough evidence of your unsound mind and enough contacts at the club to get you committed if you push me. Don't think I can't do it either."

"Oh, I'm sure your buddies would back you. It is especially important to get your wife locked up if she would rather sleep with a woman than one of you big, manly studs. That is a sure sign of insanity."

I stood there, very still, very angry, not taking my eyes off him. He had messed with me long enough; he thought this was *Survivor* and he was going to get me voted off the island. Outwit, outplay, outsmart me? Game on. We'd see who survived this challenge.

He had no idea he was dealing with me—Cotton Claymore. I, who had tasted death and come back out of the fog. Me, not his brain-damaged little wife. He had never played Texas hold 'em with a street fighter who only looked like butter wouldn't melt in her mouth. I was about to call him with a bluff of my own.

"You're making a mistake, Gregory." Gloves off. "If you think I'm going to let you threaten me, listen very closely."

He smirked.

"I have more money than you. I have more imagination than you. And I have a major advantage if you try to double-cross me."

"Yeah?" He was mocking me. "What do you think you can do to stop me?"

"I can ruin you. Do you think I don't know what you've been up to?"

"I have no idea what crazy ideas you have." His Adam's apple bobbed as he swallowed hard.

A "tell," they called it in poker. A little tic, a little fear. A "tell." Any man who would threaten his wife with commitment in order to get her money had to be up to something. Time for a raise.

"You try to bully me or make one move to control me and I will ask for an audit of all the accounts you have handled for me over the last four years. I intend to get my lawyer started on it as soon as I leave here."

Sweat bullets appeared on his upper lip. They could have been caused by the heat and humidity, but if he was the kind of gravy-sucking pig he had been behaving like, I didn't think so. I check-raised him—all in.

"Even if you get me locked up, I would be willing to bet the accommodations I have will be a lot nicer than those in prison. Stock fraud, theft, embezzlement—I'm sure they'd find something." He stepped back. "Oh, yes, they would, wouldn't they?"

"And Greg?" He looked at me as I got in my car and fastened my seat belt. "Care to bet that I'd be out on the street again at least twenty years before you?"

CHAPTER TWENTY

Calling Gregory's bluff got him off my back for the moment, but it gave me things to think about until my head hurt. I didn't believe for one minute that the creep was going to suddenly change his ways and walk the straight and narrow. Nope, he would only get more desperate and more deceptive. It was the nature of the beast—the knuckle-dragging beast cloaked in a Versace suit and Rolex watch.

I had to protect myself, as well. Cover my assets and my ass. The first thing I did was make a stop at his office to see John Allen White, my banker—remember the guy protecting all the zeros? He welcomed me as if my frantic visit was all in a normal afternoon's work, and he was more than happy to offer the name of a firm to look after my interests. He excused himself a moment, picked up his cell phone and stepped outside the door. I could hear his voice, but he spoke too softly for me to eavesdrop. Within a minute he had an appointment for me to talk to the head honcho at Greenly Inc., which conveniently was located two floors above where I was sitting at the moment.

John insisted on personally escorting me and hand-delivering me to Sean Greenly himself.

Himself, as I christened him in my mind after hearing his Irish brogue, was a combination of Gaelic charm and Dublin street fighter. He was ruddy-faced and a touch too charming at first glance, but it didn't take long for me to realize this was a guy I wanted on my side.

"John Allen says you need a little looking after."

"Well, I'm not sure exactly what that means, but I guess that's why I'm here." I looked around the office, impressed by the lack of frills. It was minimalism carried to the extreme of sparseness. Tables, chairs, desks, bookshelves with enough leather law books to start a small library, a beyond-state-of-the-art computer center—all very expensive, but not geared to impress with artsy sculpture or decorator touches. "This isn't what I expected a private investigator's office to look like."

"Oh, this isn't a PI firm," Sean informed me. "We do have people who handle investigations, though, should we need them. And a team of lawyers who specialize in divorce. We have forensic accountants, foreign contacts, personal protection, general hand-holding, all available as the situation requires."

I'm sure my puzzled expression was comical. I could feel it myself, but Himself's rollicking laugh was confirmation.

"Don't worry, darlin' girl," he soothed. "You are literally and figuratively going to be in safe and discreet hands. Greenly Inc. isn't printed on the building directory or listed in the phone book. We are a very exclusive resource for very discerning clients. We do what needs doing to make your life easier in these difficult times."

"I'm not sure that shouldn't scare me," I said, only half kidding. "I feel like the theme song from *The Godfather* should be playing in the background."

"I can arrange that if you like." He smiled. "I'm not a hit man, Ms. Strickland. I don't so much work outside the rules as I work around them. We find out where the bodies are buried that you need found. Or not found."

"Good to know. Right now, I have a long list of questions and a short list of answers. I may not even know yet, everything I need you to look into."

"Let's talk for a while," he said. "We'll know where to go after that, no worries."

After spending an hour talking to Sean, I was a lot less worried. He took notes when I mentioned Dewayne and warned me about making any promises or giving away any cash, suggesting I try to avoid talking to Dewayne for a few days.

With a nod, a raised eyebrow and a lot of nosy questions, many of which I either didn't know or couldn't explain how I didn't know, he managed to make me feel he had a better grip on my reality than I did. I left out all the Cotton Claymore details though. He didn't look the type to believe in anything he couldn't verify. Still, after our talk I felt like a good Catholic had to feel after going to confession—cleansed and filled with equal parts of remorse and hope.

Sharks smelling blood in the water were pussycats compared to this guy. It was more than having private investigators on retainer who were used to dirty, upcoming divorces, more than crackerjack accountants and hard-nosed lawyers. I got the feeling that standard operating procedure for the firm was far from standard.

It was going to be interesting to see Gregory on the other end of an investigation. Sean Himself promised me that in a week I'd have a dossier on Gregory that would make the guys from Homeland Security jealous. Good to know they were on it. I had something more important to deal with.

* * *

Jo Keesling. Jo. The black-haired woman who had filled my sleeping dreams and waking thoughts.

It was driving me crazy that I couldn't remember her. Jo— for the love of heaven! She was the woman I loved—the one who I had been killed for loving. Aggie had practically made us into a legend—a warning to avoid the fatal attraction of love.

What kind of true and eternal love could be blocked by a stupid head injury?

I hoped her voice would be the key that would open the stubborn door to my memory, so I called Keesling Consulting to set up a meeting. All I got was a bland machine message inviting me to leave a brief message and telling me my call would be returned right away. I did as instructed, feeling awkward as I tried to think of any real reason I needed to hire a media consultant. Mumbling something about a fundraiser for a charitable cause took me past the time allowed for the message. I had to call back and leave a second message explaining why I didn't leave my name and number on the last message. I barely got the phone number in before I was cut off again.

Smooth operator that I am, I sat holding my cell phone and wiping flop sweat from my face. The phone was clutched in my still damp palm when her return call came. I recognized the number, but was too scared to talk to her so I let it go to voice. Coward. Idiot and coward.

I waited ten minutes before I had the nerve to retrieve her message. The low-pitched, husky drawl sent shivers down my spine. If someone born and raised in the South says someone has a drawl, you better believe it's a beauty. Wait-for-it slow, singsongy rhythm, maple syrup over hot pancakes—that was the effect. Central nervous system meltdown.

No one had ever mentioned to me that Jo Keesling wasn't from Texas. Way Deep South, for sure. Georgia, if I had to guess. Wherever—it was the sexiest voice I'd ever heard.

Unfortunately, I didn't remember ever hearing it before.

I listened to it probably ten times, willing myself to recognize it, imagining, hoping, finally cursing that it was still only the sexiest voice I'd ever heard, but nothing more. Well, actually... it did make me pretty damn sure I was Cotton Claymore, that the memories growing stronger every day were not a delusional fantasy. My response to the voice wasn't visceral—it was purely and unexpectedly sexual. Liquid heat that I certainly never felt as Jennifer Strickland reminded me that being a lesbian wasn't first and foremost a political decision. Hormones kicked into overdrive, unleashing a flood of knee-weakening longing. I understood the cliché of guys taking a cold shower. Instead, I decided on taking a steamy, soapy bath before I returned the call. It was a *very* long bath.

When I called back, I was braced to withstand the drawl. Instead, it was answered by a nasal teenager who was very easy to talk to, if somewhat less thrilling. She confirmed a meeting with Ms. Keesling for the following day. Yes, one thirty would be fine. Did I need driving instructions?

* * *

Aggie wasn't thrilled with my initiative.

"You did what?"

Aggie and I were closing down the ground floor area of the Outreach for the night, locking the office and food bank and making sure all the coffeepots were turned off in the cafeteria. We'd already cleaned up in the gym. I ran the big rectangular dust mop over the hardwood floor while she put the basketballs in the hopper by tossing them from as many angles as she could manage. She wasn't beyond showing off.

"J.C., what kind of business do you have with Jo Keesling? I've about had it with all your weird shit. Another message from the great beyond?"

"No, a message from here." I waved my arms to include the whole building. "This place needs help."

"You got that right. Like it needed a couple of new cars and pickup trucks." Aggie looked at me, waiting for a response. I didn't offer one.

"It needs more money for food, for repairs, for hiring more staff."

"No lie. What does that have to do with you running over to see Jo? I think you got some bug up your butt about Jo and Cotton and you figure that talking to her is going to make a difference to whatever's going on in your banged-up brain."

"I heard she helped with the last time we...they raised any cash around here. I wanted to see if she was available again."

"Oh, if it's a big enough deal, Jo will make herself available."
Aggie sounded less than a fan. "If you can attach a party with
lots of lights and cameras, you can count on it."

"What's that supposed to mean?"

"Nothin'. Just being a big old bitch."

"No argument from me. I got the impression you and Jo
were close."

"No. Cotton and Jo were close. Cotton and I were close. Jo
was a fact of life I was having to get used to."

"Why would you talk like that?" I said, halfway pissed. "I
thought you liked Jo. I thought you liked working with her
here."

"Who you been talkin' to?" Aggie stomped across the floor
and skidded to a halt right in my path. "Nobody said anything
about Jo around here, did they? Where you getting your
information?" She eyed me suspiciously. "Jo never worked here.
It was all in the talking stage—just Jo and Cotton. And me."

"I don't remember who told me." I stammered a bit.
"Someone had to though. How else would I have known?"

"I don't know how you know so much shit you can't know
on one day and then you can't remember shit when you get hit
with a hard question." Aggie glowered at me, but there was a
tiny bit of something else in the look as well. "You mess with my
head, J.C. Rich society chick from waaay uptown, come down
here tight and green and a month later you're chasing a woman
who could be big trouble, acting like you own the place."

"I know very well I don't own the place." *Anymore.* "Someone
needs to do something to get things moving and I have the
ability to do it. And the money to hire a consultant to help see
that it gets done right."

"Lotta consultants in Dallas, s'all I'm sayin' to you." She
flipped off the overheads and left me standing with only the
shaft of light from the hallway framing her outline. "And who
are you to take it on yourself to do this?"

"Aggie, if you ever want me to tell you who I think I am, just
ask. I'm not sure you really want to know."

CHAPTER TWENTY-ONE

My old Cotton fashion sense was returning, but I was in a quandary over what was the perfect outfit to wear to meet the love of your past life.

The mirror had been not much help. Jennifer had left me a great body and a pretty face, but it was far from the face and body of Cotton Claymore. Not that I wanted to show up looking like my old self. Giving Jo a heart attack wasn't in my plan.

The real problem was, I had no plan to speak of. Raising money for the Outreach was a good idea, but in reality I could have written a check for more than we were going to raise in my wildest dreams. If all else went down the tubes I was still likely to do just that. No way I was going to let the Outreach go unfunded.

There was a loyal and underpaid staff who counted on their jobs. And there were too many people who had no other place to go, no other place to turn to. This was a temporary oasis for those who needed a way station on their journeys out of hell.

But, crass as it sounds, I was not above using the place to have a reason to meet with Jo. Busted—*cherchez la femme*—I'm not so noble as to pass up my best shot.

I'm beginning to doubt I have much of a claim to nobility in any case. My brain, as it recovers, seems to have a distinctly pragmatic, if not always strictly moral way of dealing with situations. Buy my way in. Lie my way in. As long as I get in, I'm afraid I am a pretty results-oriented kind of a girl. Rationalization, I'm finding, is something I excel at. That and dressing for success.

I finally decided on a great khaki suit, tailored as all get-out, proper for a business meeting. Did I know the white shirt under it was just a little sheer and snug across my breasts? Hey—I'm brain-injured, not brain-dead. A woman has to work with what she has to work with.

The traffic was unusually light. I arrived half an hour early and had just enough time to make myself nervous—no, I got to nervous in fifteen minutes. After which I was a wreck. I pulled in to the convenience store across the street and bought a pack of cigarettes and a seventy-nine-cent lighter. I don't know what made me do it, but at some point, either Jennifer or Cotton had had the habit.

The paper and tobacco crackled faintly as the flame ignited the tip. When the acrid smoke hit my lungs, it was fabulous. I looked around—feeling like a crack whore as I stood just outside the door of the store, not even waiting to get out of the flow of traffic. Everyone in Texas dashed from house to business to car—anything to get out of the heat and into the air conditioning. I didn't notice the melting asphalt of the parking lot or the burning rays of the sun. Just stood there smoking.

The fierce rush of nicotine was as soothing as a tranquilizer dart to a charging rhino. My knees nearly buckled as I inhaled. It was so good that when I finished smoking, I felt that after-sex, sated feeling that called for a cigarette. So I smoked another one.

Then I went back into the store and bought a pack of extra strong breath mints. I popped one in my mouth and crunched it, rubbing it around my teeth with my tongue. I had no inclination to have a second one of those. I went back into the store and came out with a bottle of water. I rinsed and spit. The clerk was starting to look at me funny, so I got in the car and drove back across the street to face my destiny, self-conscious now that I probably smelled like a very minty ashtray.

* * *

It's funny how your brain can carry on without you sometimes, have conversations, respond coherently to situations and to people, and you sort of come to in the middle of it all, realizing only then that you were having an out-of-body experience all the while. Let me explain.

I was fine walking in. Keesling Consulting was on the second floor in an end suite. It looked a lot like a successful lawyer's office, if the lawyer had great taste and a sense of whimsy.

The receptionist desk and waiting area was filled with books and plants and a few oversized, overstuffed chairs. A low glass-topped table rested on the back of a bronze dragon. There was a conference room with the requisite long wooden table and high-backed leather chairs. And there was a full-sized merry-go-round horse, complete with the pole and the brass rings hanging just out of reach.

The horse was hot pink with a wild black mane and tail, lacquered to a shine. I walked to it and ran my hand over his nose. We knew each other, this fiery steed and I. Calliope music played in a distant part of my brain and laughter echoed with it. I wanted to kiss him, but the receptionist was already waiting impatiently, tapping her toe silently on the carpet, but too well trained to rush a potential client.

They were tearing down the rides at the state fair when Jo spotted him. The carnies were loading the merry-go-round on the truck, piece by piece. The horse was leaning up against the operating machinery housing, looking for the world like he had escaped from the herd.

Jo ran to him and threw her arms around his neck, nuzzling and fondling the carved pony.

"I have to have him, Cotton. Get him for me."

"They hang horse thieves in Texas, ma'am," I said, thinking she was playing.

"No really. I want him. Make them sell him to you."

"They aren't going to sell me that horse, Jo. I'll call the antique stores and find you one, promise."

"This one please," she wheedled. "I love him and he doesn't want to go back in that truck. Besides, he hates all those grubby little kids."

"He told you he hates kids?"

"Not exactly. But he has an earful of cotton candy and it didn't get there by itself." She removed the offending gunk and tossed it on the littered fairway. "This is no place for a lord of the prairie, Cotton. Make them give him to us."

It took more finagling than I'm going to admit, but the guys who loaded the trucks and I had a serious talk. They didn't take American Express, but they did know where the ATM was. Money did change hands. They did deliver. That's all I'm going to confess to because I don't know if the statute of limitations on horse theft can be transferred along with a memory.

It was worth it all—then and now. The first time seeing Jo's delight and knowing I had put it there was my reward. Now, before I walked in her office, I finally remembered. I remembered Jo.

I remembered it all.

CHAPTER TWENTY-TWO

Presto chango!

That's how quickly it happened. One minute—okay, six months—I'm wandering around being lost except for the increasingly frequent glimpses of my life as Cotton. Then all at once, everything is clear except how it happened. All of my life is my life again. Every joy, every screw-up. What I like for breakfast. Where I hid Jo's birthday present.

And why I'm here. My God, Jo's here. Just follow the girl down the hall and open the door and…And then, she's not going to know me. I can't grab her and hug her. I can't tell her about all this crazy, crazy stuff. She won't know me from a stranger on the street.

The air bursts from my lungs, and I realize I've been holding my breath, as if I had literally gone off into the deep end and sucked in one big gulp of air until I could get back to the surface. Inhale. Exhale. Inhale slowly. Breathing is supposed to be an automatic function. But did you ever notice that as soon as you start thinking about it, it isn't easy to do without being very aware of it? Exhale. Inhale. Until something takes your mind off of it, you keep thinking about it. Exhale. Inhale.

"Right in here." The girl motioned me to enter the door at the end of the hall. "She's waiting for you."

That did it. Breathing awareness over. The knob turned in my hand. The door swings open and there she is, rising to greet me, smiling politely, extending her hand. I reach out and *Zap!* Our fingers touched and we both snatched our hands back, stung by the electricity that arced between us. I would have liked to believe it was destiny, chemistry, two souls being made one.

"Static electricity," she laughed. "Sorry. One day I'm going to have that carpet yanked and install a rubber floor. Come in. Sit."

I sat down, sinking into the deep cushion of the client chair, and looked at her as if I hadn't seen her in a lifetime. Which was true, at least for me, in a manner of speaking. The time away, wherever and however it happened, had sure been good to her.

Her hair was longer than I remembered it, a silky black curtain framing her face and curving just past her shoulders. She reached up and tucked one side behind her ear, showcasing a slender hand with short polished nails. She had rings on her fingers—more rings than she had fingers—and what looked to be a dozen thin bangles on her wrist. I smiled and glanced at the other hand—more rings.

Some expensive—emerald and diamond and lapis—some flea-market treasures of cut glass that ended up turning her fingers green. It never mattered to Jo, not if she liked it. She was like a magpie—drawn to bright glittery loot that filled several jewelry boxes to overflowing. And she loved necklaces. Today she had on a silver rope that twisted and held a chunk of unpolished green stone.

The rock was not as bright a green as her eyes. Thick black lashes, green fire flashing, slightly almond slant. How could I have ever forgotten this face?

"Are you feeling sick, honey?" Her Georgia drawl was as thick as bread pudding with whiskey sauce. She pressed a button and asked her assistant to bring us something cold to drink. "Iced tea?"

I nodded, sure that it would come in a crystal glass with slices of orange and lime and lemon. Her specialty. I never really cared for the sweetened tea, but it was my little secret. She was so proud of it, I drank it and she thought it was my favorite.

"It's this heat," she said. "I don't know why civilized people ever settled here in the first place."

She was chattering away, trying to put me at ease. It gave me a chance to soak her in. Lightning in a bottle. Effervescent as a shaken bottle of champagne. Gypsy hip, city slick. My girl.

The tea came, just as I remembered it. Too sweet, too fruity—I drank it as if it were nectar. She nodded her approval.

"See how much better you feel? The color is coming back into your face."

She sipped her tea and half sat on the edge of her big desk, showing off legs a dancer would have been proud of, ending in a pair of heels even I recognized as Jimmy Choo. I used to laugh at her stilettos, telling her it was clear she hadn't been a lesbian long. It was an old joke—before it was okay to say gay, we were women in comfortable shoes.

"I love those shoes," I said, unable to stop myself. "Do they hurt your feet?" I waited for the usual answer and it came right on cue.

"Only when I walk."

My girl, still my girl.

"Your call said you wanted to get some help with a charity fundraiser." She walked behind her desk and flipped open her planner. "Want to give me some details? What kind of charity are you working for?"

"Outreach Oaklawn. We help women and children who are in abusive relationships."

She didn't say anything for a minute, but her body language changed. The open, easy warmth cooled a few degrees, and she crossed her arms over her chest. *Get back. No closer.* I'd read that message before and knew exactly what it meant.

"I don't think I'm the best person for this job," she began.

"Why's that?" I kept my tone light. "You got something against women and kids? Forget them. I could change the place. Turn it into a refuge to save the fire ants. That's a mistreated species that nobody else has claimed. Lots of places helping those darned women and kids in the first place."

"No, that's not true. Everyone else is income-based or they have too many rules about who they allow in. The Outreach—" Her defense was automatic, her smile, sheepish. "You were setting me up."

"Damn, I'm good," I said. "Look how well it worked."

"I've had some dealings with the Outreach before. They do good things down there." She bit her bottom lip, pulling it slowly through even white teeth. I had to tear my eyes away from her mouth. "It's a personal matter. I don't think I can go down there."

"Why not?"

"I lost…someone. I lost a friend who used to run Outreach Oaklawn." She flipped pages in her day planner, stalling until she could speak. "It's hard to explain, but I don't think it's safe for me to be hanging around the place. Especially not with you."

"What's wrong with me?" I was flabbergasted. She didn't even know she knew me. How could she not want to be around me?

"Not a thing." She looked up at me, peering through a few inky strands of hair that had fallen over one eye. "I don't want you to take this the wrong way."

"Okay. I'm the soul of open-mindedness."

"You are a very good-looking woman."

"How can I take that the wrong way?" I smiled and leaned forward, noticing her glance flicker over my shirt, then quickly away. "Thank you."

"The last time I got involved with a good-looking blonde from the Outreach, it ended badly. Really badly." She gave me a look that made me a little jealous of myself. "I won't go into details, but it was dangerous."

"Don't be afraid. I'll take care of you."

"That's what she said." Her eyes clouded, lost in an old memory. "That's what Cotton said."

CHAPTER TWENTY-THREE

"Your friend Cotton let you down."

"Don't you dare say that!" Jo glared at me. "What do you know about Cotton anyway?" Her eyes narrowed and she lifted her chin defiantly. "Why did you choose me for this project? Something isn't making sense here."

"I got your name from Aggie Burke."

"You may have gotten my name from Aggie, but she doesn't know where I am. I didn't contact anyone from the Outreach after—" She shook her head. "After Cotton died."

It hurt to see her like this, sad and angry and uncertain. That was everything Jo wasn't. The only time I had ever seen her upset was when we had decided to live together. She had gone into a panic that her husband—soon-to-be-ex-husband before I was in the picture at all—would never let her go.

"He's a jealous maniac. When I moved out, he told me if he ever caught me with another man, the guy would be a dead man soon. I think knowing I was in love with a woman would be even worse for his ego."

"He was just trying to scare you, Jo," I had soothed. "People don't go around killing people because they move on after a divorce. If they did, we wouldn't have to wait for a table at any of the good restaurants. Half of Texas would be six feet under."

She wasn't mollified.

"You don't know Max. He's used to getting his own way about everything. When I moved out, he laughed and said I should have a nice vacation. I'd be back soon."

Suddenly Jo looked at me and uncrossed her arms, relaxing the totally rigid posture, opening the gate a tiny crack.

"This is so wrong—telling you about my private life. Not at all professional." A small, apologetic smile made me want to comfort her. "There are certain rules in business that I'm not doing very well with."

"I'm not that big on rules, Jo. You can talk to me."

"I haven't known you for fifteen minutes and I'm spilling my guts. I've told you things I never talk about to anyone."

"Maybe we knew each other in another lifetime," I said in a teasing tone, testing the waters. "You believe in that sort of thing?"

"It's a nice thought."

"Haven't you had that feeling before?" I coached. "You meet someone you have never seen and there's something familiar about them. Something inside them that you recognize?"

"I do feel like I know you," she said grudgingly. "I feel too much, too close. This isn't right."

"Maybe we're soul mates."

"Maybe you're coming on to me," she said. "Do you use this line a lot?"

"Not a lot." I smiled at her. "Is it working?"

"Maybe a little."

She was flirting with me—with J.C. Winters. Part of me saw this as progress—I was getting through to her; we were connecting on a higher plane. Another part of me, the more earthbound, realistic part, said, "Bullshit. She's flirting with some chick she just met. Not exactly pining for old Cotton. At least not for too long."

"Will you reconsider helping me with the project at the Outreach? I really need your help. The misunderstood little fire ants need your help."

"No one will ever donate money to help fire ants. Low cuddle factor."

I laughed. She smiled back. Progress.

"Longhorn cattle are already taken," she mused. "What the heck—since you already have a place for them, maybe we should stick to women and children."

"*We?* Do I dare to hope you've changed your mind?"

"Why don't I put together a couple of ideas and we can go over your budget. What kind of event do you have in mind? A-listers or general public?" She was already into the project. Typical Jo. Once she set her sights on something she was tenacious. "Any time frame you're locked into?"

"No time frame. No budget cap. I'm open to any fabulous idea you have to pitch me."

"You may be the easiest client I've had in a long time."

"No doubt about it. Easy is my middle name."

"Nice to know." Jo laughed. What a sound. My legs turned to jelly. "I have a tendency to get carried away. I should warn you, I've been known to go a little over the top."

"As long as there are no clowns or elephant rides, I think I can handle a few surprises. I like surprises as long as I don't know they're coming. Then they make me crazy."

"That's spooky. That's exactly what my friend Cotton used to say about surprises."

"Lots of people feel that way, I'm sure."

"I guess." She stood up, indicating very discreetly that our time was about over. "There is something about you I can't quite get my head around, J.C. You are a mystery, aren't you?"

"Especially to myself." I followed her lead and stood too. As she passed me, I caught a whiff of her cologne. "Coco. You still wear Coco."

"Still?" Suspicion was on the rise again. "How do you know I've always worn this scent?"

"It's unusual. I meant I didn't know they still made it." Lame excuse, even to my own ears.

"I don't believe you." She opened the door and we walked out into the hallway. "You act as if you know me. You know my cologne. Something is too creepy here. Awfully strange."

"I never said I wasn't strange. I'm not dangerous though."

"I wouldn't bet on that."

We were beside the carousel horse and I reached over and rubbed his nose for luck, like I'd done so many times in passing.

"Happy trails, Pal."

I didn't know I'd said the words aloud, until she clutched the fabric of my jacket collar and yanked me around.

"Stop right there." She was frightened. I could see it in her eyes and feel it in the tremor of the hand still on my shoulder. "Nobody ever said that but Cotton. No one knows his name but us."

"Ssh," I soothed. "I know Jo. Don't be afraid."

"Who are you?" She pushed me away and stepped back, holding her hand up like a traffic cop when I moved in her direction. "Who are you?"

"If you listen to me, I'll explain—"

"No. I want you to get out of here."

"Jo. Let me explain."

"No. This is crazy—some kind of con job, isn't it?"

"I thought I was crazy too," I said urgently. "But if you will listen to me—"

"You are crazy. Get out." Her voice was edging toward hysteria. "Get the hell out of here, right now!"

The girl who showed me in stepped into the hall, looking concerned.

"Is everything okay, Jo?"

"It's fine, Sherry. Ms. Winters will be leaving now." Under her breath, Jo hissed, "Get out now or I'll have her call the cops."

"I'll go. Please think about letting me explain."

"Go." She looked terrified and angry.

"Let me try to explain, please," I begged.

"No, just get out of here." Anger edged terror into second place. "And keep your hands off my horse."

CHAPTER TWENTY-FOUR

I spent a long chunk of sleepless night kicking myself for being a total screw-up. What was I thinking?

Just because I finally knew who I was didn't mean I could go around expecting to be recognized and welcomed back with open arms. That whole prodigal son story probably wouldn't have worked so well if he had been coming back from the dead instead of just out sowing a few wild oats in Nazareth or Samaria or somewhere.

After my big memory breakthrough with Jo, I should have been sitting on top of the world. Instead I was more afraid and confused than ever. How the hell was that even possible? Could I ever trust anyone enough to tell them what I believed had happened? What if no one ever believed I was really back? What if Aggie and Jo wrote me off as some spooky weirdo and moved on?

My head was a mess—inside and out, backward and forward, on this plane or in some other foggy dimension. Overload. I did what I always did when my brain turned to blueberry jam.

I called Dr. Carey. I don't know if it was my unique situation or a last-minute cancellation, but I got an immediate session with her and Andrew.

Andrew was dressed as if he were on his way to a hospital board meeting, all spiffed up in a suit and power tie—what Saint Nick would wear to a meeting with The Donald. Dr. Carey was surprisingly a bit of a mess—in the nicest sense of the word.

Her auburn hair was down around her shoulders. She wasn't wearing any makeup except for a token swipe of lipstick. Instead of her usual polished professional attire, she had on jeans and a gauzy print shirt. I was surprised, but not complaining. She looked kinda hot. I think Andrew must have been thinking the same thing because we were both content to sit and stare. The way we both loved to talk, our silence spoke volumes.

"If the two of you have had a good enough look, can we get on with the session?" She sounded all business, but she was smiling as if she enjoyed the attention. "I do have a life outside these walls, you know."

I honestly had never given the idea any thought. Dr. Carey was always in her office in my thoughts. Like my third grade teacher was always in school writing on the chalkboard.

I had a flash of a memory of Mrs. Todd, with her black bun and cats-eye glasses, hugging us goodbye the final day of school. I had held on to her and cried. When she asked what was wrong, I said I was sorry we were going to be home all summer and she'd be alone until school started. She laughed and said she was going to Mexico with her husband and children, not to worry.

It had been a revelation, not an entirely welcome one. The world didn't revolve around me. People had lives that didn't include me. The price of tea in China wasn't dependent on me. What a concept.

"I remember that my third grade teacher was Mrs. Todd," I said. When they both looked at me as if expecting more, I went on. "I remember everything."

"Hmmm." Andrew smiled, but he looked a little doubtful. "I'm impressed. I couldn't recall where I parked my car yesterday and you remember everything."

"Not that kind of everything. I remember everything from when I was Cotton." I was excited and trying to explain the magnitude of my recovery. "I know Aggie and I know Jo and I know what I got Jo for her birthday. And when I saw the carousel horse—"

"Slow down," Dr. Carey said, shooting a look-what-you've-done-now glance in Andrew's direction. She didn't seem happy with my progress. "Take it easy. We'll listen."

"And I remember I like pumpernickel bagels. And I'm allergic to shellfish. I remember it all."

"When did your recollections start coming back in such detail?" Dr. Carey asked. "And how and when did you find Jo?"

"Let me tell you what's happened."

They listened. They nodded. Occasionally Dr. Carey looked up from her yellow notepad to interject or clarify a point. Andrew never said a word. That worried me. Maybe it was only my perception, but from day one I always felt that he was on my side. He had defended my sanity and pointed me in the right direction to reclaim my life. Today he seemed distant and not altogether happy for me.

"Andrew, aren't you excited?" I called him on it. "I have my memory back. It's only a matter of time until everything is back to normal."

"I'm very encouraged, J.C. You've had a major breakthrough." He unbuttoned his jacket, freeing his belly from the Italian silk prison of his suit. "However, it might be wise to slow down a bit and give yourself a chance to get back into the flow of traffic gradually."

"I don't want to slow down," I snapped. "I've been living in the slow lane for months now. What I want is to step on the gas and get where I'm headed faster. I am damned tired of caution flags and detours."

"Of course you are. You'd have to be, J.C.," he said. "You wouldn't be human if you weren't frustrated. You need to understand that we want that for you very much."

Andrew was quietly encouraging, as usual, but not afraid to give his opinion, also as usual. Not that he could just give his opinion. Way too easy. Better to lead me to his lair after a round of sneaky questioning.

"What makes you think you remember everything?"

"Because I remember it. Who would know better than I do?"

"What if you only think you know everything? If you don't remember it, how do you know?" he asked. "Would it be so terrible to find you have things yet to discover?"

"Not terrible no. But I felt it all come back to me in a rush." I was convinced. "It was wonderful to be back in control."

"Aaah control. Now we're getting somewhere." He nodded sagely, making me fantasize about punching him in the stomach, burying my fist in his fat, jiggly paunch. "What were your parents' names, Cotton?"

"John Claymore and Charlotte Bailey," I answered without hesitation. "He was a professor of history and my mother was an attorney." I volunteered the information, proud of knowing who they were, what they did.

"Where did you go to college?" he asked.

"Southern Methodist." I said, happy to show my knowledge. "Go Mustangs!"

"Where do you live? Your address?"

"I live in an apartment on Turtle Creek."

"No, J.C. Winters lives in an apartment on Turtle Creek. Where does Cotton live?"

I had no answer. There was a total blank spot.

"What kind of car do you drive?" He fired the questions, one after the other. "Tell me your driver's license number? Your phone number?"

Nothing. No idea. Less than no idea. I stopped trying to answer, wishing he would stop talking. Then he did, and I felt the walls closing in on me.

Dr. Carey intervened.

"That's enough, Andrew. Let her catch her breath." She put down her notebook and gave him a meaningful glare. "J.C.— Cotton," she corrected. I looked up to see her smiling at me. It was the first time she had called me Cotton and it steadied my wobbly world. "Don't worry about remembering every detail of your life. We all have things that we forget—sometimes that's a good thing. Protective. Everything important will come back in time. Don't be so worried that the pieces don't all fit at once."

"Do you think they will eventually fit together, Dr. Carey?" I felt lost again, two steps forward, one step back. "What if I'm like Humpty Dumpty?"

"Things are going to work out," she said, sounding more optimistic than I was used to her being. "All the king's horses and all the king's men are fine, but I think you have a better chance with me and Andrew. Humpty Dumpty never had the advantage of a couple of great therapists."

CHAPTER TWENTY-FIVE

Fairy tales are an excellent analogy for my life. This is not so comforting as it sounds. Oh, I know they all start out "once upon a time" and end up "happily ever after," but some pretty horrible stuff happens in between in a lot of those stories. Curses, spells, ogres, wicked witches, poisoned apples—not a few of my favorite things. Of course, being beaten to death and coming back in another person's body did have a certain macabre twist that might have interested the Brothers Grimm.

I was having enough trouble with my own cast of characters without trying to keep up with the three little pigs. I didn't know any magic words that would change straw into gold or make Aggie and Jo recognize me again.

I don't think I would have believed Jo was back if the circumstances had been reversed. I'm not a very spiritual person even now. The whole idea of souls flitting around without bodies and coming and going and all that misty-moisty stuff still seemed like superstitious claptrap. Stuff they make spooky movies out of, not the kind of thing modern, educated people could give credence to.

The only problem was, here I am—a modern, educated woman—walking around in a loaner body without a clue of how I got here. Kinda hard to argue with that.

I couldn't get Jo to return my phone calls. She was probably considering a restraining order. I'd left about five messages on her voice mail, trying to get her to give me a chance to explain. I was kind of vague about what I was talking about, not sure if competency hearings might be able to use the recordings against me if anyone decided to put me in a rubber room. Instead I begged her to listen, to consider that there were things in the universe we couldn't always understand. Sounded nuts even to me.

When her call came a couple of days later, I was more than a little shocked. It was a strange message, but one that gave me hope.

"J.C. Winters or whoever you really are, this is Jo Keesling." As if I didn't know. I held my breath.

"I don't know what to think. You freaked me out. I talked to Aggie Burke about you yesterday, and I ended up more confused than ever. Then I had the strangest dream about you last night. You and Cotton. If you know where to go, meet me at three today in the first place Cotton and I went out together. If you're there, I'll know...If I don't see you there, I'll know...Oh, I don't know what I mean. I'm starting to think I may be crazier than you are."

Click.

I threw on my clothes. Okay—after I picked out something that made me look incredibly hot—I threw on some clothes and headed for the Outreach. Aggie had talked to Jo about me. I wanted to get some idea of what she had asked. I wanted to know what she said about me.

Aggie was sitting at her desk doing paperwork, a most unusual sight, as I walked in the front door. Now that I was back in charge of my brain—of Jennifer's brain—I remembered that Aggie was legally the head honcho. For all her shooting hoops and hanging around the gym, Aggie was responsible for operations and had never mentioned it to me. Of course, there was no earthly reason she should have bothered to tell a lowly volunteer the details of the business.

Just how Aggie got control of everything wasn't something I could ask her without sounding nosy or strange. The Outreach had been Cotton Claymore's main public project. Although I don't know how or why it was my life's work, I wanted it to stay strong and independent. I keep forgetting that I—Jennifer Strickland/J.C. Winters—am only a volunteer around here.

I keep forgetting I'm dead, if you want to get picky about little things like that.

"Aggie, have you got a few minutes to talk to me?"

"Talk to you?" Aggie sounded mad. "And who are you today? A volunteer? A psychic? A fucking ghost? Just who am I talking to?"

"Somewhere private please?" There were several other people at desks in their cubicles across the room. The last thing I wanted was to provide entertainment and food for gossip for the whole staff. "How about the gym?"

"How about wherever I want?" Aggie snarled at me. "Outside."

I followed meekly as she strode from the building, halfway jogging to keep up with her as she kept going for a block, staying a few steps behind to keep from getting lashed by one of her long braids, which were whipping the air as she went loping along. Mad was understating the case. She was pissed, royally pissed. And I was the cause. Not an entirely comfortable feeling.

"Okay." She wheeled to a stop and faced me, looking for all the world as if she were guarding her team's basket during the playoffs. "Talk."

I moved very slowly, hands up, palms open in the universal symbol for *I come as friend, unarmed, please don't kick my ass*. I'd seen her leave strapping six-footers sitting on their rear ends when they tried to make a move on her territory. She looked at me as if it could still go either way.

"Aggie, I got a message from Jo this morning. She said she talked to you. What did she say? How did she sound?"

"How do you think she sounded, you stupid idiot? She was a mess, askin' me about you, wanting me to make sense of this mess for her."

"What did you tell her?"

"That you were a Grade A nut job, that's what I told her." Aggie stepped back and looked at me, shaking her head as if she'd never seen me before. "Nah, that's what I should have told her. I told her I didn't know what was goin' on." She shrugged. "This is some strange shit. She said she thinks you are Cotton."

"And you? Do think I'm Cotton?"

"How is that possible, girl?" Aggie was angry, lashing out at me like it was my fault the world was wobbly. "You're an uptown white chick with a lot of money who came slummin' down here to help the disadvantaged. That's who you are—that works for me. Then, you start bein' all weird, sayin' stuff, knowin' stuff, feelin' like my old friend."

"I am your friend, Ag. I swear I am."

"Nah, look at you." Aggie pushed me with the flat of one big hand, nearly knocking me off my feet. "Don't you know I saw Cotton dead, held her body. I saw her beaten to where her own mama wouldn't know her. Now you show up talkin' like her. How am I supposed to think it's you when I'm looking' at... *you*?"

"I don't know. I don't know how it happened." My voice was ragged. "What do you think it feels like for me? I thought I had lost my mind. Now I get a second chance and my best friend and my girl treat me like a mud sandwich. Instead of hoping it's true, you act like I'm doing this just to screw with you."

The more I talked the madder I got. Evidently there was no universal law preventing me from being here. Maybe there was even some cosmic reason it was supposed to happen. Hell, I don't know. Whatever. Who were these two to make me come crawling, explaining, begging them to take me back?

"Screw both of you! I've had it, trying to ease back into your life—trying to ease back into *my* life." I spun around, flipping her the bird as I walked off. "Bye, you big dummy. I can find some new friends. You two go ahead and write me off."

I was muttering to the world at large, not caring who was listening or watching me. Maybe I was crazy, but I was rich and crazy, so I could suffer in style and buy as many friends as I wanted. Better caliber of friends than the ones I was trying to hang on to, that was for sure.

"Cotton!"

I heard Aggie yell my name and I stopped automatically. My stomach lurched to hear her call my name again after so long.

I turned to find her standing three feet behind me, tears running down her dark cheekbones.

"Cotton?"

I felt the dampness on my own cheeks and wiped it away, surprised to find I was crying too. Aggie covered her mouth with her hand, stuffing the sobs back where they wouldn't embarrass her in public. She was tough stuff, and crying—in public or otherwise—wasn't her style. After a long minute, she reached over and barely brushed my face with a balled-up fist.

"Cotton. Girlfriend, you're lookin' a damn sight better than when we buried your ass."

CHAPTER TWENTY-SIX

One down, one to go.

The two touchstones of my life as Cotton Claymore were my best friend, Aggie, and the love of my life, Jo Keesling. Aggie reminded me I had somewhere important to be and I needed to stop sniveling and take care of business. Silver-tongued devil that she is, she was on the money.

"You do know where to go, right?" Aggie looked a little worried, still a teensy bit uncertain that the two of us hadn't slipped into some parallel universe or were sharing some particularly strange delusion. "You can't be guessing about this. Jo will be waiting for you."

"Not if I get there first." I grinned, confidence growing by the minute. "I'm going to be waiting for her this time. I want to have the element of surprise on my side."

"You *are* the element of surprise, stupid." Aggie gave a raucous hoot of laughter. "Playing Lazarus isn't enough of a surprise. What are you planning for an encore? Jugglin'? Walkin' on water?"

"I was thinking more along the lines of pulling something out of a hat. I need your help."

"Uh-oh. I'm always in trouble when you need my help."

"No, just a shot in the dark," I said. "Knowing you, I bet you didn't throw all of my stuff out of my desk after—as you so delicately put it—you buried my ass."

"I wasn't hired as a housekeeper," Aggie said with a lopsided grin. "Your stuff is in a big box in the equipment storage locker in the gym. What's in there that's gonna help you straighten out this mess?"

"Come on. I'll show you."

It took half an hour for us to unearth the box. Most of the stuff in it must have been work-related. There was an ancient Palm Pilot left over from who knows when and my wallet. I flipped it open and stared at my driver's license. Not a bad picture. There were still a couple of twenties in there as well as some photos and two keys tied with a piece of string that intrigued me. I put the keys in with the money and stuffed the wallet in my back pocket.

I dug through the paperweights and coffee mugs and paperback books until I located my old Rangers baseball cap. I snapped the bill of the hat back and looked inside. With a flourish I pulled out a crumpled wad of red tissue paper.

"And abraca-freakin-dabra, there it is!"

I held my treasure in the air like the sword Excalibur pulled from the stone. Aggie's eyes were practically bugging out of her head, astonished that I really knew what was in there. I think it was solid proof—the icing on the cake that I was back.

"I'm out of here," I yelled over my shoulder, not bothering to share my find. "We'll celebrate later."

* * *

There wasn't a crowd at the Nasher Sculpture Center this time of day, especially with the heat still breaking records. I paid my ten dollars and went in. Since I had my old wallet and ID, I could have gotten in free with my membership card if they didn't look too closely at the photograph. I decided not to chance it. No complaints though. Ten bucks was a small price to pay for the reward I hoped was to come.

I loved this place. Located in downtown Dallas, the Nasher held a collection of some of the world's greatest sculptures on display in a building and garden that were as much art as the exhibits themselves. Today I scarcely saw them as I positioned myself in the trees just behind the Barbara Hepworth *Squares with Two Circles* sculpture, waiting for Jo. It was one of her favorite pieces so I knew she would come here.

There were a couple of people taking pictures and a small group of what I assumed was an art class, sketching intently. I didn't have much of a wait. Maybe she wanted to be early too. I watched her walking, thinking how lucky I was to get a second chance to be with her. Lord, I pray I'm going to be so lucky.

She was a knockout, so full of grace and energy that I was certainly not the only one watching her. She wore white capri-length jeans and a pink pullover shirt that stopped just above the low-rise waist of the pants. The toenails peeking out of a pair of strappy high-heeled sandals were an exact match for the shirt. As she got closer, I could see the silver ring in her belly button. Her hair blew across her face, the black strands glinting almost blue in the sunshine.

When she saw me standing there she hesitated, a stutter step, uncertain. I was afraid to move toward her when it was what I wanted so much to do. She came closer slowly, slowly, until I was beginning to think she would never cover the few feet separating us. When we were perhaps three feet apart, she stopped.

"I didn't know if you would be here," she said in a near whisper. "How did you know?"

"How could I forget?"

"This isn't possible." She stared at my face as if trying to see inside me. "You know this isn't possible."

"I know." I didn't have any answers that would make sense to her. "But I'm here anyway."

"It really is you, isn't it? Inside your mind."

I nodded.

"How?"

"I don't know the answer to that, honey." I didn't move, not wanting her to bolt and run. "I know I'm here. I know I love you. It's been a long battle to find you again."

"So what took you so long?"

"Jennifer had a bad head injury—"

"Jennifer? Who's Jennifer?" A sudden snap of jealousy sharpened her voice.

"It's a long story, but it's thanks to Jennifer that I'm here talking to you right now." I thought the proprietary moment was a good sign. "Trust me, you can put the green-eyed monster back in its cage."

That made her smile, which made me smile. We stood there, the two of us, not touching, just grinning at each other. It wasn't the first time the green-eyed creature had made an appearance. Jo had been jealous of little old ladies in the supermarket when the planets all lined up just right.

"It *is* you, Cotton," she said, still smiling. "And whoever this Jennifer is, I'd give her a kiss myself to say thank you."

"Then I'd have to be jealous." I laughed. "Or would I? This is very confusing and I know more of the story than you do."

Neither of us had moved so much as an inch closer, and it was beginning to feel strained. I wanted to grab her and hold her, but there were too many people close by. The world is changing, but this wasn't one of the places where a public display of affection would go over big, even after a trip back from the dead.

"I'm kind of scared of you." Jo took one step, then another toward me. "I can feel it's you in there, in that body, but it's not the body I know." She reached out and cupped my chin lightly with the tips of her fingers, so delicately it tingled. "This isn't the face I've missed every second you've been gone."

Too much, too much, too much.

"Jo, baby." I pulled myself back one step. "If you make me cry like a sissy, with all these people looking, I'm not going to give you your present."

"Present? Now that's what I like to hear." She blinked back her own tears and rubbed her palms together in mock greed. "When did you get me a present? It's not my birthday."

"I missed your birthday." It had been a week after I had been killed. "I had this made for you."

It was still wrapped in the crumpled twist of tissue paper. She grabbed it and shook it next to her ear as if it were in a box.

"What can it be? Not a CD. Not a harmonica." She tore it open and held it in the flat of her hand. "What...?"

It was a brass ring, smaller than the one from the carousel, with two keys attached. I took it from her and dangled it from my finger.

"Let me explain. This one—" I held up the first key. It was made of shiny gold-looking metal and had a custom-designed grip, with our initials engraved in it in fancy swirled letters. "I had this made to give you before; it was the key to my apartment to celebrate our new life together. I was sure you'd take it."

"In a heartbeat," she whispered.

"And this one—" I held up the second key, a plain cheap silver one I'd had copied in ten minutes at a hardware store. "I had this one made today; it's the key to my apartment to celebrate our new life together. I'm sure hoping you'll take it."

"In a heartbeat," she whispered.

Then she was in my arms, all juicy and warm from the Texas sun. She kissed me, full on, no holds barred, right in front of God and everybody.

CHAPTER TWENTY-SEVEN

There are worse things in the world than routine. It wasn't something I had ever really valued, tending more toward faster, newer, shinier. Being settled down had seemed like settling. After all I'd been through and all I'd fought through to get back to my life, settling into a routine was a dream come true.

Jo and I were happy. True, it wasn't easy at first. I felt like Lucy when Ricky said, "You've got some 'splainin' to do." While I had benefited from many sessions with two shrinks guiding me through the psychological and metaphysical maze, Jo had to get a crash course from me.

She seemed to accept it more easily than I had, but then again, she was a genuine believer in anything too good to be true. She had half a warehouse of stuff she bought on late-night infomercials. Amazing Spot Remover, Peanut-shell Pillow, Sunless Tanning Tablets—she bought them all. And when she got holes eaten in her carpet, a stiff neck and two weeks' worth of carrot-colored skin, she never even asked for the guaranteed nineteen ninety-five refund. I was a shoo-in deal—The Remarkable Recycled Girlfriend.

The new house key worked just fine, but we were still keeping two separate apartments. I wanted us to move in together right away, sort of being in the making-up-for-lost-time mode—lost time in ways I never knew time could be lost.

Jo was the voice of reason, which, in itself, struck me as a little strange. I never knew her to be all that reasonable. "Impulsive" had always been her middle name. Sort of like Lola from *Damn Yankees:* Whatever Lola wants, Lola gets. Delayed gratification wasn't a concept Jo found appealing. But now she starts being reasonable—go figure.

"Sweetie," she drawled. "I think it's too soon to start living together full-time. We don't want to be the tagline of that old joke."

"What joke is that?"

"You know the one—What does a lesbian bring on her second date?"

"Flowers and a U-Haul," I answered, but I wasn't amused. "That might be funny if we hadn't been together long before this week."

"That's what it looks like to other people though. They think we just met. They don't know I live with a walk-around."

"Walk-in," I reminded her. "I explained Andrew's theory to you."

"Kidding," she said with a laugh. "You are so easy."

"Just because I can be had doesn't mean I'm easy."

"That's exactly what it means. And I have enjoyed having you."

"If you moved in, you could have me all of the time." Subtlety was never my strong suit.

"You need some time to yourself, baby," she cooed.

She did a lot of cooing lately. And singing, which—as much as I loved her—I never encouraged. Jo has many talents, domestic and otherwise, but she couldn't carry a tune if you put it in a bucket. Fortunately for someone with no ability to stay on pitch, she was also blessed with a tin ear. Thank goodness she never knew she was singing so badly that people thought she was doing it as a gag.

When she's happy, she sings. When she is happy, I am happy. I am very good at tuning out anything I don't want to hear. A couple put together by the Fates, no doubt about it.

"I don't need time to myself. I've been isolated for months. Enough quality alone time to last a lifetime or two."

"You haven't had a chance to get settled into your new place," Jo said. "I don't think all of my things will even fit in here. Besides, it's fun to have two apartments to play in. Romantic."

"This is plenty romantic. C'mon Jo. You've got a million reasons for us not to live together," I pressed. "A girl could think maybe you've had a change of heart while I was out of the picture."

"Not a smart girl like mine."

"Why not put me out of my misery and move in then?"

"Well, technically, you are still a married woman. This Gregory person—he could use this against you in court." Jo waved her hand, stretching an imaginary banner in the air. "I can see the headlines now: 'Loyal Husband Abandoned While Wife Frolics in Lesbian Love Nest.' We are tabloid material, no doubt about it."

"Puhlease," I scoffed. "That whole husband thing's about to change. Besides, Gregory said I needed someone to move in here and take care of me." I arched my eyebrow and gave her my best suggestive leer. "And you do a great job of taking care of me, if you know what I mean."

"You are bad." Jo burst into laughter. "So bad. Do you suppose the pay is decent? This could be a sweet deal for me if Gregory is interviewing for the position. Move in with his wife *and* get paid for it."

"I'll ask him about benefits next time we have lunch."

"You need to stay away from him." Her laughter subsided. "If he finds out about us, he could be dangerous."

"Gregory hasn't got the balls to be dangerous. He doesn't care about Jennifer, just her money. Unless there's a buck to be made or a snob to be impressed, he's not interested enough to turn off his laptop."

"Don't bet on it," Jo said. "I lost you once because of a jealous husband—mine. I don't want it to be because of yours this time."

"You really think your ex could be a killer? He seemed like a fairly nice guy," I said. "Full of himself, for sure, but a murderer?"

"I know he did it. He always said he wouldn't let anyone else have me." She pointed her finger at me for emphasis. "Cotton—you—wouldn't listen when I said I was being followed. Listen to me now. I sure the hell don't want Max to know I'm with another woman after what happened before. He got away with it. He got away with murder." She was as indignant as she was frightened. "There's nothing to say he wouldn't try it again."

"Max wouldn't kill me," I said, trying to lighten the mood. "First of all, it would look really suspicious if you had two girlfriends in a row get knocked off. Secondly, and most important, he can't afford to kill anyone who buys four cars in one day. I'm his best customer."

CHAPTER TWENTY-EIGHT

There are four seasons in Dallas, Texas: early summer, summer, late summer and winter. Late summer was upon us. Instead of broiling every day, twenty-four seven, we were down to merely hot, with an occasional coolish day and evening. The whole city was giddy with the break in the heat.

Occupancy at the Outreach was way down. The cooler temperatures had a calming effect on the hot-tempered creeps who took their discomfort out by pounding on their wives and kids. Everyone here was happiest when we were needed least.

The whole staff took the opportunity to use the big kitchen and dining room to get together and eat and visit. The people who worked here were dedicated beyond belief. They sure weren't in it for the money. Aggie was in her element, working the crowd, making certain everyone was getting plenty to eat and taking time to talk to people in a more relaxed way than was possible when everybody was doing a full workload. She was popular with everyone and had a natural gift for making them forget she was the boss.

I had been welcomed into the Outreach, if not like a long-lost child, at least like a distant relative. I guess they'd figured out I was hanging around for the long haul, instead of playing do-gooder for a week or two before disappearing back to the more rarified air of the snooty rich.

I had more or less slid back into making center decisions, sometimes without remembering that officially I should clear them with Aggie. She knew this place was my baby, my creation. Now that I was back, if something needed to be decided, she happily let me ramrod the situation. Everybody else put up with my slightly bossy attitude because Aggie put up with it. If I was okay with her, they figured I had to be okay.

I walked up behind Molly Rayner and put my hand on her shoulder.

"I heard someone has been out painting the town in my old ball gowns."

"Yeah. I figured since you were taking over my territory, I'd even the score." She patted my hand and gave me a warm smile. "I'm thinking about putting in a few hours at the gym though. Some of these society ladies are a lot tougher than I gave them credit for."

"You can't always judge a book by its Monique Lhuillier, can you now, Molly?"

"Not even if I could spell it." She snapped her fingers. "I forgot. The other day some guy came by the delivery dock asking about you."

"What guy?" I wondered if cousin Dewayne was skulking about, since I'd been avoiding his calls, each a little more impatient than the last. It had made me uneasy to find he had managed to get my number. How he'd figured out where I was working was another disturbing question. "Tall blond guy, a little seedy?"

"Nah. Dark and maybe five ten or so. Not a grifter, for sure. Dressed rich enough to go out with one of your old evening gowns. Funny thing. He had a picture of you, but he kept asking questions about Jennifer Strickland. Guess he hadn't heard you were getting divorced."

"What kind of questions?" Probably one of Gregory's stooge investigators. I guess I didn't scare him as much as I thought.

"Where you lived. How long you been working here. Who you're hanging out with." She shrugged. "I told him you were a snooty bitch who didn't have time to talk to the likes of me."

"Molly—"

"I'm poking fun at you, J.C. I didn't tell him anything. I figured if he was up to any good he would have walked in the front door and talked to you himself."

"Thanks Molly." She was solid—the kind of person I liked having my back. "If he comes around asking any more questions, would you let me know? If anyone comes around?"

"Sure thing." As I turned to walk away, she called me back. "J.C., when we were unloading all the boxes of stuff you donated, I found a few things I was pretty sure you didn't mean to include—pictures, a journal, stuff like that. Want me to drop it by tomorrow?"

"Anytime. Thanks, Molly. Nice of you to notice."

When I told Aggie what Molly had said about the guy at the dock, she wasn't happy at all.

"That worries me."

"I'm sure it's one of Gregory's trained monkeys trying to dig up dirt for the divorce."

"If that's the case, why would he be asking where you live and how long you've been here? Gregory knows the answer to all of that."

"Yes that's true." I didn't like the idea of being asked after. "Do you think he could be working for Max Sealy? Jo's terrified of his finding out she's involved with someone again. She's really scared of him."

"I think she has good reason to be. She was almost killed herself."

"Don't you get paranoid too. There's a good chance the whole thing was a gay-bashing hate crime."

"You think using a stun gun to get Jo out of the way and then a baseball bat on—" Aggie's voice faltered. "On *you* wasn't a strange setup for a random hate crime?"

"I'm beginning to wonder if anything in the whole damn universe is random. Too many coincidences for my comfort."

"I'll have a few friends do some watching around the parking lot and alleys. And I want you to be more careful; no more breezing in and out of here at all kinds of hours. I want you to be more cautious, no matter where you are."

"Aggie, we don't need to overreact." I didn't like the idea of tiptoeing through my life. "This could be a reporter or something like that. We can't go jumping to conclusions."

"Sure we can," she growled. "And we can be ready for trouble if it comes."

"And how are we going to get ready? Buy a gun?"

"Good first step. Then we teach you how to use it and get a permit."

"I was *not* serious, for God's sake."

"I am. Dead serious."

"Oh, come on Ag." I laughed, but she didn't crack a smile. "Can you really imagine the two of us 'packing heat'?"

Aggie grabbed my hand and put it on the waistband of the sweatpants she was wearing. Under the baggy shirt was a hard metal shape even a novice like myself knew wasn't a cap pistol. I snatched my hand back.

"Christ Aggie. That's a real gun. How? When?"

"Of course it's real. It's also legal."

"Why haven't you shown it to me? Or told me about it?"

"That's why it's called a concealed handgun permit. You aren't supposed to go around showing it to everybody." Aggie lowered her voice. "There are a lot of dangerous fools walking around this town who aren't happy we've helped their wives and girlfriends get away from them. It's not smart to have no protection against guys like that."

"Oh Lord. If Jo finds out about this, she will go ballistic."

"Jo asked me about getting a permit two weeks ago."

"No way. Jo's about as likely to use a gun as she is to suddenly rise and fly."

"I think you underestimate little Jo." Aggie cocked her head to one side and shrugged. "She's not the delicate little flower you picture her as. Jo has a long history of taking care of Jo."

"And exactly what is that supposed to mean?" I didn't like her to have such a suspicious mind where Jo was concerned. "This isn't the first time you've made a crack about her. What's she ever done to you?"

"Not a thing."

"So why don't you like her?"

"Like her just fine." I could see she was lying through her perfect white teeth. "Nothing wrong with noticing someone might have a tiny fault or two."

"That still sounds like a veiled criticism. Stop bullshitting and tell me what you've got against her. I won't be mad."

"Yeah right," Aggie drawled. "You are so crazy 'bout that woman you think her farts don't stink. Always have been. So you imagine I'm gonna dis her to you?"

"I think I've been in the dark so long about so many things, a little clue here and there couldn't hurt."

"Uh-huh. Ain't comin' from me, s'all I'm sayin to you."

CHAPTER TWENTY-NINE

Jo left me. It was only for a couple of days, but it felt like a long time. She was heading up a big benefit for the gubernatorial campaign in Austin. The dinner was A-list, strictly for the cream of the crop, that being anyone who could come up with the five thousand for a plate of ribs and beans. I know the rest of the country has rubber chicken at their political fundraisers, but Texas *is* cattle country after all.

I watched her pack, drove her to the airport and kissed her goodbye, wishing I didn't feel so alone. Aggie was out on the town and asked me to come along, but being a third wheel to a perky redhead didn't appeal to me, especially when the evening included a movie at the Angelica, a local art film house. Any movie that required me to listen to Chinese while I read English subtitles took the evening from fun to fat chance.

I decided to have a quiet evening at home, reading a book or doing something constructive. Times like this I wish I recalled a hobby—a knack for macramé or a passion for bowling, maybe. Instead, I picked up an order of extra-spicy garlic chicken from a neighborhood Thai place and a six-pack of Kirin to soothe the burn.

The Thai food was a good idea. The book was a chick lit paperback Jo had left, and it was so dull it made watching grass grow seem exciting. Nothing like boredom to encourage dealing with unpleasant matters. I had an upcoming meeting with Himself to see how my divorce proceedings were proceeding. I wanted to give him the journal of Jennifer's that Molly Rayner brought me.

I glanced through the first few pages. Not a word about giving cousin Dewayne a hunk of change; no mention of him at all. The notebook was mostly a rehash of her fabulous shopping and spa-ing adventures, with a few gripes about Gregory scattered here and there. Even Jennifer was beginning to suspect that Prince Charming was hiding a little frog DNA.

She was especially interested in some details she found while snooping—I mean, while checking her email—on Gregory's precious laptop. It seems she was the designated driver to and from the dentist after Gregory had a little happy juice for a root canal. He was so stoned he hadn't locked down his system, and Jennifer hadn't been able to resist the temptation of browsing his files.

Not being as unskilled at the computer as I am, when she found some information that aroused her curiosity, she sent the files to her email on her own computer for later review. Trusting soul that she was about Gregory managing her money, Jennifer knew enough to doubt that she and Gregory owned property in the Caymans. She certainly didn't have access to a pass-protected bank account in Costa Rica.

She also wondered why her parents' last travel itinerary was on her husband's computer. She had barely known Gregory at the time, having only met him because of some paperwork she needed to sign when her parents were setting up details on estate planning. Her folks hadn't seemed to know him much better, certainly not well enough to share private details of their vacation with him. Not until after her parents' tragic plane crash had the handsome young broker offered her a shoulder to cry on and become a source of financial advice. When he proposed to her after only a few weeks' courtship, it seemed natural to accept.

Jennifer had written page after page—wondering why she and Gregory were drifting apart, planning things that she could do to keep him. It made me sad to think the previous owner of my body had wasted tears and other bodily fluids on trying to keep the slimeball in her life. I wished there was some way for her to know he wasn't worth a single second of her concern.

Without a golden parachute, Gregory wasn't about to dive out of the jet-set wealth of the super rich into the more scaled-down style he could manage on his own. Gregory could afford to fly first class on his own income. Jennifer could buy the airline. *I* could buy the airline now, if the mood struck me. Crazy that.

I wish I knew what made Jennifer decide to let me have her body, to give life up without a fight. She didn't have to let me in, I know that much—she had the original claim. I don't know why she left; poor little rich girls have problems too. If I'd had to spend years living with Gregory, I think I'd have been looking for an exit sign myself. But all that money could have bought a lot of freedom without going literally out of this world.

Reading her journal was like reading about a stranger and, since I looked in the mirror at Jennifer's face every morning, that didn't seem right. I owe her so much, I wish there was something I could do to make the balance sheet more even. I get a buttload of money, a nice body, a way to reclaim my life— Jennifer gets dead.

There was a fair possibility that my sensitive musings were in large part due to the three bottles of beer I had downed with dinner and while reading Jennifer's memoir. I thought about making a pot of coffee to chemically balance my blood alcohol level. I thought about taking a hot bath and watching TV. What I did was fall asleep on the couch, surrounded by empty beer bottles and holding the journal on my chest.

I dreamed of the fog for the first time in a long while. Not too surprising considering my reading material and curiosity about why Jennifer left and I came back. Booze is a wonderful guide dog to blind dreamers.

My sleep was filled with fog and fury. Jennifer was there, demanding justice. The voices were shrill and the impenetrable whiteness hurt me. Hurt my head.

When I woke, my head was pounding, the overhead light glaring white and blinding. I blinked and was a little surprised to find myself still balancing Jennifer's journal on my chest. I stood on unsteady feet and let it fall to the floor. This had been a bad dream and a bad trip. Booze may be a guide dog, but let me tell you, she's a bitch.

CHAPTER THIRTY

At the risk of sounding trite, there are two kinds of people in the world: those who wake up smiling and chipper the morning after having too much to drink and those whom a compassionate God should let live. I am not a chipper person. God let me live, and being merciful, along with light, He let there be coffee.

I had a pot before getting into the shower on my way to Starbucks. It was substandard compared to my usual latte, but strong enough to let me withstand the water crashing against my skull and the supersonic roar of the blowdryer. I had an appointment with Himself at ten and with the help of half the lethal dose of caffeine and more than the recommended two aspirin tablets, I hoped to get there looking vaguely human.

I grabbed Jennifer's journal and headed out for the offices of the mysterious Greenly Inc. Judging from the small fortune this firm was charging me, I expected miracles. Well, not get-your-name-in-the-Scriptures miracles, but something impressive. If not a burning bush, maybe a houseplant that didn't die if you forgot to water it for a month. That would do me a lot more good than parting the seas, especially in Dallas.

Sean Himself was waiting for me with a big easy smile and the offer of a cup of coffee, which I declined. The gallon or so I'd had earlier was starting to kick in and I was so wired, I could feel each hair on my head vibrating.

"I brought something I thought you might find interesting," I began. "This is Jennifer's diary." He wrinkled his forehead, looking puzzled. I realized what I had said and corrected myself. "*My* diary. Jennifer before the accident—me before the accident," I stammered. "My diary."

I presented it to him, wondering now why I didn't just tell him what it said. I was getting so used to being Cotton again to Jo and Aggie it was easy to talk about Jennifer in the third person. My shrinks had accepted the notion, but no way was I going to try to explain it all to a virtual stranger.

"It has a lot of information about suspicious behavior by Gregory. I thought it might be of some use in your investigation."

"Glad to have it." He took the book and put in on his desk. "Truth to tell, very glad to have it. This is turning out not to be your garden-variety divorce. Lots of interesting people involved. And a few situations we're going to have to decide how we want to handle them should they become common knowledge."

"Let's give it a go." He pulled a manila file folder out of his top drawer; it was remarkably thick. "Doyle Dewayne Winters. It seems you have good reason to doubt your cousin's story. He's a flimflam man, through and through. Mostly petty theft, but he seems to be escalating in intensity."

He looked up from the file and shook his head.

"He would have been paroled earlier, but he beat the bejesus out of his cellmate. Don't let him fool you. He's already been a bad boy since he got out of jail, racked up a sizeable gambling debt. The man holding the marker is rough trade, so Dewayne may be desperate for cash. If he hasn't already been tagged by the cops, it's only a matter of time. If you see him or he starts squeezing you, one call to me will take care of it.

"My next piece of advice is for you to stay as far from your husband as you can possibly manage."

"That's not a plan; that's a done deal," I said. "Besides giving me the creeps in general, I'm starting to get scared of Gregory. He'd be sitting pretty if anything happened to me before I get my will changed or the divorce settlement goes through."

"We'd better get the legal eagles cracking on the paperwork then," Himself said, jotting down a note on the folder. "Don't be afraid; just be cautious. I'm serious about this. I have a few more things that have to be verified before I can present you with hard facts, but don't assume anything when you're dealing with him. After combing your financial statements, I have every reason to believe your husband is capable of some pretty underhanded activities."

He opened the file and pulled out a couple of pages.

"I don't know that you want the authorities involved, but it's more than clear that Mr. Strickland has been skimming quite a lot of money from your accounts since the day he married you. Before then, actually, if you want to count all the money he embezzled from your parents."

"He was stealing from my parents?"

"Hand over fist." Himself pantomimed as if he were pulling a rope in. "I don't know how he thought he was going to get away with it, clumsy bastard that he is. Begging your pardon." I waved him on. "He's not even a very clever thief, just a very lucky one. If your parents hadn't died so tragically, God rest their souls, he'd have been done for. Double lucky, because you evidently gave him *carte blanche* with the funds and must have never looked at a statement in your life."

"So it seems. As you figured out pretty quickly, I'm not much of a financial whiz, but my father was. He'd have figured out if he was being stolen from." A shiver of something nasty ran down my spine. "I think you may want to do a more in-depth investigation of Gregory after you read the journal. Something very strange is on his computer regarding my parents and their final trip."

I gave him a brief idea of the contents of Gregory's laptop according to Jennifer's foray into hacking. "I don't care about the money. I'd happily give him a chunk to get rid of him, but I'm not going to let him get away with murder. Do you think he could have been involved in my parents' deaths?"

"That's a big leap on short evidence, but I promise that I'm not going to allow you to become another victim." He scribbled something on a yellow Post-it note and stuck it on the front of the file folder. "Tomorrow, I'm getting you a bodyguard."

"Oh, I don't think that's necessary," I objected. "We don't have a shred of real proof yet that Gregory is dangerous, just crooked. He's too big a sissy to get his hands dirty with anything violent. This thing with my parents' trip information may have been less incriminating than I thought."

"After all I've told you, how can you close your eyes to the possibility he's bad news? Women are such fools over men." He was exasperated. "Under the circumstances, I hardly expected such typically female behavior from you."

"The circumstance being?"

"It would seem men in general and your husband in particular would have no sway over you now that you are involved with a woman."

Despite his professional skills, Himself, it seemed, was a little bit of a caveman. I hadn't seen that coming, but as long as he kept it out of my business, no skin off my nose. "That's pretty judgmental of you. I don't see how my having a girlfriend impacts my ability to interact with the men in my life." Wait. How did he know about me and Jo? Only one way he could have. "I didn't hire you to investigate me, by the way."

"I can't protect you if I don't know everything I can find out about you."

"Just do your best. I'm not fooled by my soon-to-be-ex-husband nor impressed by his macho charms. I just don't want to be followed around everywhere I go."

"Which brings us to another issue," he said. "You are already being followed around. At this point, if you don't want a bodyguard, I suppose we can follow the guys who are tailing you. Watch the watchers."

"Gregory's goons. He's trying to get proof that I'm a danger to myself. If he could lock me up somewhere and not have to divorce me, he would be a very happy camper."

"We already have enough dirt on him to dissuade him of that plan. What I want to make sure of is that he isn't into something so bad he has no way out. Cornered animals are mindless and dangerous."

"So what's the plan?" I asked. "I let him follow me around until you catch him?"

"Something like that." He picked up the journal and fanned the pages. "Give me a couple of days to go over this and I think we can have a clearer idea of how we want to proceed."

"Okay." My head was throbbing like crazy. "Are we done for now?"

"Not quite." He looked uncomfortable, rather like a man having to knock down a hornet's nest—certain that it was necessary but not looking forward to the job. "I have to talk to you about Jo Keesling, and I'm afraid you aren't going to like what I have to say."

CHAPTER THIRTY-ONE

"If I'm not going to like what you have to say, Mr. Greenly, maybe you ought to consider not saying it."

He was watching my face intently—looking for a sign that it was safe for him to proceed. I was, after all, the paying client. I could feel the blood rush to my cheeks, knew they had to be flushed and red. *Red light. Danger. Stop.* He didn't.

"Sometimes in my line of work, you discover things you have to deal with whether you like it or not. Things that are in your client's best interests to know—however they choose to deal with it." He was choosing his words carefully, not a good sign. "There are sensitive issues that have come to light." He cleared his throat and started from a different direction. "You've been protected all of your life, Jennifer. Your parents had the means to shield you from having to act out of need or desperation. Everyone isn't so lucky."

"I realize that having money makes life easier, Mr. Greenly." I wasn't in the mood for a discourse on the advantages of being rich. "How does this have anything to do with my divorce or my girlfriend?"

"Your divorce is only a part of what I see as a potentially harmful situation. How much do you know about your friend… about Ms. Keesling?"

"What about Jo? Is she in danger?"

"Maybe, but my bigger concern is that I think she puts you in danger. Her partner in her last relationship was killed, some think by her husband." He shrugged. "I'm not so sure of that myself. The police never had enough evidence to arrest him."

"I am very aware of the circumstances. Max Sealy shouldn't still be walking the streets. Jo's terrified of him."

"I understand that. However, Ms. Keesling is not exactly the innocent victim that you might suspect. She was involved in a situation with a local psychologist, Dr. Cotton Claymore, that didn't paint either of them in the best light. Jo's involvement may have been a factor in her lover's death."

"Of course it was a factor. Her affair made that big jock into a raving manic killer. That wasn't her fault." I was getting angry. "An affair doesn't justify murder."

"The affair was only the final straw, as the saying goes. There may have been much more complicated things going on than it seems at first glance," he said. "I haven't got enough evidence to make a direct accusation, but you might not want to be so quick to trust a woman you haven't known all that long."

"Long enough," I snapped. "What do you have on Jo to ask me to keep her at arm's length? Not that it's likely to happen, just so you know."

"Ms. Keesling came from a very unfortunate background. Dirt poor, alcoholic single mother—pretty grim." He spoke quietly, sympathetically. "She was a great beauty from the time she was a teenager. It was the only currency she had to trade on to get out of that place. She became skilled at using her charm."

"Hold on a minute." I held up a hand to keep him from speaking right away. "Be very careful what you imply about Jo. I won't have you trashing her to me."

"And I've no desire to do so. You need to know that she developed a pattern of—shall we say—attaching herself to people who had money or fame or notoriety and used it to her own benefit."

"She was a gopher for a local publicity firm in Atlanta." He opened the folder again and took out a sheaf of pages and photographs, which he handed to me. "She left town with an aging actor who was in Atlanta doing a film. She was young and beautiful, if not too sophisticated."

Her face in the picture broke my heart. Eager and vulnerable—a target for the fading star who had his arm around her. She was cheaply dressed and unpolished next to him, but she had a spark that lit her up. I recognized the actor from an old legal drama that had made him a household name for two seasons before he went straight to the daytime television melodramas that ran night and day.

"He was her ticket out of Hicksville," he continued. "A couple of years in LA and she made a bit of a name for herself doing publicity for a handful of beginners on their way up and feeding inside items to the tabloids. Better haircut. Better clothes."

"Stop it. This is none of my business unless she decides to tell me. I don't give a rat's ass how she got to be who she is."

"Then she met and married Max Sealy. She didn't have to worry for money any longer. No more hustling gossip. She was able to set up her consulting and public relations firm and had access to all the introductions his name could attract. When they settled in Dallas, he was a big fish and she swam happily along."

"I get the picture." I tossed the material he had given me down on his desk. "I don't care how she started out or where she came from. What part of that are you having trouble understanding?"

"Then Sealy retired and started selling cars and renting himself out as a guest at public functions. Jo moved on. She dumped him for a local media darling named Cotton Claymore. The situation caused a lot of buzz and got her a lot of publicity."

"That's enough." I stood up, intent on leaving. "You're making her sound like a gold digger. That's not true. Jo is a successful businesswoman, a really gifted fundraiser."

"That she is," he soothed. "But she made a mistake when she got hooked up with Max Sealy and his cohorts. A few of these men are involved in some under the table deals that make Enron look like a Sunday picnic. They just haven't been caught yet."

"She's not with Sealy anymore, as you very well know."

"No, but she's still doing business with a lot of the same people," he said. "And a few of them are very bad guys, no matter what color hats they wear in public."

"For your information, right now Jo is working with the man who may be governor in a few more weeks."

"Like I said, they haven't been caught yet." He leaned forward and lowered his voice although we were the only ones in the room. "Yours isn't the only case I'm handling. Let me tell you a secret. Quentin Biggs may be the next governor of Texas, but if you shake hands with him, count your fingers when he lets go."

"Okay, say that's true. I wasn't planning to vote for him anyway." I stood and gathered my things. "What has this got to do with Jo or me?"

"That's a question I'd like you to think about," he said quietly. "I'm on your side, Jennifer. Instead of asking me about it, ask Jo about how she met Cotton Claymore. Ask her why she's still involved with Biggs. Then ask yourself what all this social climbing has got to do with Jo's involvement with you."

CHAPTER THIRTY-TWO

I never asked Jo any of those questions. I picked her up at the airport, gave her a couple of welcome home kisses and told myself to leave well enough alone. Something in the misty reaches of my memory warned me that maybe I had forgotten these details for a reason. I had decided that all I needed was the present. The past was turning out to be way too complicated. I was worn out with meetings and intrigue and warnings of dire things to come.

I decided to pretend I was Forrest Gump. Simple is as simple does or something like that. All I wanted to do was listen to Jo describing all the fun and chaos she had been part of in Austin. I decided it was time for me to have some fun too. We needed a break, maybe a few days out of town—maybe Vegas or a bed-and-breakfast with massages and facials. I decided to call Aggie and see if she and some lucky woman wanted to join us.

It turns out Forrest was wrong. Simple never is that simple. Aggie had other plans for us. I vaguely recalled Jo and Ag advocating that we needed to get a gun for protection. I never thought of it again. She had taken that casual conversation and translated it into something I never wanted to do in the first place. Seems I was living in a fool's paradise, thinking I had any say about my life.

The Weekend of the Drugstore Cowgirls would have made a heck of a reality show. Aggie drove Jo and me to Bullet Bazaar, a gun store and shooting range for a day of practice before we went to our class and testing for a license to carry a concealed weapon. Jo was upbeat, if not enthusiastic. I was present in body, but definitely not a happy camper.

The place was my worst nightmare—filled with the reek of testosterone and rows of glass-topped cases filled with Colts, Smith and Wessons and Glocks. They had revolvers and semi-automatics and laser sights. There were shooting targets with everything from a plain bull's-eye target to human outlines to seated, smiling photographs of Osama bin Laden.

They had books on shooting in self-defense and home protection. There were thin volumes on gun-cleaning supplies and how to pick the perfect holster, comparing the merits of leather versus canvas with Velcro. It seemed all the authors were particularly worried about the Second Amendment and paranoid that the United Nations was a big front to remove guns from the hands of every law-abiding citizen, something which would then presumably leave only criminals with all the fun toys.

Cookbooks were popular, although I didn't look closely enough to find out if the recipes were how to prepare what you shot or foods to eat while sitting in a deer blind. Probably both. And they had bumper stickers touting the joys of gun loving for every occasion. I think I even saw one for Mother's Day. Pinkie swear.

We had to rent guns and goggles and ear protectors. Aggie knew the guys who owned the store, so they made us feel right at home. I tried to pretend I wasn't really there, but before I knew it I was dressed like one-third of an inept SWAT team and herded to the indoor practice range.

I don't know if it was the same as getting seated near the kitchen in a nice restaurant, but we were at the very last booth, down three spaces from a guy with a mullet carrying a custom-made crocodile-padded case. He made a big show of opening the case and pulling out a gleaming phallic monster that Clint Eastwood would have died for in the Dirty Harry movies. When he fired it the first time, I screamed like a cornered piglet and thanked the guys up at the rental desk for insisting on the heavily padded earmuff-looking things I had resisted wearing.

I watched as Aggie demonstrated loading the gun and not pointing it at anyone else and how to pin up the target and move it down range. The din of two big whirring fans blowing the gunpowder-drenched air around and an intermittent barrage of gunfire on top of my headgear made it virtually impossible to hear any of the words she so earnestly was saying. Lip reading and sign language wore thin for me in about five minutes.

Jo went first. She was almost as bad at shooting as she was at singing. She squinted and closed her eyes when she fired, and it was a miracle we weren't tossed out the way she waved the gun around. Considering she'd brought up the possibility of getting a gun in the first place, Jo sure wasn't having the best time of her life. Aggie finally had her sit on a metal folding stool by the fan while I took my turn.

Aggie decided I should go with the Glock for practice and during my proficiency testing. I argued when she said it was a semiautomatic, thinking that sounded much worse than a revolver. It seems a revolver is a simpler gun, but a semi was faster to shoot especially if more than one round was needed. She explained if you qualified with a revolver, that was all you were able to carry legally; using a semiautomatic during qualification meant you were good to go with either one.

I used the Glock. It was functional, simple, easy to use and didn't have a safety, evidently something to be desired during the timed practice shots for the proficiency testing. All I could tell you is that it's black, metallic and intimidating. Add to that the bullet casings flying around and the hot acrid smell of gunpowder and you've pretty well summed up my version of hell, except in hell, there also was no caffeine.

My first shot missed the target altogether. Aggie consoled me, encouraged me and made me try again. I don't know what happened, but as it turns out, I'm a crackerjack shot. I put the next seventeen rounds in an area the size of a saucer. Kinda liked the way it made me feel, seeing those ragged holes pepper the paper target. Maybe I was Annie Oakley before I was Jennifer or Cotton. Aggie was slack-jawed with shock and then proud as if I had won a blue ribbon.

Anyway, it was seriously crazy how much I liked it. It wasn't about bloodlust or penis envy or mere marksmanship. There was a poetry about it, a purity of the connection between intention and results—a philosophical clarity. I think, therefore I shoot. I think part of the thrill was also a control issue. After so long with no conscious control of my own mind, the ability to massacre paper tigers made a pretty convincing demonstration that I was in charge for the moment, at least if the targets weren't shooting back.

And I liked showing how good I was in front of my girlfriend. A little who's-your-daddy butch thing.

Despite her initial enthusiasm, Jo wouldn't let me buy her a gun, not even a little one. She also announced that she wasn't taking the classes and generally swore off firearms in general. She said they gave her the creeps and winced visibly with every shot that was fired.

I, on the other hand, finally found a store I could really let my latent shopping skills run amok. I left the store with a Kimber semiautomatic pistol, a leather holster, two boxes of ammunition, a gun-cleaning kit and an incipient case of carpal tunnel syndrome.

After a two-day course of classroom instruction and written testing, I completed my proficiency training. I was then fingerprinted and background-checked within an inch of my life.

Two days before I had been a peaceful, unarmed woman with not a hint of knowledge of stopping power or caliber. Without too much arm-twisting, I had become that rarest of all creatures: a liberal lesbian with a license to carry.

CHAPTER THIRTY-THREE

Fall was on its way. The temperatures in the mornings and evenings were finally comfortable enough to get outside and into the streets. Jo and I walked a lot. On the mornings we stayed at my place—which was virtually all the time—we'd circle the park before heading to Starbucks to kill an hour or two sitting outside, Jo working the daily Sudoku puzzle while I tackled the *New York Times* crossword. The puzzle taught me a valuable lesson: you may forget your own name and the faces of your nearest and dearest, but obscure three letter words like "qis" and "suq" are resilient even against the ravages of death.

In the evenings it was fun to drop by one of the girl bars and have a glass of wine and shoot a game of pool with Aggie or Molly. Sometimes there were cookouts—or call-ins, as Jo referred to her special talent for having people for dinner without cooking a thing.

"Marty's delivers booze and cheese plates and desserts. The rest can come from Eatzi's and *voila!* Dinner is served and I have time to get my pedicure." She was a girly-girl from tip to toe; a bad toenail day was out of the question. "You get to pick out the music."

"I live to serve," I said humbly. "Do I really get to choose the music or just load what you want into the player?"

"Of course you get to choose it," she said reasonably. "I left a whole stack of CDs on the counter and you can pick anything you like from that pile."

"You make my life such a joy. Whatever would I do without you?"

"You always have good old Gregory to fall back on." She walked behind me and pulled my head back against her breasts. "Of course I'm a lot softer to fall back on than he is."

"Hmmm," I mused, testing her softness and agreeing wholeheartedly. "What a hard choice—a beautiful sexy wench who is bossy as the day is long, but a *fabulous* roll in the hay— or the illegitimate spawn of Medusa and Microsoft?" I grabbed Jo and twirled her around the room before gently pushing her onto the sofa. "You are so lucky I'm not into hairy knuckles. Besides, I think Gregory has been screwing me so thoroughly in the bankbook, anything in the bedroom would be redundant."

"So how is the divorce coming—not that I'm being pushy or anything like that? Any word from the lawyers?"

"I have a meeting scheduled tomorrow. Maybe I'll have some news."

I had been vague about the details of my divorce proceedings. I hadn't explained about Himself or the mysterious Greenly Inc. to Jo. Hadn't mentioned it, in fact. I wasn't really ready to get in to the whole mess Himself had stirred up. I was avoiding him by avoiding talking about it.

I loved Jo, but a tiny part of me was still a little unsure of how much to trust her. I had enough holes in my memory to use it as a strainer. Until all the pieces fit tighter, I was leery of giving anyone too much control.

Besides the nightmare at Greenly Inc., all of Aggie's snide jabs about Jo had planted their own seeds of doubt. When the day came that I was sure I had my memory back in full and no more surprises were lurking in my gray matter, maybe I'd be ready to share all of myself instead of hiding and not trusting anyone. Maybe.

"It's nice paying other people to do my dirty work." I stood looking down at her as she stretched provocatively on the couch. I gave her a guilty shrug. "Never having had the pleasure of being filthy rich before my little adventure in Jenniferland, I had no idea how much work it would be to get a divorce. On the bright side, it does provide jobs for a whole lot of people."

"Any idea how long it will take to get finalized?"

"Why the hurry?" I asked. "It's not as if that marriage is really any part of my life, except on paper."

"He's trying to get more of your money," Jo said. "You know he's after your assets."

"Who cares if he gets a few bucks? It's not like I'd care if he wasn't such an obvious prick about it." I didn't share my growing suspicion that Gregory was a dangerous man. No need in her having to worry too. Better to change the subject. "You know, it might be easier and faster to have him knocked off—God knows I can afford it."

"Cotton, you better stop talking like that, even to me. If something happened to him, you'd end up in jail yourself."

"You better stop calling me Cotton, even when it's just the two of us," I warned. "You're going to slip and people will think you've gone nuts. Are you ever going to call me J.C.?"

"If I must." Her dramatic sigh would have been overacting all the way to the second balcony. "Couldn't you have picked some other name, something a little like closer to Cotton?"

"Linen? Woolen?" She giggled at my suggestions. "Would you rather cuddle up and whisper, 'I love you, Cashmere' in my ear?"

"As long as my baby is back to cuddle, I can even manage J.C."

"You think so?"

"Come here and let me whisper it in your ear and show you."

She beckoned me with a crook of her finger and a come-hither smile. I took a flying leap to land on the couch beside her. I was more than willing to be convinced and she acted as if she wanted the job. My God, was it good to be me.

I was ninety percent persuaded and one hundred percent exhausted when the phone rang. It was likely Cousin Dewayne again. His calls were getting less kissy and more urgently demanding, if not outright hostile. I was thinking of having my number changed again.

"Let the machine get it," I begged, not able to make my shaky legs carry me across the room to the phone. "They can leave a message."

"What makes you think I was going to crawl to the phone myself?" Jo pushed the tangle of black hair out of her eyes. "And I don't care if they leave ten messages. I'm not moving from this spot until tomorrow."

The phone clicked over to silent after four rings and was transferred to a voice mailbox. After a couple of minutes it rang again. Four rings—voice mail. And again. And again. Again.

"Oh crap. Let me get it so whoever it is will stop." I wobbled toward the phone, kicking our scattered clothes out of the way as I went. "It can't be Aggie. She'd either use my cell or be banging on the door by now." I punched in the number for the voice mail service and entered my password. "Five messages. Aren't we popular?"

"Who is it?" Jo asked after I listened to the first message without saying anything and went on the next. "What's wrong? You better tell me."

She came to stand beside me and put her ear next to mine as the third message came on.

"*You bitches are an abomination to the Lord.*"

Jo sucked in a sharp draw of air.

"Holy shit," she swore. "What did the first ones say?"

"Pretty much a warm up for this one." I was surprised my voice came out so evenly. Inside I was quivering like Jell-O. "Let's see what comes next."

I pushed the button for message four.

"I can see you. Both of you—you disgust me." The next words of the raspy voice sent me running to the balcony, phone dropped to the floor. *"Naked on the couch, making a mockery of decency."*

I yanked the curtain across the big window, not trying to cover myself. What was the point after providing the floor show for some pervert Peeping Tom? Jo had picked up the receiver and was listening to the last message. Her face was paper white and her hand shook as she held the phone out to me.

"Honey," I soothed. "Don't let it scare you. It's some nosy watcher in one of the apartments across the road. We'll keep the curtain closed next time. Let him get his jollies on his own."

She shook her head.

"Listen to the last one," she whispered. "My God, Cotton. It's happening again."

CHAPTER THIRTY-FOUR

"The dirty bastard." Aggie was the first person we called. She was at the apartment in fifteen minutes flat. "Sneaky little window-peepin' bastard."

She was holding the phone in a grip she would obviously rather have had around the perpetrator's throat as she listened to the fifth and final message: *"I'm watching you every day and every night. Watching you both. You can't be allowed to live among normal people. You don't deserve another chance."*

"How sick is this dude?" She looked at me, then at Jo. "I know this is doctored, but anything about his voice sound at all familiar? Any phrases sound like anyone you know?"

Acknowledging our headshakes with a nod, she listened to the messages once again and then looked at the two of us as if the whole thing was our fault. We sat, side by side, on the sofa, looking like a couple of guilty schoolgirls who had been caught in the act by the headmistress. We had thrown our clothes on and fluffed the pillows on the couch, but it was obvious we had been doing the nasty. Even threatening phone calls by a nutcase couldn't wipe the goofy-eyed satisfaction off my face.

"What am I going to do with you?" Aggie asked. "I can't leave you alone for a minute without worrying about you getting into some kind of a mess."

"Sorry we're causing so much trouble—making out on the couch in our own living room. What were we thinking?" I said. "It's not like we sent out an engraved invitation to this guy to join us."

"Don't be sarcastic with me," she snapped. "I'm not blaming you. I'm just really scared."

"Scared?" I was honestly not expecting fear. "It's nothing to be scared of. I wanted some help figuring out which window he was watching from so we could…maybe we should…" I stammered, running out of anything to say. I had no idea of what we could do. "Call the cops or something."

"Hell, yeah, we'll be calling the cops. Like you should already have done." She reached in her knapsack, pulled out her cell phone and tossed it to me. "In case you don't remember it, the number is 911."

"I'm not stupid." I was pretty sure I would have known that on my own. "I can manage to report this by myself, thanks," I said, turning my back and walking a few steps away to the kitchen as I called in the incident.

That'll show her.

"They'll be here in a few minutes." I said as I walked back into the room.

"Good deal. That will give us time to look around ourselves."

She pulled a pair of binoculars from her backpack. Always prepared. If I had called her with a fishing emergency, I had no doubt she could have pulled a rod and reel or bucket of bait out of her wizard's bag.

"First, though, turn off the lights in here and let's scope out the view."

I flipped off the main lights. In the darkness of our living room, she cautiously pulled back the curtain far enough to slide the balcony door open and squeeze outside. I followed her, glancing back where I could see the dim outline of Jo's body huddled on the sofa. She made no effort to join us and I let her stay there, thinking she needed a few minutes to herself. Her nerves had gotten the better of her, not that mine were in much better shape. I just handled it in a different way.

Aggie and I were doing our own Nancy Drew number on the case. Aggie slowly scanned the high-rise building across the street. There were at least ten floors of windows that could have seen us if their occupants had been so inclined and willing to spend hours watching and waiting for an opportunity.

"This is creepy, Ag. Knowing someone was watching us." I cringed. "No telling how many other people he's been peeping. I'm calling the manager to tell everyone be on guard. Then—"

"This isn't a problem for everyone, J.C." Aggie put down the binoculars and lowered her voice. "I don't want to scare Jo more than she already is, but this is no random pervert."

"What do you mean? He's watching us—us in particular?" I didn't like where this was heading. "Don't you think that's a stretch?"

"You aren't thinking clearly. The calls."

"So he calls to threaten us. Probably how he gets off."

"You're not listed."

"What?"

"You have an unlisted number, babe. No random creep is going to be able to make a dirty call without a lot of digging around for that information. Still think this is a smutty joke?"

"It's happening again."

Jo stepped out onto the balcony, her bare feet quiet as she joined us. Her tone was a whisper, almost without inflection. Fear had leached the color from her voice, taken away all the animation that was her trademark.

"I knew there was danger." I had to strain to hear her. "Since I was a little girl, I've always known when something bad was happening. I knew it the last time. No one would listen to me then either."

"Shh. It's going to be fine, sweetheart."

I put my arm around her shoulders, but she shook it off and hissed at me, actually hissed like an angry cornered wildcat.

"It's going to be fine? Everything's going to be all right?" Hysteria was gaining on anger. "'No one is following you, Jo.' 'It's all in your imagination.'"

"Come on back inside, Jo," I said softly, trying to keep the fear from my own voice. "Let's go back inside and we'll decide what to do."

"I warned you last time. I warned you and you laughed at me." Her voice was a mournful echo. "And now it's happening again."

The hairs on my arms and the back of my neck were at full attention.

"Jo, Aggie and I are going to take care of this. The police will be here soon. We can get protection."

"He got away with it before. He's going to do it again." She was crying now. Her whole body was shaking with the sobs. "Cotton. Don't let him do this. Find him. Find Max."

"We're fine tonight. Tomorrow we'll take whatever steps we need to make sure he's caught. Let's turn these tapes over to the police—"

"Trust the police? That's a good one. They were so much help arresting the killer before." She cried so hard I could barely make out her words. "He's going to kill you again. He's going to kill us both this time."

"Honey. Ssh. It's okay. This time we believe you. We won't let anything bad happen. It's going to be okay," I soothed, promising more than I was sure I could deliver. "This time we'll be okay."

"Yeah, maybe we're going to be okay this time," Jo said. "It's next time I'm worried about."

CHAPTER THIRTY-FIVE

Our visit from Dallas's finest wasn't all that fine.

The two officers sent to handle our call looked as professional and reassuring as you could ask. Their dark uniforms were crisp. Their badges were shiny, as were their black cop shoes. In fact, they could have been on the recruiting poster for the City of Dallas Police Department.

Sergeant Teague was well built, if not too tall, maybe five ten or so. He looked as if he spent a lot of his free time in the gym. Officer Maples was almost the same height, but dark to his blond, and rail-thin to his stoutness. She had a little spiral notebook and scribbled furiously every time anyone spoke. I don't think I heard her utter more than a dozen words during the interview.

"Dispatch said you received threatening phone calls," Officer Teague began. "I need to get your authorization to copy the calls. And we'll send tech people out later to set up a tap in case you get more calls."

"Not a problem."

"Did you recognize the caller's voice?" I motioned to include Jo. "Neither of us did."

"Have either of you had any trouble with co-workers or any family disputes?"

I thought about mentioning Dewayne, but it seemed a stretch. I'd learned to erase his messages without listening. I didn't like that he had grown more demanding and much less charming, but his interest was financial, not peeping, and I don't think he had a clue about my relationship with Jo. Then there was Gregory; he was certainly watching me closely.

"I'm getting a divorce," I began, only to be cut off by the next question.

"Any conflict with your neighbors?" He might have been reading a checklist. I shook my head. "Noticed anyone following you or showing up in casual situations enough to make you aware of them?"

"I haven't seen anyone," I said, "but in case you didn't hear me before, I'm going through a messy divorce. My soon-to-be-ex-husband has been having me followed—strictly for my own good. I don't think even he's this sick, but I would love you to question him."

I gave the name, address and phone number to Officer Maples. I wish I could be an invisible observer when Mr. High and Mighty had to be interrogated like a mere mortal. The officers asked Jo the same question.

"Not lately." Jo's answer made Officer Maples look up at her, expecting more, but with a shrug, Jo went on. "Not really, but there was a problem several months ago—"

"Let's say in the past six months," Sergeant Teague sounded less than concerned. "A nice-looking woman is going to get watched—pardon me, but you ladies are the types likely to attract admirers. That isn't the kind of attention I'm talking about."

"Not to dismiss your compliment, Sarge, but I think some weirdo watching you through your window and calling to say you don't deserve to live is a touch more than being an admirer." I didn't like the way he was looking at us, not a lot more respectful than the night peeper. "But thanks for the concern."

"One other idea." He looked at the couch again and raised an eyebrow. "It might be a good idea to close the curtain over the balcony or turn off the lights if you don't want to put on a show."

"I'll make a note of that." I was sugar-sweet. "Maybe you should listen to the calls now."

They listened to the messages. Sergeant Teague's eyes focused on us, then slid to the couch and across the street to the building facing our windows, then back to the couch. Officer Maples had the decency to keep any lascivious wonderings hidden. Her cheeks flushed noticeably and she cleared her throat.

"Ms. Strickland." Her tone was comforting. "In most cases these callers are only trying to scare people."

"Then mission accomplished," I said. "We are scared out of our minds."

"Yes ma'am. I'm sure you are." Teague regained control of the interview. "Have you had any other calls or any other threats? Letters? Anything of that nature that might have fingerprints?"

"No. Just the calls last night." I was trying to be helpful. "Can't you check the phone records and see where the calls were made? They do that on all the crime shows."

"This isn't a high-profile crime, ma'am. It's a nuisance call, not a murder investigation." He had the temerity to smirk. "We don't need to call the guys from *CSI*."

"So until there's a body, you aren't going to do anything?"

"Of course we're going to do something, ma'am. We're going to investigate and follow up on it," he said. "If I were you, I'd have my number changed and be careful who I gave it out to. These calls are usually from someone you know."

"I didn't know this guy," I replied.

"The voice was altered," he said. "That's why it sounded so mechanical."

"Don't you have some kind of technology, something at the lab to run it through?" I was out of my element, but damnit, I had seen *CSI* a lot and no one had to beg Marg Helgenberg to do her job. "Voiceprints, databases, secret decoder rings—anything?"

"I'll turn the tape we made over to the lab people, but anybody can buy stuff to distort a voice from the Internet or even local surveillance stores. Not likely to track him down by that."

"What if we know who it is?" Jo had been quiet until now. "My ex-husband—"

"Lady, not to be rude or anything, but we hear that accusation every time. And here—" he pointed an accusatory finger at each of us. "We have two exes to consider. Do you have any proof your ex is involved?" He asked the question politely enough, but the twist of his mouth and the sideways glance at his partner said, "Here we go again."

"Nothing more than the fact he murdered one of my friends last year and threatened me if I got involved with anyone else."

Sergeant Teague—I probably should change the name to protect the guy's reputation and to keep me from being sued— snapped to attention at Jo's accusation. He glanced at Officer Maples to make sure she was getting everything on paper. He shouldn't have worried; she was scratching away, transcribing his every word in her little notebook.

"Your ex-husband killed someone last year? What's his name?"

"Max Sealy."

"Max Sealy, the baseball player?" His voice rose noticeably and Maple's pen came to an abrupt halt. "Your ex-husband is *that* Max Sealy?"

"That's the one."

"I remember the case." Teague looked at his sidekick. "Local gay woman beaten to death. Everyone liked Sealy for the murder, but nothing stuck. There was a big investigation, then it was kicked to the Hate Crimes unit. Probably in the cold case files by now. No evidence Max Sealy had any connection at all, except the ex-wife here was the vic's girlfriend."

"We *are* still here, Officer." I was getting steamed at his lack of respect and I didn't care much to be pigeonholed as "local gay woman." "So does this mean you'll talk to Sealy?"

"We will check all leads, ma'am." He gave me a business card with his name and some department numbers on it. "If you have any questions or have any more trouble, call us. Or call 911 if you feel it's an emergency situation."

"Like if one of us ends up dead? Would that be an emergency situation?" I was talking to their retreating backsides. "Don't worry, officers. We can check out the leads on our own."

"I don't see your badges," the cop said in parting. "Stay out of the way and let us investigate." He turned and added a word of advice before stepping into the elevator. "Don't be stupid, lady. Let us do our job."

* * *

I was stupid enough to confront Max Sealy the next morning, but I wasn't stupid enough to do it alone. Aggie rode shotgun, almost literally. We were both carrying weapons, nice legal, registered and loaded weapons. My small Kimber forty-four caliber felt like it weighed a ton in my shoulder bag. Aggie was used to hers and never seemed awkward about it at all.

"I feel like I'm walking into the O.K. Corral, Ag. Carrying this gun makes me feel more afraid, not less."

"Forget it's there," she advised. "You aren't going to need to use it."

"Then mind telling me why the heck you insisted that I bring it?"

"You need to get used to having it around. The time may come that you wish you had it on."

"That day isn't today," I said, tugging the gun out of my purse with one hand and thrusting it across the console toward the passenger side. "Put it in the glove box. I can't deal with it right now."

"You're gonna have to deal with it, sooner or later."

"I choose later."

"I just hope it isn't your funeral. Again."

"One more thing, Ag." As we were walking up the ramp toward the building, I thought it was time for me to clear the slate with her about my previous visit here. "I better tell you something before we go in here."

"What's that?"

"You know those vans and pickups that got donated to the Outreach?"

"Uh-huh."

"I bought those."

"Do tell."

"You knew?" She was making fun of me in her own none too subtle way—outright rubbing in how dumb I was. "How did you know it was me?"

"Well, I was pretty sure it wasn't Santa Claus. Too early for that. And you were new at the center, with so much money it was burning a hole in your fancy pant's pocket." Aggie waved her hand impatiently. "Don't keep me waiting all day? Are you telling me you got them here? You went by yourself to look up Max?"

"I was trying to find Jo."

"Seems like there might have been an easier and less expensive way to get that scoop than buying half his lot. Not to mention less dangerous."

"I wanted to look him up. I thought he might be more forthcoming if I laid out a bunch of cash." The way she shook her head didn't look like she understood where I was coming from. "Besides, my brain had more holes in it than a cheese grater at that point in time. I wasn't making the best of decisions then."

"Unlike now, I guess." Aggie held the front door open for me. "Come on then. Let's get this showdown on the way."

CHAPTER THIRTY-SIX

Nelda was at the reception desk, her crowning glory teased to bountiful perfection. She looked at me, then up at Aggie.

"Good afternoon." She nudged her purse farther under the desk with the toe of her shoe. "How may I help you ladies?"

She obviously didn't consider us ladies. At least not ladies who she didn't worry might steal her purse. I didn't want to speak for Aggie, but my feelings were hurt.

"We'd like to speak to Max."

"I'll see if Mr. Sealy is available."

"Tell him it's Jennifer Strickland," I said. "I promise he'll want to talk to me."

Max came storming down the hallway, not attempting to hide his rage.

"I want you out of here, right now," he snarled. "Both of you."

"Max. Max," I chided. "Is this any way to treat a good customer like me?"

"I don't want your damn business, bitch. I want you to get off my property."

Spit droplets sprayed from his lips, giving the impression he might start foaming at the mouth at any minute. His usual ruddy complexion was a dangerous purple.

"We need to have a serious talk, Max. You and me and my big friend here." I stepped toward him. "Why don't we go to your office, where it's more private?"

"I could have you arrested for slander," he spat. "Sending the cops out here to question me. Who do you think you are?"

"I know who I am, you asshole. I'm someone you do *not* want to screw with." I lowered my voice and asked more reasonably than I was feeling, "Do you want Nelda telling every soul on the lot that you were in a screaming fight with your ex-wife's lover? Want everyone to know exactly why the police were talking to you this morning?"

He glared at me for a couple of seconds, then turned and stomped off down the hall, leaving us to follow. Nelda was making no attempt to pretend she wasn't watching every bit of the drama. I'm sure the car business usually didn't provide such a steamy show.

Max was already barricaded behind his big wooden wall of a desk when we strolled in and sat in the two chairs facing him. He didn't ask if we wanted a cup of coffee even though there was a fresh pot on the table by the door. So much for Southern hospitality.

"So you're Jo's latest conquest?" If looks could really kill people, I would be ready to be embalmed.

"Yes, I guess that would be me. As if you didn't know."

"You might want to be careful, Ms. Strickland. Has anyone told you how her last little honey ended up?"

"I know more about it than anyone except the killer." I looked in his eyes without blinking until he broke contact. "The police may not have done a very good job, but trust me, payback's a real bitch. Take it from another real bitch, Max."

"What do you want with me?"

I wanted to punch his headlights out, but I decided to play cat and mouse for a while. "As if you didn't know, Mr. Peepers."

"I've got better things to do than peeping in windows at night."

"For an innocent man, you seem to have a pretty good idea of the circumstances."

"I had no idea and didn't give a crap until today. I'm not interested in what that black-haired slut is up to. Not until I get dragged in to it." He reached into his top drawer and pulled out a legal-sized manila envelope. "I found this on the front step when I opened up this morning."

He tossed the envelope across the vast sea of oak between us. I saw the notation in big square letters: **MAX SEALY— YOUR EYES ONLY!**

"Go on," he urged. "Take a good look."

There were photographs inside—half a dozen or so in grainy black and white and two in living color. The black and whites were of me, getting out of my car—going to the bank, carrying in groceries. One might have been at Lee Park. Another couple at the Outreach. One of Aggie and me walking arm in arm coming out of a bar one night last week.

The two colored shots were as crisp and clear as studio portraits. The first was of me and Jo at the Nasher Sculpture Garden, wrapped in our passionate reunion kiss. We were framed so artistically we might have been in an ad for *Girlfriends* magazine. The second was of the two of us from last night—a telephoto shot of another more intimate embrace in the apartment living room.

"You slug." Aggie growled. It was the first time she'd said a word since we walked into the showroom. "I ought to—"

"Not me. I had nothing to do with these," he said. "I'm being set up."

"Yeah right." Aggie was on her feet beside me and she didn't look at all convinced. "Give me one reason we should believe you, you lying sack of Siberian snake shit."

I was astonished by her alliteration in the middle of an out-and-out threat. Max didn't seem to appreciate her poetic talents, but the threat must have come through loud and clear. He scooted his leather chair so far back it hit the wall with a thunk and raised both hands in a defensive gesture.

"I told you I had nothing to do with these. Why would I want the cops questioning me? I've had enough problems because Jo can't stay away from chasing pussy."

Aggie was around the desk and grabbed him by the front of his jacket before I could blink.

"You want to rephrase that?" She sounded serious. "I really think you can find a nicer way to make your point."

Max was panting so hard I was afraid he was going to have a stroke on the spot. I wouldn't have cared except I didn't want Aggie to be blamed for killing the creep.

"Let him go, Aggie." She tightened her grip, lifting him nearly to a standing position so she had more leverage to throw him back down in his chair. "I don't think he took the pictures."

"What? He's guilty as hell."

"Oh, I think he's guilty of plenty, but I bet someone is giving him a nudge in our direction this time." I snatched the photos and stuffed them into my shoulder bag. "We have one more stop to make."

I slapped my hand flat on his desk to get his attention. He didn't take his eyes off Aggie until I smacked it a second time, harder. He licked his dry lips and his eyes skittered back and forth between the two of us.

"Don't think I'm forgetting about you. If you so much as cross within a block of me or Jo in traffic, I'll show you what a little pussy can do to a big, fat rat."

CHAPTER THIRTY-SEVEN

"Whoa, this isn't the Texas Motor Speedway," Aggie yelped as I made a corner on three wheels, spinning out of Sealy Motors onto the main highway. "Stop driving like a fool and tell me where we're going in such a hurry."

"We are going to meet my soon-to-be-ex at his fancy downtown office tower." I stomped on the accelerator and got us into the thickening traffic on LBJ Freeway. "And you are going to keep me from shoving these pictures up his creepy, back-stabbing ass."

"He took the pictures?"

"Not personally, I'm sure. Gregory hires people to do his dirty work for him." I threaded the Beamer in and out of the cars, making my way to the faster-moving HOV lane. "He's been having me investigated."

"He's doin' what?"

"He's been having me followed."

"Since when?"

"Since I moved out of his house. Said it was for my own good." I laughed, remembering his holier-than-thou attitude before he went ballistic on me in the restaurant parking lot. "His story was he was worried about me—what with the head injury and all. Right. He was gathering evidence to get me locked up so he could get away with stealing Jennifer blind. I knew he had some pictures, but—"

"And you're just now getting around to tellin' me about it?" Aggie banged her fist on the dash. "Did it not occur to you to let me in on this?"

"If you hit that any harder, the air bag is going to blow up in your face," I said calmly. "I warned him what would happen if he didn't call off his dogs."

"She warned him." Aggie raised her hands to heaven. "Sweet Jesus, she warned him. Isn't that enough?"

"Evidently I underestimated him. I thought he was only a thieving cold-hearted creep." I yanked the wheel to avoid an eighteen-wheeler trying to get in front of me from a side ramp. "Not today buddy. I'm in a hurry."

"If you get on the tollway, it will shoot us right downtown," Aggie directed. "The late traffic will all be headed in the opposite direction."

"He's going to wish he had listened to me. He's not going to push me around and that's what's making him crazy."

"Lotsa crazy goin' round. Regular epidemic."

"You haven't seen the king of crazy until you meet Gregory. He looks normal, but he has a microchip where everyone else has a heart."

We were zipping through the normally pokey stream of cars and slid to a halt at valet parking in record time. The elevator ride to the twentieth floor seemed to take longer than our flying trip downtown. When the doors slid open, we walked into a reception area so posh the queen of England would have felt right at home.

The young woman sitting behind the tall, circular desk was as sleek as the area she was guarding. No Nelda Highhair here. Butter blonde, caramel silk dress, pearl earrings—she would have been a perfect fit for the North Dallas house I came back to life in. You had to give it to Gregory: he was consistent, if nothing else.

"May I help you?" she purred.

"I'd like to see Gregory Strickland."

"Did you have an appointment?" She was polite, but not quite ready to give us the golden ticket. "Is Mr. Strickland expecting you?"

"No he's not expecting me," I said sweetly. "But I have something better than appointment. I have a trust fund and the deed on his house, so I think he'd like you to show me in."

"Pardon me?" Blondie was confused. "May I get your name?"

"Tell Gregory his wife is here."

"Mrs. Strickland, I'm so sorry," she stammered. "I didn't recognize you." She looked at me as if I had been replaced by an alien. "Uh, you have a new haircut since the last time I saw you. Go right in. I'll let him know you're here."

We started walking down the hallway as she was whispering our arrival into the intercom.

"A new haircut? If only she knew." Aggie snickered. "Which office?"

"I have no clue. If I've ever stepped foot in the place, it must have been way before Jennifer abandoned ship." The heavy wooden doors on the offices were unmarked. "I guess we can start with the first one and—"

It proved unnecessary to guess. The door at the end of the hallway opened and Gregory stood waiting for us to arrive, watching with disappointment darkening his face.

"Jennifer, won't you come in? And please introduce me to your new *friend*." He was disgustingly polite. "You should have let me know you were coming. I'd have made more time in my schedule to visit."

"Last-minute decision to drop in, Greg. This is my *best* friend and head of the Outreach, Aggie Burke." Neither of them made any pretense of wanting to shake hands. "We won't keep you long."

"Would you like me to get Brenda to bring you something, coffee or a soft drink?"

"No."

"Come in and sit then. What can I do for you?"

"I think you should ask what I can do for you, Greg." I pulled the envelope out of my purse and handed it to him. "I want the negatives to those, for starters."

He didn't even have the acting skills to look surprised. Maybe he thought he was above being bothered; maybe he was stupid. But the one thing he shouldn't have done was exactly what he did.

"Oh my." He ran a fingertip over the colored photos and smirked. "These are going to be embarrassing for you in the divorce settlement. I'm afraid most of the judges aren't tolerant of alternative lifestyles."

"Bad way to start, Greg. Threatening me?"

"She hates that, man," Aggie said. "I think you should give her the pictures."

"I have nothing to do with these, although they are quite artistic."

"And I suppose that you had nothing to do with the obscene calls that went along with them?" I wanted to wipe the smarmy smile off his face. "Any idea how these got into Max Sealy's hands this morning?"

"Of course not," he swore. "It would be next to inviting murder to give a madman like Max proof that his wife was at it again. With my own poor wife, who probably isn't capable of realizing who she has gotten involved with." He grinned. "Why, he could be dangerous."

"He's not the only one who could be dangerous, Strickland." Aggie stepped close to him and snatched the pictures out of his fingers. Although he was a couple of inches taller than she was, he gave her ground. "What kind of man tries to put two women in that kind of situation? You better watch your back and pray nothing happens to either of them."

"Are you trying to intimidate me?"

"No Gregory," I interrupted. "Thank you, Ag, but I want to handle this."

"You go, girl." Aggie moved away from Gregory, but only a step and her fists were still balled up.

"Greg. 'Intimidate' is such a nice word. Make no mistake: This is not intimidation; this is a threat. I'm the one who is *threatening* you."

"Jennifer—" He began to speak, but I didn't let him get a word in edgewise.

"No. I talk, you listen."

"You can't come into my office and dictate to me—"

"Yes I can. Here's the deal." I outlined my plan in short sentences, little words. "I want the photos. I want the negatives. I want a divorce with no fault and no attempts to play games about my mental health. I want you to talk to Max and get a leash on that dog."

"And what do I get out of it?" Gregory asked defiantly. "What makes you think you can—?"

"Here's what you get, Greg. The house in North Dallas and all the furnishings. The paintings except for the ones my parents left to me. The Porsche. A more than generous cash settlement."

He still looked ready to jump in with an argument. I had a couple more things that I thought might seal the deal.

"You also get to keep the beachfront house in the Caymans that you diverted money from my stock portfolio to buy." He turned a little pale under his tanning-bed bronze. "You get to keep the cash you've stashed in Costa Rica." He looked as if he were going to puke.

"You have one week to make this a done deal or I swear to God you won't know what hit you." He stepped behind his desk and slumped into the chair. "And because I'm such a nice person, as an added bonus, maybe, if you're really nice, you get to stay out of prison."

CHAPTER THIRTY-EIGHT

"Now *that's* what I call a good day at the office!" I was delirious with my ambush of Gregory. "Did you see the look on his face? He's lucky I don't have him arrested—the pervert. I didn't think even Gregory could be so disgusting."

"Think again," Aggie said. "You know, I understand the blackmail notion." She touched the envelope of photographs. "But how did he know to put the dirty deed off on Max Sealy? You know about it from me and Jo, but none of that made the papers."

"When he found out that I was volunteering at the Outreach, he was all snotty about the company I was keeping—all those liberals and homosexuals, don't you know?" I laughed aloud, recalling his horror. "He said his buddies at the country club gossiped that Max had gotten away with something seriously bad."

"You think they meant Cotton's—make that *your* murder?" Aggie shook her head so hard that her long braids whipped the air. "Girl, do you know how crazy that sounds? Drivin' around town with my dead best friend—well, let's just say I've made some weird adjustments for you." She rolled her eyes. "Do you believe Max could have been the killer?"

"That's what Gregory implied." I shrugged. "Don't underestimate him. He's a real jackass, but he's smart and very devious."

"Yeah maybe," she said, "but I wish you could have seen how righteous you looked up there when you handed old Gregory his walkin' papers. Fierce! You surprised me almost as much as you did him," she said. "You never told me he was stealing from you. How did you figure it out?"

"Little bit of information from my bank. Little gut instinct. Lots of bluffing."

"Remind me not to play poker with you, girl," Aggie said with a laugh. "And I thought I was good."

"Just glad it's over. If I never see him again, it'll be too soon for me."

"You better want him to stop making Sealy mad." Aggie whistled through her teeth. "I could feel the hatred. Having the cops grill him got him all macho about Jo leaving him for you. I don't think he's playing with a full deck."

"I'd say he's one sandwich shy of a picnic."

"One brick short of a load."

"His cheese has slipped off his cracker?" I loved this little word game. Ag and I had spent years collecting the corny sayings, getting points for any new ones we found.

"His bread is still doughy in the middle," Aggie responded.

"Good one. Five points." I lost this round and gave the award gracefully. "Where did you find that one?"

"Made it up."

"No you didn't."

We were interrupted in the contest by my cell phone playing the distinctive opening bars of Barry Manilow's "Copacabana."

"Girlfriend, you cannot keep that ringtone." Aggie groaned her disapproval as I dug my phone out of my pocket. "I'll be embarrassed to be out in public with you. If that phone rings in front of anyone cool, I swear I'll walk right by like I never saw you in my life."

"Walk on, sister." I laughed as I flipped it open. "I'm an unrepentant Fanilow."

I tuned out her groan as I answered. It was Jo—rattling on so fast I barely got a word in edgewise before she hung up.

"The romance must be winding down," Aggie teased. "You look like you got dumped."

"Just for the evening. Seems Jo has been summoned to stem a crisis at the Biggs' campaign headquarters. She was flustered and said not to wait up. She's going to have to get some papers from her place and she'll probably stay there tonight."

"Yep, it's over, all right."

"Like hell it is." I laughed. "If you heard what she promised me to make up for being gone…"

"No please. I'm not able to handle the graphic details without a drink or two."

"Okay, since I'm off my leash for the night, let's go get a great meal and I'll get you loopy." As much as I liked the evenings with Jo, the notion of a night out with Aggie sounded great. "After the day I've put you through, I'm buying."

"Honey child, with the money you have, until further notice, you're always buying."

"Sounds like a deal to me." I grinned and goosed the car into high gear. "Let's go spend my money and think of something different to do tonight."

CHAPTER THIRTY-NINE

"When you said let's do somethin' different, I was thinking you meant eating at The India Palace or somethin' like that." Aggie was slurring her words a bit, which wasn't surprising after the pitchers of beer we had with our pizza. "This is a whole 'nother somethin' you got us into."

"It seemed like a good idea at the time," I said, not so sure I had made the right call. "You weren't trying to talk me out of it."

"Of course not. I'm drunk. What kind of buddy passes up an adventure like this?" She waved her flashlight around, casting eerie shadows in the dimly lit hall of the indoor storage facility. "I didn't know we were going to have to bribe ole Norman Bates at the front desk to get in, though. I swear you better not have a body stashed in a freezer or I'm outta here."

As I'd pulled out my wallet to pay for the pizza, the two keys I'd found in the box of my stuff Aggie had stashed in the equipment locker fell out. It was Aggie who figured out that they were keys to this storage place, but I couldn't remember whose idea it was to get a cab, stop for flashlights and go treasure hunting in the middle of the night. Sounded more like me.

"Don't be an idiot, Ag." I was trying to seem more certain than I was feeling. "Just because I had a couple of keys with the name of this place printed on them doesn't mean you have to act like this is a Hitchcock movie. It's probably a box of receipts or some old furniture. You remember more of my life as Cotton than I do. What would I have to hide in a place like this?"

"Beats me, but you always had a devious streak," she said. "Not bad usually, but this is probably where you stashed all the corners you cut to make everything work."

"Sssh," I giggled. "You're going to wake Norman's mother."

We both thought that was funny, but I think you had to be there to appreciate the humor. Oh, yeah, and you had to be tipsy.

There was enough light in the hallway from the row of dim bulbs to find space 117. Even though the building was advertised as temperature-controlled, it must have meant temperature-controlled for hanging meat. I couldn't see my breath fog up when I breathed, but after coming in from outside, it felt freezing.

To be truthful, although it would have been a nice, spooky touch, the door didn't squeak when we turned the key but slid open silently. It didn't look any more promising once we got inside and shut the door. In the center of the room was a single large black backpack. Other than a few less than spectacular cobwebs, that was it. No furniture. No boxes. No body.

"This is kinda weird," Aggie said. "Who'd pay for a whole room to stash a backpack?"

"I've got a weirder question." I glanced around the dimly lit room, shining my flashlight into shaded corners. "Since I've been out of commission for a while—who's been paying the rent on this space?"

"Sure as hell wasn't me. Didn't even know about it until an hour ago."

Aggie stepped closer and put her light beam right on the bag. "Pretty dusty, so I'd guess no one's been here since you left it. Maybe you paid ahead."

"Not likely since I was always scraping to get a few bucks for the Outreach. I wouldn't waste money on something like this." I hesitated. "Would I?"

"Not without a good reason," she hedged. "What could you possibly have in there? And a backpack was definitely not your style. If you couldn't stash it in your back pocket, it was too big."

"Not one of the things I remember, but I'm getting a bad feeling about this." I moved closer and we stood staring down at the backpack as if it were a live thing. "The best thing is to open it and look inside instead of playing twenty questions. Here, hold this." I thrust my flashlight at her. "It's not like it's a bomb."

"Heavy." I lifted it slightly to find the front and unsnapped the clasps on both sides of the big canvas tote. "Okay, here we go."

"Let's have a little light." I flipped the top back and motioned for her to come closer. "C'mon now, Aggie. Whatever's in here isn't going to bite."

Aggie focused the flashlight on the interior of the bag and neither of us had much to say for a long stretch. It wasn't that we'd never seen anything like it before—just not so much and not so unexpected. We continued to stare until Aggie reached in and pulled out a bundle of hundreds.

"Holy moly." She was beyond cursing. "Where did you get this kind of money?"

"I have absolutely no fucking clue." I wasn't kidding. "My God, do you think it's real?"

"I don't think you'd be hiding it in here if it was Monopoly money, do you?" She broke one bundle open and fanned out the stack of unsmiling Benjamin Franklins. "This is freakin' me big-time, Cotton."

"Me too." I pulled my hands back and moved back a couple of inches. "No way this is mine. Maybe we're in the wrong unit."

"Yeah. I bet your key will open any lock in the place." Aggie dumped the money back in the bag. "We need to get out of here now."

"Don't sound so scared, Ag. It's making me nervous."

"You need to be nervous, woman," she scolded. "We're in a creepy room in a bad part of town in the middle of the night, half drunk and elbow deep in dirty money. Be very scared."

"First of all, calm down." I was thinking, still fuzzy from the beer, but making an effort not to panic. "We didn't break in—we have the key. We aren't driving so being a little over the limit is no crime. It just seems creepy because the lighting isn't so good."

"And you got an explanation for why this money is here instead of in your account in a nice well-lit bank?"

"Not at the moment, but it's not like someone is about to jump us and grab it. It's been here a while, safe enough."

"You sure about that?" Aggie swept the flashlight beam around the room. "See that little red light up there?" I followed the pointing light beam.

"Yes. It's a security camera. What's so strange about that?"

"It's *inside* the unit. Security is to watch the hallways for intruders." She grabbed my arm and tugged me toward the door. "Let's get out of here now and think about why later. I don't like our faces on some stranger's camera fingering a stash we don't have any business with. And I don't know that Norman Bates out front hasn't already tagged us to whoever's bugging this place. Let's go."

"I'm coming." Her reasoning swept away any lingering beer-fuzz. "You really think someone is watching this place still? After all, as far as anyone knows, Cotton Claymore's been dead almost a year. Why would you think they're still watching?"

"They haven't taken their money back yet, have they?" She was half-dragging me down the hallway. "Whatever you did, they obviously are keeping an eye out for someone. Maybe they think you had an accomplice."

"You think they'll be looking for us?" I had enough on my hands without this development. "Gregory. Max. The peeper. This is getting ridiculous."

"You want ridiculous?" Aggie pushed me into the waiting cab and told the driver to go. "We've been blaming Max for bashing you all this time. Could be we have another contender for the dirty deed." She looked down at the flashlights she still held in her hands and clicked them off. "Any other little surprises you haven't told me about?"

"Now how the hell would I know of any more surprises, if I can't remember them?" I was finding this situation a little absurd now that we were putting distance between us and the storage facility. "For all I know a bunch of space ninjas from the fifth dimension has me under surveillance for crimes against the Mother Ship. Unless I tell you otherwise or the hit squad shows up, I'm calling it a night."

CHAPTER FORTY

Ten days passed without the ninja hit squad's arrival, so Aggie and I let down our guard and drifted back to our routine at the Outreach. We still glanced around to make sure no one was listening when we talked about the stash of cash or wondered who it belonged to and why Cotton had gotten involved in such a risky situation. Mostly, we tried to forget about it. Talk about not thinking about pink elephants.

"Molly had a good idea about the kitchen remodeling," Aggie said. We were going over a list of projects for repair and updating that were looming for the Outreach. "Her cousin has a hook-up with an appliance dealer. Thinks he might donate a new stove and dishwasher for a tax write-off."

"Any idea when he thinks he might?" I asked. "If we wait for maybe-so's to make up their minds, people are going to be eating cold cereal with plastic forks. Get the stuff in here by next week. I'll cover it."

"Yeah, you know where you can get your hands on some money, don't you?" Aggie grinned. Time and distance made big worries seem not so bad.

"I've got a checkbook. I don't have to go scrounging. You—"
The dulcet tones of "Copacabana" floated from my cell phone. Ignoring Aggie's groan, I checked the caller ID.

"Hello sweetie," I began, noting that it was Jo's number, but I was cut off by her near panic-stricken monologue. "No, don't go back in the building…call 911. We'll be there in ten minutes." Aggie was hanging on my every word. Hearing only my end was enough to let her know the trouble was serious. "Five minutes then. Don't touch anything. Call the police and keep the car door locked. It'll be okay, baby."

I snapped the phone shut and grabbed my keys. Aggie was out the door before I was. We were in the car and on the way in less than a minute. I put my foot nearly through the floorboard, stomping hard on the accelerator. The Beamer leaped forward at the demand.

"Jo went shopping for a couple of hours. When she came back to her car, there was a bunch of dead flowers under her windshield wipers."

"That's spooky, but calling 911 may be overreacting a little bit." I could always count on Aggie to be the voice of reason, thank goodness. "Did they leave a note?"

"Not on the car, but when she got to the apartment and went upstairs, someone had spray-painted the hall and left a couple of stuffed animals—toy cats with our names pinned on them."

"Okay, kinda crazy, but not enough to get too uptight. Stuffed kitties are pretty tame as stalkers go."

"Not when they are nailed to your door and dripping fake blood." A new wave of fear hit my stomach. "My God, it better be fake blood."

When we got there I was relieved to find it was nail polish. Blood-red nail polish.

The color of the polish was repeated in the spray-painted message scrawled on the wall halfway down the hallway and onto the door to my apartment: *DIE LITTLE PUSSY LOVER'S*

I know something is seriously wrong with me, and I wouldn't have admitted it to a living soul under penalty of death, but my first thought was not of the safety of my lover or imminent danger from a deadly stalker. It was the apostrophe. I had an almost overwhelming urge to get something to cover up the apostrophe.

It was awful enough to be the target of a deranged mind, but an illiterate, deranged mind was somehow too low a blow. There was also a missing comma after DIE, but I was willing to let that slide.

* * *

"They were about as helpful as the last time," Jo fumed, closing the door on the retreating backsides of two members of our local constabulary. "Am I being too critical or did they basically tell us they couldn't do anything until someone was injured or dead?"

"Oh, no, honey," I reassured her. "They dusted for fingerprints. They took the poor crucified plush toys. They made a report."

"I'm sure that has Sealy shakin' in his thousand-dollar ostrich boots." Aggie was furious. "I'm not waitin' for him to get a new baseball bat this time around." Her hand rested on the gun nestled in its holster at her waist. "I'll probably get to jail before he does, but if I catch him snoopin' around this part of town, he'll make it to hell before I do."

"Ag, you can't go around shooting people, no matter how much fun it would be." I loved her for being willing to do it though. "I think a second visit from the police will make Max very aware that they're keeping close tabs on him, too close to continue this."

"You don't know him," Jo said. "He's gotten used to being able to do anything he wants to—he was a sports star in Texas. Don't you understand what that means? He spent his whole life having people handle things when he screwed up. Can't pass that exam? No problem. Make that speeding ticket go away? Happy to do it, son. Look the other way when you bash your wife's lover in the head? We all know how that went."

"I think the smartest thing we can do is get out of town for a few days—have a little fun and let things cool down around here." And let me work on a plan that will end this for good, I said to myself. "Who's up for a long weekend in the country?"

"Last time you dragged me to the country, I had sores on my ass for a week," Aggie said. "If you think I'm going back to that rustic bed-and-breakfast and horseback riding hellhole, you have another think coming."

"No horses, I promise. And totally modern and luxurious. Luckily I have a therapist who thinks of me as a friend after all we've been through. Dr. Carey said during our last session that she thinks I could use a break. She has a house at Cedar Creek Lake that could make the front cover of *Texas Monthly*, according to Andrew. He's stayed out there and says it's paradise. What say the three of us go up tomorrow and spend a week fishing and hanging out?"

"We can't run away from this forever," Jo said. "He's not going to suddenly get religion and give us his blessing."

"We don't need his blessing. What we need is time to regroup." Aggie and Jo were stubborn as two mules, but I was persistent. "What harm will a little vacation do? I personally think a lot clearer if I have a belly full of fried bass and hush puppies."

"And who do you think is going to clean and fry those fish?" Jo shook her head. "I don't do cooking, much less cozy little fish fries. And I've eaten your cooking, honey. Not that I love you any less because of it."

"That's why I invited Aggie. She has her old Baptist granny's cast-iron skillet and the secret hush puppy recipe." I was practically begging. "C'mon, Ag. Save us from our own lousy cooking? I'll let you drive the boat."

"You think I can be bribed to be your cook by making me be your chauffeur in the bass boat? If you can sell that deal, they need you at the United Nations, negotiating a settlement between the Israelis and the P.L.O."

"If I didn't have so damn much money, I might apply for the job."

Aggie laughed.

"Do I have to actually fish?" she asked. "I hate that more than playin' those dopey board games."

"Okay, we'll give you a pass on the fishing." I grinned back at her. "But we have to have something to pass the time in the evenings. The TV reception sucks down there, so I had really looked forward to a smokin' hot game of Monopoly."

"I'd rather fish."

"Okay then. Trivial Pursuit."

"When pigs fly, girl. Don't push your luck."

"We'll get the All Sports edition." I laughed. "Seriously, Ag. You'll go with us?"

"I can't go up with you in the morning, but I can meet you up there tomorrow night." Aggie flipped her braids back. "Speakin' of my old granny, her birthday celebration is happenin' tomorrow. I have to go find a nice gift. Granny believes in getting birthday presents. It's what Jesus would want. Comes right after the Beatitudes." Perfect deadpan delivery.

"I can't argue with Jesus. Tomorrow night will be great."

I got ready to walk her down to her car, telling Jo I'd be back in a couple of minutes. She said goodnight to Aggie and picked up her day planner and iPhone.

"Okay, but if we're really going to do this lake thing, I've got to make a couple of calls. There's a cocktail party next week that I have to check with the hotel on." It was good to see her mind switch back to work and off the events of the past couple of days. "We'll have to drop by on our way out of town and let me leave an itinerary at the campaign headquarters. Tricia Biggs is a nervous Nellie who has to have every little detail nailed down. I swear I don't know how her husband hasn't strangled her yet."

I nodded my agreement and turned my attention back to Aggie. When we stepped into the hall, reality smacked me across the face. No matter how much I wanted not to think about it, the sight of the graffiti there yanked me back into the moment. The rough block printing was startlingly blood-like in the bright lights of the late night.

"Cotton, do you really think leaving town is going to solve anything?" Aggie asked. "You can't stay gone forever. It doesn't send a strong enough message to Max or whoever is responsible for this behavior."

"What kind of message does staying here and letting him terrorize us both send? He's a pissant who hides and makes up for his little prick by scaring women. I'm not going to pander to his ego by crying or running to the police every time I think he's lurking in an alleyway or parking garage. I'm not going to stay here and look over my shoulder every day either."

"So instead, we're all running away?"

"Sounds like a plan to me."

"Okay, I'm on your side, babe. I'll pack my skillet and be there before midnight tomorrow." She got in her old Jeep and I shut the door for her. "But you do know what they call people who run away from their troubles, don't you?"

"There's two schools of thought on that subject, Ag. Some people call them cowards. I call them survivors."

CHAPTER FORTY-ONE

The morning was the kind of day that made poets write odes to nature. Skies so bright a blue it hurt your eyes; the horizon spreading out so far and wide, it could have been a backdrop for the set of *Oklahoma*. An optimist would say, "God's in his heaven and all's right with the world." All I could think was our stalker probably wouldn't have any trouble keeping us in his sights.

So much for optimism—I think that whole glass is half full stuff is pretty much sleight of hand, a mental diversion to set the gullible up for the con. If someone convinces you that your glass is half full, pretty soon you lose track of the fact that half your water has been jacked. Ah well, the lake is full of water; I'll get a refill.

Jo packed pretty light for her, which meant I had room in the Beamer for an overnight bag and my own opinion, just barely. We were ready to head out of town as soon as she made nice-nice with the First-Lady-of-Texas-wannabe. I knew Cotton had been very politically active before I moved into Jennifer's head, but that part of me had either stayed in the fog or I had yet to unearth whatever section of my psyche made it marginally intelligible, much less a subject for passion.

Politics in Texas isn't a race; it's a demolition derby. Only in the Lone Star State could you have a white-haired grandmother and a Jewish country western singer/humorist/detective novelist running in a serious election against a polished incumbent with the blessing of his party and still have there be a question about the outcome. One past governor who later became president of the United States might never have considered the Oval Office if he could have been named baseball commissioner. For the life of me, I couldn't manage to care these days.

I put my apathy aside and drove Jo to a strip mall near the SMU campus where the Biggs for Governor campaign had its main Dallas headquarters. They had other storefront branches in Plano and Frisco and other outlying suburbs of the Metroplex, but this was a smart location for the core of the network. The college campus was a great place to find earnest young volunteer workers who often got a bonus in poli sci for a few hours of answering phones and eating doughnuts.

The West Village area was a designated hip area, full of students with pockets full of Daddy's money to spend in all the shops. My favorite sighting in the Virgin record store was a teenager wearing three hundred dollar jeans, a Tag Heuer watch and a T-shirt that proved being rich didn't mean you couldn't have a sense of humor. While people in the Texas capital celebrated their city's reputation for being a bit bizarre by sporting shirts saying "Keep Austin Weird," this kid of casual privilege was wearing the message "Keep Dallas Pretentious."

Besides its cool factor, the location made sense geographically. It was minutes from the downtown business area and convention centers, not too far from Love Field airport and ten minutes from the old money section of Dallas where Biggs lived among his fellow millionaires—protected behind rock fences and steel gates as if they were an endangered species.

The big glass-fronted windows were so covered with campaign posters and stickers and Texas flags that they might as well have been brick for all the light that got in. Jo grabbed her papers and got out of the car, saying she'd be back in no more than fifteen minutes. I was content to sit and wait, intrigued by the huge smiling photographs of the poster boy, Quentin Biggs.

If Hollywood had sent out a casting call for a rich, handsome, middle-aged man to play the part of governor, they would have hired Biggs on the spot. He was store-bought white bread, no crusts. A full head of silver hair, earnest blue eyes and a smile that had to have cost a small fortune in porcelain veneers.

He was photogenic; I'll give him that. From the artfully posed hand-on-the-back-of-a-chair blowups of him to the folksy shirtsleeves rolled up, shaking hands with the common man ones, the camera loved the man.

Biggs exuded charisma with a capital C. He inspired confidence with his solidness. He promised fiscal knowledge with his air of wealth. He even loved animals, as you could see as he walked down a country road with his loyal golden retriever. Why then did I get a knot in my stomach just looking at him?

I'm not being dramatic. Something about Quentin Biggs made me really uncomfortable. My palms were sweating and I felt a touch of queasiness and fear and guilt. It didn't make sense at all, but the longer I looked at the posters, the more I thought I might be sick. Luckily Jo came breezing out just then and smiled at me, taking my mind off the whole thing.

"Ready to hit the highway?" I asked. "It's going to feel great to get out of this town for a while."

"If it ever happens." She was irritated. "Her Majesty isn't here. We have to take this stuff and deliver it to her at home." She told me the address. "It's only a few minutes from here. We won't be there long."

"No way," I said with a groan. "Since when do you have to be a delivery service? Can't someone here take it over?"

"This isn't an everyday situation, honey. I'm wearing a lot of hats on this job, but it's a huge project. If it will make Tricia Biggs happy for me to bring this by, it'll be well worth the detour."

"Is it that important to make her happy?"

"If she's happy, Quentin is in a generous mood, which is a very good thing for everyone concerned."

"Quentin? You're on a first name basis with the candidate?" I grinned at her as she fastened her seat belt. "Very cozy."

"I've known Quentin and Tricia for years. Max used to do some parties for Quentin's business."

"'Do some parties'? What does that mean?"

"Oh, you know," she shrugged, "celebrity stuff. Wining and dining with big clients. Taking pictures for the magazines and papers."

"And he got paid for it?" She nodded. "So Max was pimped out for Quentin Biggs and you were just along for the ride, so to speak?"

"That's a nasty way to look at it." She wasn't amused. "You used to hang at parties to raise cash for the Outreach. Doesn't that put you in the same boat?"

"Yeah, I guess it does. So much for throwing stones."

I turned into the driveway of a house on Beverly Drive, stopping at the gated outer wall. I started to press the intercom button, but Jo gave me a code to punch in. The huge wrought-iron barrier slid silently open and we entered the fortress.

The Biggs's house was big indeed. I know Jennifer had money, but she didn't live large. These were the people who put their money where it would be seen, at least if you had the code to get in the gate. The grounds surrounding the mansion were manicured and vast, leading up to a white-pillared structure that made Tara seem a poor relative. If it was built to impress people, the architect had overachieved his goals.

"Pull right up to the main door," Jo said, casually enough for me to know this was far from her first visit here. "We can leave the car for the few minutes we'll be here."

"I'll wait for you here."

"No," she said. "I can use you as a hostage. Tricia won't be able to insist on keeping me talking if you stand there and look upset."

She half-dragged, half-escorted me to the massive front doors and rang the bell. I don't know if I expected to be let in by a liveried footman or what, but when the door opened, Tricia Biggs was standing there to let us in.

I took one look at her and remembered the last time I saw her. The ground beneath my feet quivered and I felt the forces of doom mustering their troops. This woman was no stranger to me. It was due to her that I had blackmailed the man who was likely to become the next governor of Texas.

CHAPTER FORTY-TWO

I think that remembering I was a crook was more of a shock than remembering I had come back from the dead. While there had been the occasional hint that Cotton Claymore might not have revered convention and had cut a corner or two when rules and regulations got in the way, it had never occurred to me to consider that I might have actual go-directly-to-jail criminal tendencies. Seeing Tricia Biggs was a wake-up call that I didn't have everything figured out yet.

The first time I laid eyes on her I didn't know her name. Didn't have a clue as to who she was. I was used to women who hid from violent lovers and husbands and who were humiliated enough by their situation that they didn't want to give out their real names.

This woman was far from a typical case. She was wearing an outfit that cost enough to feed a family of four for a week. The rocks on her ring finger were at least four carats of high quality ice. Not the usual banged-up housewife with no place safe to sleep. But she *was* banged up. Banged up by someone who was careful to put the bruises where they weren't readily visible.

"Mary Smith" was the name she gave the evening she showed up at the Outreach. She had rung the after-hours emergency bell. I was on call that night so I did the intake interview. She was almost doubled over in pain, holding her midsection and biting her bottom lip to keep from crying out.

She wouldn't let me call a doctor, but did allow the on-staff nurse to examine her. Despite being told she needed X-rays to rule out internal bleeding, she refused to go to the hospital. There were records there, she said. He could find her. The ice pack we gave her to hold against her ribs was a poor substitute for a doctor's exam and a sizeable shot of painkiller.

The bruising was a sick purple and darkening blue against the whiteness of her stomach and ribs. She was a redhead with the kind of alabaster skin that only natural redheads have. There was a clear shoeprint on her lower back. What kind of man could kick and beat a woman and still have the cold presence of mind not to leave a mark on her arms or face? As much as I abhorred animal rage, this was worse. Rage didn't have the cruelty or the patience it took to do this kind of calculated damage.

"Mary, is there anyone you want me to call?"

"No please don't." Panic edged her words. "This place is supposed to be confidential. I can't go where he can trace me. I don't have any money and I can't use my credit cards. He'd find me and send one of his men after me. I'll be dead."

"We're not going to let that happen," I assured her. "We'll keep you safe here. There are laws to protect you. If he's that dangerous, you need to press charges, get a restraining order in place."

"You don't know who you're dealing with." There was a curious note of pride in her voice, even with the pain and fear. "My husband is a very powerful man. He's not afraid of the police."

"Then we'll find something he is afraid of," I said, more to have something to say than having any real intent to do anything. "Has this happened before?"

"Only once." She looked down at her hands and twisted the wedding band back and forth absently. "It was a long time ago and he felt so badly about it. He's treated me like a queen since then. Until today."

"Wife beaters always do it again," I said, matter of fact in my long experience with the breed. "The only way you can be safe is not to put yourself back in harm's way."

"My husband isn't a 'wife beater.'" She was horrified at the term. "I know he did this and once before, but he's under a lot of pressure right now and I made it worse. I—"

"Please stop defending him," I said as kindly as I could manage. "You let him use you as a kickball and you still make excuses for him. Why?"

This wasn't the first time I'd heard the same old story, and it wasn't the first time I'd asked the question. I didn't understand these women. If some guy had done this to me, I'd find a way to make him pay.

"You don't know him." She gave a nervous grunt of what might have been mistaken for laughter. "Well, you don't know that you know him. But the good he's doing in this state far outweighs the outbursts. Sometimes he has to do things other people wouldn't approve of, for the greater good."

"Yeah, that's a new excuse for beating on people—the greater good." I wanted to scream. "Sounds like a politician."

"Oh my God. You know it's Quentin." She leaped to her feet, yelped in pain and sank back into the chair with tears flowing down her cheeks, leaving little rivulets in her still perfect makeup. "Oh God, he's going to kill me."

"No one's going to kill anyone. It's all right."

Quentin? Politics? My brain was spinning like a dust devil. Could it be true? The multicolored bruised proof was sitting terrified and not two feet from me. Lieutenant Governor Quentin Biggs, the Gray Eminence of Texas, protector of the oppressed—Quentin Biggs was an abusive husband. It boggled the mind.

"Please, I've got to go. You can't breathe a word of this to anyone." She was getting to her feet, wincing, but not giving in to her injuries. "I'm going now."

"Mrs. Biggs, you can't leave. Not in your condition."

"Mary Smith." The words were through gritted teeth. "My name is Mary Smith. If you let anyone know otherwise, I'll sue you. My husband will see that this place is razed to the ground if you bring us in to it."

"I'm not going to bring you into anything, *Mary*," I soothed. "I want you to go upstairs and sleep where you're safe tonight. Tomorrow, we'll figure out what to do."

"There's nothing to figure. I'm going home." She was more terrified now than when she arrived. "He's a good man, no matter how this looks."

"He's not a good man," I said, shaking my head at her blind loyalty. I'd seen men from ditchdiggers to—well, to lieutenant governors, I guess—protected by women with broken noses and bloodied faces. "He's like a hundred other men who hurt women. You need to make him pay for what he's done to you. I'll help you."

"I don't want your help." She had made it to the front door, obviously a hard trek; every step had to hurt like hell. "He's my husband. I don't want revenge. I just want him to love me." She slipped out the door and into the night.

"I just want him to love me," I whined to the empty room. "What kind of crap is that? These testosterone maniacs all need to be taught a lesson. They can't keep doing this and leaving me to clean up their mess." I kicked the ice pack that had fallen to the floor across the room. "I'm going to make an example out of you, Mr. Quentin Biggs. You get to pick up the check for all the bullying sonofabitches in this whole damned town. I am personally going to see that you pay."

CHAPTER FORTY-THREE

Judging from the hotel-sized house Jo and I were ushered into, I obviously didn't make Quentin Biggs pay enough to hurt his lifestyle any. The place was magnificent. As Jennifer, this was the kind of home I could afford to live in. As Cotton, I'd have been lucky to be invited for cocktails for a charity fundraiser.

Tricia Biggs led us to the study—a room so filled with books that I was tempted to see if I could use my library card to check a few out until next week. She was so gracious and poised she would have probably said yes just to be polite.

She bore little resemblance to the battered woman I had encountered at the Outreach in my last life. If not for the vibrant red hair and patrician face, I'd hardly have recognized her. She was the lady of the manor, gracious and dressed to impress. I wondered if there were any new bruises beneath her flawlessly tailored Escada slacks and jacket?

Of course she had no memory of me. She'd never met J.C. Winters before. She had no knowledge of the amateurish blackmail note I had cut out of magazines and pasted together while wearing rubber gloves so I didn't leave fingerprints. My idea of smart was wetting the glue on the envelope with a sponge so as not to give up my DNA in spit. The real miracle was that the damned letter actually reached The Man himself. Who'd have believed Quentin Biggs would actually open his own mail, even if it was marked "personal and private"? The world was a funny place.

In Tricia Biggs's world, I was a stranger to her and the dark secrets she and Cotton shared. She had no idea of the revenge I had exacted on her behalf. I don't think she would have thanked me. At a bare minimum I'm sure her offer to get me something to drink while I waited wouldn't have happened. While Tricia Biggs and Jo went over their paperwork, I discreetly cased the joint. The furnishings in this room alone were worth a small fortune. A cluster of Fabergé eggs nestled on a table lit by a small Tiffany lamp. I'd be willing to bet the farm that the pair of Chinese Fu dogs on either side of the fireplace weren't replicas. The rug covering most of the floor had traveled across the world to end up beneath our feet. I'm not sure where or when I had gained my knowledge of fine objets d'art, but someone had ingrained a little culture in me along the way. Maybe someday I'd know who to thank.

In fact, the more I looked around the house full of treasures, the more I realized my big sting was more like a mosquito bite to old Quentin. Of course, the real danger from a mosquito wasn't the bite, but the risk of being infected with something serious the pesky bug was carrying. Cotton had been carrying information that could have poisoned his political career. Simple solution: Swat. No more mosquito, no more problem.

The real question was, whom did he use as the swatter?

A man like Biggs didn't take a chance on losing this kind of life to a pissant little blackmailer. What the hell was I thinking when I pulled my little "if you don't want the world to know you beat your wife, put five hundred thousand dollars in a briefcase and leave it in the last bathroom stall at the lower level of the mall" trick? Yeah, Cotton was a real gifted grifter.

I didn't really expect the money to be there, but it was and I congratulated myself on the con. But just because I thought

I was clever dumping the bricks of money into a trash bag and stashing it in my backpack didn't mean I had gotten away with it. Just because I hadn't seen anyone following me didn't mean they hadn't been watching the whole time. Stashing the money in a self-storage unit hadn't protected me from having my head bashed in.

I didn't think I'd share the details of my returned memory with Aggie. It was bad enough that I'd possibly put her in danger without making her an accessory after the fact. Better that only I knew that backpack with half a million dollars was a result of my felonious ego. Let it gather dust from now until forever. Good riddance to bad garbage was a saying to live by. Literally.

I looked over at Jo and Tricia, chatting away as if they'd known each other for ages. Exactly like they'd known each other for ages—at least for a long time before I met Jo. I hated fundraisers, but I was always begging for money to fund the Outreach. I had leapt at an invitation to mingle with this deep-pocketed crowd. My knees got rubbery and I sank down on one of the antique armchairs by the window.

What a coincidence that Max and Jo and I had been among a few dozen guests at the same party. Or…maybe someone knew about my taste in women and Jo's attraction to the limelight before the invitations went out. How convenient for Biggs and what a coincidence that I started dating Max's wife within a month of my little shakedown.

A jealous husband, a wife looking to trade up, and a womanizing lesbian. Someone was bound to end up dead—I was just beginning to think it was no accident that it turned out to be me.

How could Biggs have managed to set us all up? He would have to be a master magician, pulling levers behind the curtain like the great and powerful wizard of Oz. He couldn't have been sure Jo and I would gravitate to each other, although now that I look back, the other women at the party had either been over sixty or pushing two hundred and sixty.

I am a seriously flawed and shallow person, so getting me involved with a hottie like Jo must have been easier than selling dollar beers at a Rangers' game. Getting Jo to flirt with me wasn't that hard to predict either, all modesty aside. What he couldn't have known was that the two of us would really fall in love. I doubt he cared one way or the other.

As for getting Max Sealy to do the dirty work with the baseball bat, it wouldn't have taken much to prime him with a few tidbits of gossip, a hint of being cuckolded, a blow to his ego. With his temper, it would have been all too easy to send him roaring into the foggy night intent on murder.

Of course, there was always the possibility that poor Max was only a perfect red herring for a smart silver shark. There are professionals who serve at the beck and call of the wealthy and powerful. Most of them are in less dangerous lines of work, but exterminators come in all kinds of guises. It must be rare to have a built-in patsy if one came to be necessary. Max had patsy written all over him. If he hadn't been famous and I hadn't been gay, he'd be sitting in a cell in Huntsville, sure as original sin.

Then again, maybe my whole paranoid fantasy about Quentin Biggs was a way of expiating my guilt for being a thief. I didn't have a shred of proof he was involved. I didn't even know if my death was connected in any way to my little stint as Robin Hood. Maybe I got away with it, clean and lucky. Maybe after my murder no one was still monitoring that camera or perhaps they plain forgot about it and had no way of connecting the dots between Cotton Claymore and J.C. Winters.

Jo and Tricia Biggs were exchanging kisses on each other's cheeks, making the fluttery goodbye sounds only produced by Southern belles. I wasn't part of the inner circle, so I managed to escape with only a handshake.

As we drove out of the main gate, I looked up and down the street, checking for signs we were being watched or followed. I hadn't forgotten why we were going out of town for the weekend. I'm not a total idiot, no matter how much that seems to be the case sometimes. I also know that everybody loves Robin Hood except the guy whose money gets stolen.

CHAPTER FORTY-FOUR

While it is true only God can make a tree, Cedar Creek Reservoir is a convincing argument that people can make a decent lake. All the major lakes in North Texas are man-made, but—apologies to God—while I know it's not on the scale of the Great Lakes up north, this was a pretty place.

During the hour and a half drive south out of Dallas, Jo and I talked and laughed and felt the worries of the last few days melt away. Maybe not melt, but shrink considerably in intensity. By the time we arrived we were tired of talking about all the crap that had virtually consumed our every waking thought all week.

Dr. Carey's house was a jewel—three bedrooms, a den with a fireplace big enough to roast an ox, a grand kitchen and a screened-in porch that wrapped around three sides of the house and looked out over the lake. A private pier led out far enough into the water for you to sit and fish all day. A little exploring led us to the boathouse, where we found a big ski boat and a pair of Jet Skis. We decided to spend the week being hedonistic and wallowing in the country life.

Country life in the exclusive community of homes carved out here was hardly a trip to *Green Acres*. Referring to the residences in the enclave as "lake houses" was like calling homes in the Hamptons "cottages." The houses were virtual mini-estates with all the comforts of the city without the traffic and more stars at night. I knew Dr. Carey charged a very pretty penny for her services, but this was a very cushy second home.

There were a couple of hours left before dinnertime, so we got back in the car and drove around the lake, looking at the scenery and getting the lay of the land. We stopped at a little store in Gun Barrel City, one of the half dozen small towns that surround the lake. Jo picked up so much junk food that if we never caught a single fish, the three of us could spend the week well fed, if not well-nourished.

"I think Ding Dongs should be a food group of its own," Jo said, licking the creamy center out of the second chocolate yummy she had eaten in the mile since we left the store. "They've proven chocolate is good for you—all those antioxidants, you know. And I think this center might be dairy-ish. This may turn out to be nature's perfect food."

"Seems like I read that very thing the other day in the *Journal of Modern Medicine*. The article had a very interesting sidebar called "How to Eat Ho Hos, Be a Big Fat Girl and Still Look Fabulous."

"Mmmm." She patted her flat stomach. "I think I would be even better-looking fifty pounds heavier. More of me to love."

"You keep shoveling those in and we'll be able to test your theory by next week." I laughed and glanced in my rearview mirror. "What does that idiot think he's doing?"

Jo turned in her seat to check what I was squinting at. The roads were narrower than the main highways, mostly one lane each direction, and carved a curving route through the trees. The guy behind us kept speeding up, then dropping back to a safer distance.

The car was a monster SUV, black and menacing and larger than life on the narrow roads. With the dark-tinted windows, I didn't know how he was able to see well enough to drive. It was getting past twilight and the numbskull didn't even have his headlights on.

"Maybe he wants to pass us," Jo said. "Kind of pull over a little so he can get by."

"I'm over as far as I can go without ending up in the ditch," I said, not wanting to accommodate such a rude driver. "Besides, I haven't seen three cars in the last five miles. He can get by any time he wants to."

"He's getting too close," Jo said. "He's nearly on our bumper."

"I'm going to slow way down." I tapped the brakes. "He can pass us or we can all drive twenty miles an hour like my Aunt Mildred used to and take forever to get home. We're not in any hurry."

"He's dropping back. Oh, wait, he pulled over to the side and stopped." She turned back around in the seat. "You don't suppose this is how the neighbors say hello around here, do you?"

"If it is, I'd rather they sent a fruit basket," I said. We drove for a minute more in comfortable silence.

All of a sudden, a pair of high beams glared in my rearview, moving up behind us at a high rate of speed. Way too fast for these twisty roads at twilight.

"What the hell?" I had read stories of road rage, but never had I been prepared to feel so much anger over so little provocation. "Someone ought to kick his ass. I'll show him." I slowed down to a crawl. He slowed even more and dropped way back. "Hah! That's right. Back off, big boy."

"J.C., stop messing with this guy." Jo punched me on my shoulder, a little too hard to be called playful. "Let's be big about this and just get home safely."

"Damn it, he's coming up again." I saw him in the mirror. "I think you're right. He's nuts."

The car was nearly up my tailpipe before I had the sense to realize he had no intention of slowing down. He was trying to run us off the road. I jammed the accelerator to the floor, but not fast enough. He tapped the back bumper of the car, not hard, but at this rate of speed it gave us a pretty good jolt.

"Hang on, Jo. I'm going to get us out of here before we get killed by this lunatic."

"It's too late," she yelped. "He's pulling up beside us."

The driver yanked his steering wheel hard to the right. The big box of a car veered in front of us so hard I stood up on the brake pedal, praying we weren't going to plow right into him.

"Hang on, Jo!"

We were skidding off into the ditch before I could say or do anything but try to keep from slamming into the crazy fool's car, which had stopped a few dozen feet in front of us.

"Are you okay?" I reached over to Jo, wanting to touch her, to make sure she wasn't hurt. "I'm going to see exactly what this guy—"

"Oh, my God. Lock your door. Hurry!" Jo screamed at me and pointed, her fingers shaking. "Hurry. He's got something in his hand. And he's wearing a mask."

"What are you talking about?" Her words made no sense until I looked where she was pointing and saw a big man in a red ski mask walking deliberately toward our car. "Open the glove box, Jo! My gun's in there."

She was fumbling with the latch on the glove box when the man reached our car. He raised his hands over his head and swung, smashing his baseball bat into the windshield.

CHAPTER FORTY-FIVE

The crash of breaking glass was almost loud enough to drown the sound of Jo's terrified scream. My heart was pounding in my ears, the pulse of blood so deafening I could feel it vibrate through my body.

Time was out of whack—moving so slowly the ragged pieces of safety glass came showering in like raindrops, yet moving so fast I barely had time to shield my eyes from them.

The second blow hit the window on my side, buckling the glass, making it sag and crackle, but not completely breaking it into pieces. The man's shadow blocked the light from my side. The next blow was coming; I could feel the back swing, could imagine the wind hissing around the blunt wood as he readied the next hit.

"The gun," I screamed. "Give it to me."

"Here. Here." Jo was shaking. I could feel her hands trembling so hard I could barely grab hold of the pistol. "God, help us. Hurry."

I don't know how I managed to pull the slide and find the safety release, but all the practice at the gun range must have kicked in. The shadow moved away from my window and was crossing in front of the car to Jo's side. His body blocked the headlights as he passed them, giving me an idea of how fast he was moving.

"Get down, Jo," I shrieked. "On the floor. Now!"

She ducked out of my way as the man passed in front of the window. It happened so fast that I wasn't sure if he broke the window with the bat or if I broke it with the bullet as I fired. It sure as hell exploded.

Jo screamed but stayed down. I knew she was all right. No one could be making that much noise and be in too bad of a shape. The man ran past our car and toward his SUV. Like an idiot I swung my door open and pointed my gun at him, firing twice, but missing. My arms were braced on the top of the doo frame and my legs were shoulder-width apart—perfect form, but with all the adrenaline pumping through my system, I couldn't hit the broad side of a barn.

I could see the man open his door and pull himself up in the SUV. I thought for a second about trying to look at his license plate, but I wanted to see if I could tell anything about him to identify him. Big. Jeans. Dark sweatshirt. Red ski mask. That alone would probably make him stand out in any crowd at the lake.

Just then a big truck, not a semi, but big, came in from the opposite direction. I could hear its brakes squealing as it ground to a halt on the other side of the road.

"Hey," a gruff masculine voice yelled. He must have gotten out of the rig because I heard the door slam. "What's happening? Is anybody hurt?"

By that time the truck driver had walked halfway across the road. He came to a frozen stop when he saw me braced against my car door, firing another round as our attacker leaped into his car and burned rubber down the road.

My Good Samaritan didn't look like he was ready to come any closer.

All at once my nerves unraveled like rope that reached the end of its strength capacity. My hands started trembling so badly, the Kimber fell to the ground, making a soft thump as it hit the packed dirt.

"Shit, lady. Are you okay?" He edged nearer, his eyes on the ground, making sure the gun was down. "What the hell happened here?"

"Cotton?" Jo was wailing my name, forgetting J.C., forgetting anything but her terror. "Cotton, are you okay?" She scrambled over the console and crawled across the driver's seat to get to me and threw herself into my arms.

"Did you shoot him?" She was trembling. "I hope you shot him."

"I don't know." I was trembling too.

"I don't see no blood," our hill country hero said. He was looking at the ground by the light of our headlights. "It's getting pretty dark though. I can't really see that well."

"Can you call the police for us?" I asked. "Will you wait with us until they get here?"

"Yes, ma'am. Do you think he'll come back?"

He didn't sound too brave all of a sudden. I looked closer at him and realized he probably wasn't more than twenty years old.

"No." I wasn't as sure as I sounded. "He's a coward. Only tries to kill women when no one is around. He's gone for now."

"Okay ma'am. I'm going to get my shotgun out of the truck anyway, just for insurance. And my cell phone." He turned toward the truck.

"You aren't leaving us here?" I needed reassurance, even from a stranger who had a shotgun in his truck. "You're coming back?"

"I'll only be a minute. I promise." He gave me a thumbs-up. "My name's Howie—yell out if you need me sooner."

Suddenly I was afraid, much more afraid than I had been during the heat of the battle. My knees were shaking so much I staggered backward, tumbling to the ground and taking Jo with me. Much to my disgust I started sobbing. So much for being a pistol-packing, badass mama. I held Jo and boo-hooed like a scared little girl.

CHAPTER FORTY-SIX

I managed to stop crying and was able to walk without my legs turning to jelly by the time the police arrived. The Beamer was surrounded by a sea of red and blue blinking lights where seven marked cars from at least three of the towns around Cedar Creek had converged. "Gunshots fired" was hardly the kind of thing the locals were used to, so it was no big surprise to find that we were quite a hit.

Our statements were taken. I noticed Jo had the highest policeman-to-victim ratio, in case anyone was counting. It could have had something to do with the fact that I had on jeans and a baseball shirt while the belle of the ball was wearing a mint-green Juicy Couture sweat suit and a teeny tank top that clearly had never been near a gym. Next time I'm involved in a shooting incident, I am for sure going to do a wardrobe check beforehand.

My gun was checked and my registration cleared. Photographs of the car from every angle were snapped, and there was a prolonged argument between two police chiefs over whether the car should be impounded as evidence and if so, where and by which town. I wanted to drive it back to the lake house, but that idea was shot down when one officer, with amazing efficiency and for God knows what reason, spotted a suspicious device while looking under the back bumper of the car with a big flashlight.

"Ms. Strickland." The officer was using what was still, unfortunately, my legal name. "Do you have any idea why there would be a GPS tracking device on your car?"

"I have On-Star security. Could it be part of that?" Like I know anything about tracking systems. I tried to be helpful. "Anti-theft or something?"

"No, this isn't anything factory. Looks like someone might be following you."

"My ex-husband." Jo walked up and addressed the issue. "My ex has been stalking us. You can call the Dallas Police Department and talk to them. We've been getting threatening phone calls and our apartment was vandalized and a death threat was painted on our door. That's why we drove all the way out here. We wanted to be safe."

The officer eyed Jo, running his gaze from her sleek black hair to her toes and all the curvy areas in between, obviously liking what he saw. She stepped closer to me and put her hand through the crook of my arm, leaving no doubt of her intentions. Patrolman Pete didn't seem nearly so approving after that.

"We'll put in a call on that, Miss." He looked down at her driver's license that he had clipped with mine to his notebook. "Miss Keesling?"

Jo nodded.

"This ex-husband of yours has a name?"

"Max Sealy." She rolled her eyes as he did the usual double take. "Yes, *that* Max Sealy. We did tell you the windows were smashed with a baseball bat, didn't we?"

"I believe I have that in my notes." He was coolly polite, maybe more a fan of baseball than ex-wives and their lady friends. "If you ladies would like to have a seat in one of the cruisers, I do need a few minutes to check on this."

We declined his offer. Tired as we were, the notion of sitting in the backseat of a police car on a dark country road was a little too much like a bad episode of one of those television shows that made me nervous. Besides, I wanted to talk to Jo for a minute, alone.

"Jo," I began, trying to have a neutral tone. "I think you have to at least entertain the possibility that someone besides Max could be doing these things. We can't keep throwing him to the cops every time something weird happens."

"You're taking up for my ex-husband? Did you get another bump on the head awhile ago?"

"No. But there could be people in my past I haven't remembered yet. People who had a grudge against me or something."

I didn't want to come right out and confess my sins. I wasn't exactly proud of being a criminal, no matter how justified I felt at the time. Jo didn't know I was on the run from the Sheriff of Nottingham by way of Texas.

"I still want them to keep an eye on Max," she snapped. "It's not like we have a long list of suspects."

"I wasn't ruling him out, honey. Just trying to cover all the bases." Her eyes cut to me, sparking green fire in the reflected lights. "No baseball pun intended," I said. "Honest slip of the tongue."

Howie was still standing at the edge of all the hoopla, so we went over to talk to him. He was like a kid at the country fair, wide-eyed and eager to join the carnies.

"Man, I've never seen this much excitement or this many cops in one place since the shootout with the Branch Davidians over in Waco." He was only half-kidding. "Probably some reporters on the way by now."

"Oh goodie. I always wanted to have my face plastered on the ten o'clock news." I was exhausted and my patience was running out. "They're going to tow the car. Any chance you could give us a lift to our house? It's only a few miles from here.

"We'd be happy to pay you for your time," I added, not wanting to ask any favors. "Fill the truck up as a thank-you."

"Acourse I'll take y'all home. I'll see if they'll let me get your bags and stuff." He motioned to the policemen still milling around the car. "And just so you know," he added with a shy grin, "neighbors don't take money for helping each other out. Y'all are welcome to a ride."

The police officer approached us, a grim expression on his stoic face.

"I talked to the Dallas department. Something strange is happening."

He was hesitating to tell us more. I took that as a bad sign.

"They confirmed your story. Furthermore..." He cleared his throat. Definitely a bad sign. "Earlier today two officers went to Mr. Sealy's house to ask him a few questions about the incident involving the vandalization at your apartment. His housekeeper let them in, but when she went to the study to tell him the officers were there, it was discovered he had left out the back entrance, leaving the garage open. He was driving a black SUV."

"So he followed us here?" Jo was angry more than frightened. "I told them it was Max. I told them from the beginning." She glared at me. "I told *everyone*. If anyone had listened to me, he would have been in jail months ago and none of this would be happening."

"Try to stay calm, ma'am. We have an all points bulletin out for him and the vehicle," the officer said. "This is a small community. I doubt he'll stick around and wait to be apprehended. We will run cars by your place every hour until he's picked up."

"We're expecting a friend to be coming in a couple of hours." I thought of how pissed Aggie was going to be. She had been bragging about what a good shot I turned out to be. "I don't need her to be busted by a posse when she comes in. I'll give her a call so she will know what's going on."

"Unless she's driving a black SUV, she won't have anything to worry about," he said. "I'll give the patrol the word she's coming so they won't be all over a car pulling in that late."

"Thanks Officer."

By the time we walked back to the car, the flashing lights were down to two cars and a tow truck. Howie was carting the last of our shopping bags and assorted junk to his truck.

We got our licenses and Jo's purse from the patrolmen. The last item returned was my gun. I tucked it into my bag, wishing I had at least winged him. Winged him? Good Lord, I was starting to sound like a detective show cop myself. Maybe after all this was over, I could see if there was an opening on the force in Gun Barrel City.

CHAPTER FORTY-SEVEN

We didn't get back to the lake house until after eleven. Howie unloaded everything for us and said he'd drop by to check on us in a day or two. The young man renewed my faith in humanity. He had been brave in the face of uncertainty and danger and wanted absolutely nothing in return. If he hadn't stopped and helped us, I'd probably still be sitting on the shoulder of the road blubbering.

Jo went upstairs to take a hot bubble bath while I got my courage up to call Aggie and fill her in on the evening. I poured us each a large glass of strong red wine; I figured we deserved it. Jo told me to bring her a refill when I got finished talking so she could get a good night's sleep.

Aggie answered her cell phone on the second ring. I could hear a party in the background, laughing and loud.

"Isn't Granny too old to be up this late?" I asked.

"Granny is the last to go down," Aggie said. "She's unwrapped a king's ransom in presents and eaten enough rich food to kill a woman half her age. Somebody brought tiramisu and she's decided it's better than banana pudding. I'm not telling her about the liqueur the ladyfingers are soaked in."

"Y'all are so going to go to hell for getting your dear old grandma drunk. What would Jesus say to that?"

"You ask him," Aggie laughed. "You're the one who does all that 'I'm here—I'm dead—no, I'm here again' stuff."

"You can get stuffed," I said. "Your granny is going to kick your butt if she wakes up with a hangover tomorrow."

"Don't I know it. She's a handful."

"And you couldn't be prouder of her."

"No way. She's a rock." Aggie cut to the chase. "Now stop buttering me up asking about my grandma and tell me what's wrong. Somethin's up, so spill it. Don't try to lie to me either. I can always hear it in your voice."

"I haven't tried to lie yet, so don't start intimidating me."

So I gave her the short version or the version that would have been short without all her interruptions. When I got to the part about whipping out my gun, she lost it completely.

"I knew I shouldn't have let you two go on your own. Shit fire, are you sure it's safe until I get there?" When Ag's cursing got creative, I knew I was in for it. "My stuff is already in the Jeep. I'm going to kiss Granny goodnight, then I'll be on my way. I should be there in a couple of hours."

"You need me to tell you how to get here? It's kind of out in the middle of nowhere."

"Nope. I already ran a map on the computer earlier today."

"Organized as always," I said. "Aggie, the police know you're coming, so they'll be looking for the Jeep. I'll set the guest code for the garage door keypad, so you can let yourself in. I'll use the same numbers as the Outreach code. We're both fried, so we may be asleep already. Just drive around the back. If you hit the water, you've gone too far."

"Funny. Try to get some rest. You know I'm gonna wake you up when I get there."

"I'm counting on it. Drive safe."

I set the code for the garage and checked to make sure all the doors were locked. There was a large oval window at the top of the stairway that had a full-on view of the pier and lake. In the darkness, the lake was an inky black, lit intermittently by a full moon breaking through scuttling clouds.

A layer of white mist was rising out over the lake, as ghostly and eerie as the fog I used to have in my dreams. I hadn't had any of those dreams since Jo and I were back together, but I was strangely happy to see it rolling in. In fact, I was drawn to it as if it were calling me, rolling me in the blanket it was throwing over the lake.

I watched for a while as it thickened, getting so dense the lake and the moon were completely enveloped in the whiteness. My hands were against the window, and the fog came right up to me, welcoming me, hiding me from the world. I wished, foolishly, that I had something to give back to send a thank you to Jennifer who stayed in the mist and gave me a chance to be here in the world with Jo.

"Thanks, Jennifer," I said, knowing how corny it would seem to anyone else and not giving a fig. "I owe you."

The sound of my own voice whispering to ghosts in the night nudged me back toward reality. I left the window and turned my back on the fog. My real life, my real partner was waiting.

In fact, waiting very quietly. I figured Jo had tired of waiting and gone to sleep. She was able to sleep through a cyclone. I could see the light from the bedroom shining into the hallway. I tiptoed in, just in case she was asleep.

And sure enough, she was. Sleeping like a baby angel, one arm thrown up over her head, the other tucked under her cheek. Her hair was damp and she smelled like Coco. I thought about the past misdeeds that Himself had implied about my angel as I listened to the faint rhythm of her breathing.

Maybe he was right—him and all his spooks. Maybe my girl had a touch of gold digger—so be it. Thanks to Jennifer, I had enough gold to keep her occupied for a very long time and she could have a jeweled shovel if she wanted it. After the things I was learning about my own past, I didn't have much room to get all holier-than-thou over a greedy streak.

No matter why she was attracted to me in the first place, I think I got the sweet end of the deal. I sipped my wine and watched her for a few minutes, thanking all the gods and goddesses for the second chance we had been granted.

As I knew better than most, life was not quite the straight shot between the cradle and the grave that I'd always thought it was. I was here now and I was going to enjoy the ride. I believed in what Jo and I had; if it changed tomorrow, I'd deal with it then.

I tried to be very careful when I moved my things from where they were sitting on the foot of the bed. My shoulder bag was heavy when I lifted it, the weight reminding me to take the gun and ammo out and put them in the drawer at my side of the bed. Annie Oakley, my ass. More like Barney Fife.

I was still grinning when I got to the bathroom. I took a fast shower and put on the oversized T-shirt I liked to sleep in. My head barely touched the pillow before I was asleep. I wanted to stay up and wait for Aggie, but I was so tired I decided I would sleep for a few minutes.

I woke at the sound of movement downstairs. Aggie had never been known for sneaking in quietly. She was a lead-footed clod except on the basketball court, where she morphed into a gazelle.

Glancing over to check on Jo, still sleeping soundly, I rubbed my eyes and yawned. No reason to wake her. I padded barefoot across the carpet and eased the door shut behind me.

Carefully I started toward the stairs, navigating in the darkness. I fumbled for the hall light switch and flipped it on. Standing on the landing with the foggy sky behind him was a tall masked man holding a baseball bat, watching me and grinning.

CHAPTER FORTY-EIGHT

I can't tell you how chilling that smile was—even white teeth showing in a ghoulish grimace through the black-rimmed slit around the mouth of the red mask. This night was fast turning into a Stephen King movie, and as much as I love his books, the movies never quite turned out the way I wanted them to.

Maybe this is all a dream, I thought; maybe I'm still in bed cuddled next to Jo and having a flashback because of the horrible attack earlier. I closed my eyes and prayed, but when I opened them, my nightmare was still standing there.

"Hello Jennifer."

The fabric of the mask muffled the voice, but there was something so frightening and familiar about it that I thought I was going to gag and throw up from the knot of fear closing my throat. It was the voice of death and it had come for me again.

Maybe there was an immutability about fate. I had cheated it once, struck a deal and came back, but here it was again—my nemesis returned to take me out the same way with the same weapon. And Jo once again unaware, left to wake and go through it again. Please let her wake again, I prayed, hoping there was a god above to listen. Don't let him kill her too this time.

"Nothing to say? It's not like you to be so quiet." He spoke in a ragged half-whisper, like an actor on stage projecting to the balcony. "What's the matter—cat got your tongue? Or should I say pussy got your tongue?" His laugh was mocking and meant to intimidate.

"You're a filthy coward." I stage-whispered too, hoping not to disturb Jo and have her walk in on this. "I wish I had blown your brains out earlier tonight. That is, assuming you have a brain."

"Sticks and stones, Jennifer." He shifted the bat, moving it to rest on his shoulder. "You aren't in any position to be acting like such a bitch. That's no way to treat a guest."

"How did you get in here?" I knew I set the alarm. The only one who had the code was Aggie. "Where's Aggie?"

"I would guess that would be the big black Amazon driving the Jeep." He hefted the bat, pointing out a smear of bright scarlet on one side. "I'm afraid your friend had a little accident. And after she was nice enough to let me slip in behind her when she drove into the garage. So sad."

Please, God—not Aggie.

"Just tell me she's alive. It's not too late, if she's still alive. You can leave and get away. Just let me call an ambulance."

"It's too late," he whispered more quietly than before. "I'm afraid poor Aggie can't join us. You may be joining her soon though. Very soon."

"Don't be stupid, Max," I entreated. In all the movies I'd ever seen with lunatic killers the intended victims kept them talking. I didn't have a better plan, so I talked on. "This is a stupid thing to do. You'll never get away with it. The police are already looking for you."

"I'm counting on that." He smiled and caressed the bat in a casual gesture. It reminded me of something, but my brain was so full of fear hormones I couldn't pin it down. "Everything is moving according to plan."

"You aren't in control anymore, Max," I hissed. "They know what you've done. They're looking for your car. You aren't going to get away with this."

He laughed. It was too loud. I glanced back over my shoulder at the bedroom for a split second. He noticed.

"Ah Jennifer. Where is our little Jo? And what are we going to do with her? Should she live this time?" He flexed the bat as if taking a practice swing. "Or die? Live?" He laughed. "I haven't quite decided."

My stomach tightened and I wished I could get to my gun. I could make a run for it—I had a few steps on him. But even if I could make it to the darkened bedroom and grab the gun from my bedside table, Jo would be completely vulnerable to his reach. I stayed still, hoping to find some answer, some tiny prayer of survival.

"Even if you kill us, you'll never get away with it. Everyone knows you've been stalking us. The police forces from every town for miles around are looking for you."

"Yes that's true." He didn't seem to care. "I haven't been very smart, have I? Of course no one ever accused Max Sealy of being a genius." He flexed the bat again and took a step toward me. "No, this time there's no one in a position to engineer a cover-up. Too many people know Max is stalking you two. It's such an open-and-shut case, they'll never even question it, will they? Lock him up and throw away the key."

"Lock him up? Lock who up?" This wasn't making sense and I didn't want to leave this life as confused as I came in to it this round. "Max?"

He laughed again, louder and with obvious glee.

"Are you working for Biggs?" No answer. "Damn it, who are you? Why are you doing this?"

"Why? Jennifer, it's the oldest reason in the world." He was enjoying this—the sadist—feeding off my fear, growing casual with his power of life and death. "Money. Freedom. Maybe a little touch of revenge."

"I can give you money." A ray of hope gave me a straw to cling to in the raging flood of fear. I had something to bargain with, something he found valuable. Maybe greed was stronger than revenge. "Listen to me. I have money. Anything you want. Any amount. Just walk out of here and let us live. I'll get the money to you safely. I swear."

"And I'm supposed to trust you? Why would I do that?"

"If you kill me, all I have here is a few hundred dollars. If you let us go, I can get you a million." He shook his head. I upped the offer. "Two million. In a Swiss bank account."

"You don't get it, do you?" He came closer still. "You can't buy me off. Letting you live would be signing my own death warrant. You can't pay me enough to make the risk acceptable."

"Yes I can." I was negotiating, still stalling for time to make a run for the gun. It was my only chance. "I'll give you whatever you say. How much do you want?"

"All of it, Jennifer. I want all of it. Years I've planned and lived off crumbs." He raised one hand to his mask to pluck the mask out of where it had slid too far down over his eyes. His fingers were long and had a sprinkling of dark hair over his knuckles. "I set this stage up so carefully. Thought about how to do it for months. Then you played right in to my hands. It was almost like you were helping me. All that's left to do is—"

"You are beyond crazy. How could I help you? I barely even know you."

"So true. And you never really did." He dropped the faintly amused tone and growled, "Get on your knees." He was in a batter's stance, and my head was obviously supposed to stand in for the ball. "Don't make me make you suffer. You don't have a prayer of getting away from me." He sounded matter-of-fact, as if cooperating in my own death was a reasonable course of action. "Make this easier on yourself, Jennifer. Just get on your knees."

The sudden weakness washing over me would have made it easy to do just that, but all I could think of was that if I let him kill me in silence, let him club me like a mute and docile animal, there would be nothing to stop him from going after Jo. If I was going to die, there would be a hell of a fight first and enough noise to wake the dead.

"You can bite me." I started backing away, planning how many steps to the bedside table. "No way I'm going to make this easy for you, you scumbag."

"We'll just go ahead and do this the hard way." He drew the bat all the way back. "All that's left to do is—"

"Freeze!"

We both froze. It was amazing how instantly that word worked.

"Cotton—get over here. Max, don't you even breathe or I swear I'll blow your freaking head off."

And there was Jo, holding my Kimber in her outstretched hands.

CHAPTER FORTY-NINE

"Jo," I said, still whispering like an idiot. "Thank God."

"Get over here and take this gun." Her voice was loud and clear. Her hands were shaking visibly, but she had the pistol trained on him. "Hurry."

I moved toward her, but it was too late. Max leaped across the landing and grabbed me by the neck in a vise-hard grip, forcing me to my knees. I could feel the carpet burn ripping across my bare skin as he yanked me backward and slipped the bat around my neck, choking me with the hard edge of the wood. I latched both hands around the bat, trying as hard as I could to move it a fraction of an inch from my windpipe. He was very strong and I knew I wouldn't last long like this.

"Shoot him," I rasped, hardly able to get enough air to get the order out. "For Christ's sake, shoot him right now."

"Put the gun down or I'll break her neck." He was calm as if he were asking for a cup of coffee. "I mean it."

"Kill the bastard, Jo." The words gurgled out of my mouth, barely audible. "It's our only chance."

"She's not going to shoot me."

He tightened the pressure on the bat. I was clawing at my throat, trying to get it loose enough to breathe, trying to scratch his hands, but I could feel the blackness closing in, swirling and sucking me into the void.

"Put the gun down or she's dead. Now!" he screamed suddenly—shrill and on the edge of complete fury. "Put it down now!"

Jo was crying, but she wasn't stupid. She pulled the trigger. *Click.*

Nothing happened.

"The safety," I gasped, but too late.

He dropped his hold on me and left me retching and gasping for air. In a split second he covered the steps between him and Jo. She was in stunned shock then, still trying to fire the locked weapon.

Click. Click. Click.

He knocked the gun out of her hands and grabbed her hair, pulling her closer to me. I was trying to get enough oxygen in me to move. I wanted to leap on him and do something heroic and brave, but gagging and gasping were all I was capable of.

He pushed her hard and she landed on top of me, the weight of her body knocking out the air I had managed to suck into my burning lungs. We clutched at each other and huddled in fear, holding on without much hope, but together. It was a small comfort. He loomed over us, triumphant, framed in the window, outlined by the swirling fog.

"Please Max." I didn't know what to beg for. "Why are you doing this? You know you can't get away with it."

"I think I can, you know." He sounded almost normal, for a moment. "When the two of you are found, the police will fall in line, especially when they find his body and a note explaining that he just couldn't take it anymore after what he'd done."

"What *he* had done?" I asked. "What *who* had done?"

"Max please—" Jo was crying. "Don't do this. I'm begging you."

"Max please," he mocked. "Sorry. Mr. Baseball couldn't make it. Previous engagement."

"Who are you?" Jo rubbed her eyes with the back of one hand and squeezed my hand with the other. "You aren't Max. I just assumed it, but look at him." She hiccupped the words around the tears and pointed in his direction. "That's not Max. Max bats left-handed."

Our tormentor took the bat from his right shoulder and put it on his left.

"Nope, not comfortable." He switched back to the right-hand grip. "Guess you got me. Max is dead." He looked down at his watch. "Or he will be in a short while. Poor fellow, so overcome with remorse, he checked in to a seedy motel and washed down a bottle of pills with half a bottle of whiskey. He was well on his way to that big Hall of Fame in the sky when I last saw him. Far too late to change his mind.

"The police will find his body and they'll find the two of you—excuse me, they'll find the three of you. No doubt this will make the front pages for a while. A tragic murder—no, make that a tragic multiple murder/suicide."

"Then why are you doing this?" I asked. "Who are you and why?"

He was high as a kite on something—drugs, power, revenge—and talking fast as he stepped in for the kill. Maybe he was revving himself into the blood frenzy he was about to unleash.

"Jennifer, I think you deserve an answer to your question before you die. This should answer who." He reached up and yanked the mask off. "Any more questions?"

"Gregory." I mouthed the words, but no sound escaped.

"My darling little wife. Why didn't you die in the accident? It would have been so much simpler for us all."

Gregory's face was a twisted mask of hatred.

"You were going to divorce me. Leave me with nothing. Then after your accident, when you didn't remember, I thought it would be all right."

He shook his head and stroked the bat with those hairy knuckles the way I had seen him stroke his laptop so many times. He looked at me as if it were my fault that he was about to split our skulls open.

"I told you to stop trying to get your memory back. I hoped you wouldn't have to die." Gregory sighed. "The divorce would have uncovered the funds I took as well as...other things. You would have ruined me."

"It's not too late, Gregor." I hoped my voice was calming, hoping against hope he wouldn't be able to dirty his hands with the bloody act of murder. "I don't care about the money."

"But I do." He sounded regretful, yet determined. "I really do."

CHAPTER FIFTY

I had a sudden moment of clarity. On that landing on my knees literally begging for my life, I realized that all the years of college, a doctorate in psychology and years of counseling at the Outreach had led me to this point. I was a professional at figuring out what makes people tick, especially angry and violent men. Since I couldn't get to my gun to kill him, I had to use my training to buy time, hoping against hope for a better ending than the one I feared was coming.

People like Gregory—fastidious metrosexuals who hated disorder of any kind—were not by nature eager to spatter blood and brain matter all over themselves. Only desperation or a provocative movement by one of us would spur him into action. He was stalling right now. Testing the bat in short little bounces, waiting for one of us to make a move that would give him the courage to attack.

I could only hope to keep him talking for as long as possible. The police had promised to drive by at regular intervals. Maybe the lights on in the hallway would bring them for a closer look. It wouldn't be hard to see we were in trouble if they paid any attention. Gregory was standing on the landing in front of a full window test-driving a baseball bat in the wee small hours. Might be something to look into.

I tightened my hold on Jo, willing her to stay still, not to make any sudden moves. She leaned closer to me, but other than that she was quiet. Probably scared stiff as I was.

"Why not get a divorce, Gregory?" I tried to sound as if that was still a viable option. "You'll get a fortune in any settlement. We don't have a prenup."

"Right Jennifer," he said. "I'm sure you'd be willing to forgive this little misunderstanding tonight and make me a generous offer." He twitched the bat, not breaking his wrist, just a wiggle. "I'm not crazy."

He could have fooled me. His eyes were bloodshot and he was blinking way too fast. Except for the wild eyes and the way he was licking his lips every few seconds, he looked normal as pie. Well, that and the way he kept twitching the bloody baseball bat.

"You were provoked." I offered him an excuse. "I was at fault too. Deserting you. Having an affair." He nodded. "If you let us go check and make sure Aggie is okay, you can walk out of here free and clear. No one has to know about anything else."

"Do I look stupid?" He obviously meant that as a rhetorical question. "You'll turn on me the second I walk out of here. You'll tell them about everything I've done. You'll tell them about Max."

"I don't care about Max. He made his own choices." I couldn't believe he was buying into this for a second, but it was all I had. I laid it on with a trowel. "Everybody knows he was guilty."

"That's true. When you and your little slut here started up, the men at the club started saying I should wait until Max found out that his whoring ex-wife was on the prowl again—he'd kill you both and save me the trouble."

"Sounds to me like he asked for it."

Gregory was awfully willing to admit his misdeeds. That didn't make me hopeful he was going to have a change of heart and let us go on our living, breathing way.

"I gave him a call that the police were on their way. Told him if we met, I'd help him prove he wasn't behind the stalking."

"Why would he believe you?" Jo asked, finally finding her voice. "Max isn't stupid. He doesn't know you from a hole in the ground."

"Not true. We played golf a few times. I told him my wife was your latest fling. Told him the police were questioning me too."

"You don't want to do this, Gregory," I said. "It's not too late to quit before anyone else gets hurt."

"Are you forgetting Max left a note confessing to this?" He waved the bat around to point at Jo and me. "There's no way to explain a confession to a crime if the crime doesn't happen. An investigation will get me eventually."

"We won't tell. I swear we won't." I tried to sound reasonable. "We want to live. You want the money. You walk out right now and you can write your own ticket. Whatever you want. Five million sound good? You could live like a king anywhere in the world on that. Someplace with no extradition. Works for me."

"I didn't actually kill Max, did I?" he asked. "I just talked him into killing himself. He said he'd never make it in prison. I did give him the pills and booze though. And sat with him until he was passed out. Does that make a case for murder?"

Yes, you crazy bastard, I wanted to yell. Instead I played cheerleader.

"Of course not. Unless you were holding a gun to his head—"

The look on his face would have been comical if this had been a movie. He and I looked at each other and I cringed. Doomed, we were definitely doomed.

"But in the end, he killed himself," Jo said, getting into the spirit.

"That's true. He said he had nothing to do with killing the Claymore woman, but he knew who did. Said no way he'd rat on him or he'd end up as dead as she was."

"Who else would have a reason to kill Cotton?" Jo asked. "All she did was help people."

"No one is a saint, baby." I loved her for her faith in me, a faith I didn't deserve. Must have been Biggs, I thought, making sure nobody knew about his abuse of his wife. No reason to try to explain about him. Since we were about to die, let her keep her illusions. "It doesn't matter anymore."

"You're right. It doesn't matter now." Gregory took a deep breath and bounced on the balls of his feet like an athlete getting primed to run the big race. "I'm sorry, but all that's left is for you two to die."

Just then there was a slight but definite sound from downstairs. We all held our breath, listening. Was it a moan? Aggie? *Oh, Lord, please let it be true.*

"Gregory. It's Aggie. She's alive." I pressed him to reconsider. "Get out of here while you still can."

"You know I can't do that, Jennifer." He at least sounded regretful. "It's too late. All that's left is—" He raised the bat high over his head and sucked in a couple of deep, ragged breaths. "It's been too late since your parents had to die. It's been too late since you got your memory back."

"No Gregory. I'll help you. I'll get you a doctor." I would have promised him anything at the moment, but I knew it was too late. "Please don't do this."

His answer was swift and merciless. He swung the bat, following through with all his might. Jo screamed as the wood connected with my shoulder, snapping the bone with a horrible crunch and immobilizing me with the enormity of the pain. I couldn't even scream through the agony; I couldn't make a sound other than a keening animal-like whimper.

Jo didn't have any trouble making sounds. She yelled bloody murder and threw herself over me, covering me with her body, as if her slight form would protect me from the next blow. I couldn't even tell her I loved her, but she knew it. We braced for the end, looking up at the blood-crazed maniac who was once Jennifer's polite, urbane husband.

None of the mild-mannered stockbroker was left in his eyes. He had gone to a place beyond all of that. Nothing left but savagery and desperation. He raised the bat high above his head again.

"All that's left is—"

There was a noise downstairs again, more noticeable than before. Someone was in the house. Gregory's eyes blinked faster. Bat poised, ready to strike again, he looked toward the stairs and froze in place. I sucked air in and forgot the blinding pain as Dr. Carey walked into view, a nasty-looking gun in her hand.

"All that's left is for you to finish what you started, Gregory. Kill them. Now."

CHAPTER FIFTY-ONE

I've lost my mind.

The lights are on, but nobody's home. That's what Aggie would say. If only she were here to say it.

I've lost my best friend and I've lost my mind.

That's the only explanation that comes close to making sense. I'm in shock from the pain and I've gone totally crazy. The wiring in my brain has short-circuited, and this is what the world looks like when you finally slip over the edge. Otherwise, Dr. Veronica Carey, the person to whom I've trusted my sanity just told my husband to finish the job and kill Jo and me.

"Kill them now, Gregory. We don't have much time."

She certainly sounded real. The gun looked genuine. It was the words she was saying that threw me off.

"The lake patrol will be by before too long. You've got to finish this and get out of here."

He was more confused than I was.

"What are you doing here?" His eyes ricocheted from her to us to the gun and back to her. "You aren't supposed to be here. Why do you have a gun?"

All the while he was questioning her, he kept the bat at the ready. He was still bouncing on his toes and licking his lips. Not stable. They wouldn't recognize this version of Gregory Strickland at the country club.

"Dr. Carey? Why are you here?" I echoed Gregory's confusion.

I knew I was truly in shock because the pain was only a nuisance when it should have been an unbearable screaming agony. That was the good news. The bad news was that I would probably pass out soon, leaving Jo to face these two lunatics on her own. She was in a near state of catatonia; the only sign of movement was the occasional spastic digging of her fingers into the arm on my uninjured side.

"Dr. Carey, what are you…you and Gregory…how is this possible?" I asked. "You're my doctor, my friend. Why?"

"Therapy isn't in session now, and you lost the right to be called my friend a long time ago," she snapped. "So shut up."

She turned her attention back to Gregory. Her voice was warm and encouraging, but her gun was pointed in his direction and never wavered.

"Gregory. If you want the plan to work, you have to kill them."

"I can't do it," he whimpered. "It was horrible. You can't imagine the sound it made. I'm going to be sick." He was shaking, losing the psychotic edge he'd pumped himself into. A witness made it even harder to keep it up—performance anxiety to the ultimate degree. "You do it. You have a gun. Shoot them."

"I can't shoot them. It has to be done with the bat. Because of Max. Don't blow your alibi." She was crisp and patient as if explaining the game plan to a six-year-old. "You've come too far to stop. Look at her. Look at your cheating wife and her *girlfriend*." She spat the word.

"She's going to divorce you and send you to prison. You won't get a penny." The bat twitched infinitesimally, encouraging her to go on. "She's not going to forgive this. It's too late to go back now. She'll send you to death row."

"I won't Gregory," I said, mentally crossing my fingers. "All I want is for us all to get out of here alive. I'll give you the money. We'll get you some help."

"Shut up, Cotton." Dr. Carey's calm therapy session voice was laced with acid. "You aren't in charge here. I am." Again, her attention and the gun turned back toward Gregory. "Come on. You can do it. Aim for her head. Hit hard. She won't even feel it." Her finger tightened slightly on the trigger. "Do it."

I can blame the pain for my stupidity—that and the unbelievable pants-wetting terror—but I was beginning to realize Gregory wasn't in charge of this scenario. He never had been.

He was a coward and a murderer, but I'd lay a wager that he outsourced the actual nasty parts. I'd lived with him long enough to know he'd never get his hands dirty. His lawn was mowed by three guys with no green cards who worked out of the back of an old pickup truck. His house was cleaned by the wife of one of the lawn crew. Heaven knew who picked up the garbage, but it for sure wasn't the stockbroker with the weekly manicure. He just gave the work orders and handed out the pay envelopes.

"You aren't a monster, Gregory." Debatable, but I'm not one of those stupid victims who bravely insist on honesty when a bald-faced lie would suit the best. "I bet you a million dollars this wasn't your plan. This is her idea, isn't it?"

"Shut your mouth, Cotton." Dr. Carey briefly turned the gun in my direction. I could feel Jo's fingers tighten convulsively on my arm. "This isn't college and all your half-baked ideas aren't going to work here. There isn't anyone here who'll listen to you. I'm the one running things now."

"Why are you calling her Cotton?" Gregory let the bat rest on his shoulder. "In charge of what things?"

The gun swung back in his direction.

"I'll explain later." She was sweating now herself, nerves melting her famous ice-queen exterior. "Stop listening to her. She's known for manipulating people. She'll use you for what she needs and move on without a backward glance."

"Cotton," Jo whispered. "What the heck is she talking about?"

"Ssh, baby. I have an idea."

Our only hope was to play them against each other and hope to stall until help came. I knew both of the sharks circling us. I had an advantage of having lived with the bozo with the bat. And I was as trained to cater to the crazy man as she was. We both had fancy degrees from SMU; mine just didn't have my new name on it. I might not be able to write a big psycho thriller and get my picture in *People*, but—

As soon as the thought crossed my mind, it knocked a gaping hole in the barricades of my memory. This is it! This is what she was afraid I'd remember. This is what she had schemed and done murder to prevent. I just remembered it too late.

CHAPTER FIFTY-TWO

I looked at Dr. Carey and then at my maniac of a husband.

"Oh, Veronica and I have known each other a long time," I said softly, noticing her mouth tighten and the defiant lift of her chin. "She was my mentor back in college. Until she claimed I used her ideas for my thesis. What a shame no one believed you, Ronnie."

"Too long a story," she said. "I don't think you have long enough to live for us to have a class reunion, Cotton."

"We wrote a book *together* back then, unless one of us has forgotten. You recall that, Veronica? The one the reviewers are calling 'a sure-fire hit of urban terror.'"

"Not how I remember it." Cool and collected. "And since you won't be around long enough to miss the royalties I decided that we should go with my name on the cover."

"You were lucky they didn't boot you out for rewriting my paper and swearing it was your own work. It was messy, wasn't it?"

"You don't have time to live in the past, Cotton."

"You're the one living in the past. Scared it will come back to destroy you and the safe little world you live in." A jolt of pain shot like electricity down my arm. "How could I have forgotten you? It must have freaked you out to have me show up during that hypnosis session with poor little Jennifer. Then, all these months—seeing me, being afraid every day that I'd remember and blow your house down."

"Hard to make threats when you're on your way back to whatever unholy place I brought you out of." She was arrogant and unrepentant. The gun made it work for her. "I should have had you locked up right then, when your brain was mush. No one would ever have believed you."

"Now you get smart," Gregory said to her. "That's what I came to you for in the first place. You were well paid to have her committed. Now all of this—" He swung the bat loosely with one hand, encompassing the whole group of us. "For what? You two are talking in riddles."

"Veronica knows what the answer to the riddle is," I said, biting at the inside of my jaw to change the focus of the pain. "Whose reputation and career would be ruined if the world knew she stole a dead woman's work and passed off as her own? Any guesses?"

"No one cares what a dead woman has to say—either time she's dead." She glanced at her wristwatch, then said impatiently, "Time to take our secret to your grave, Cotton. With any luck, it will be permanent this time."

"No one cares about your little secret but you, Veronica. No one ever did." I looked at Jo. "She'd rather kill us than have the world know she's a cheat. Her whole career has been built on deception and lies."

I could tell by the way her eyes narrowed and iced over that I had gone too far. Maybe the pain was making me stupid. What did I hope to gain by antagonizing her? The police weren't going to arrive in time. I knew Veronica wouldn't be bargained with, but I had to try.

"You can have the book. Call it your own. I don't need the money and I can't take the credit in my own name. You know that."

"Too late to try your tricks on me," she said with a rueful grin. "I took classes in hostage negotiations when you were still in braces. Try Gregory. He's more vulnerable."

Sounded like a plan to me.

"Gregory, when did you come up with the plan to kill me?" He looked to Dr. Carey for an answer, strengthening my suspicion. "Let me guess. Not long after my hypnosis sessions started. Is that right, Gregory?"

"I'm warning you, Jennifer," she hissed. "Keep your mouth shut."

"I know you wanted to lock me up in some fancy hospital and have total control of my money. That's why you hired the good doctor here, wasn't it?"

"That's enough chitchat," Veronica interrupted me. "If you don't shut up, I will shoot you, just for fun," she warned. "So help me."

"I don't think so." The room was beginning to spin, counterclockwise to be specific about it, and my shoulder was starting to throb like blue hell. "I think you're going to shoot Gregory. That's been your plan all along."

"That's a lie. She's always been a liar. Please get this over. Knock the bitch's head off."

"I can't do it." Gregory let the bat slip from his hands to land with a sort of impotent thud on the floor. "I'm getting out while I still have a chance to get away. If you want her dead, you'll have to do it. I can't."

Gregory was getting paler by the second; he looked as if he couldn't decide whether to throw up or run for the hills. The fog outside was scratching at the window behind him and Dr. Carey, swirling and banging silently against the panes.

"Pick up the damn bat right now." It was an order, but he was too far gone to listen. He turned and faced her, shaking his head in defeat. "Listen, you ass, I'm not going to go to jail for you. Either pick it up or I *will* kill you and do it myself."

"That's how it was supposed to turn out anyway, wasn't it?" I managed to keep my teeth from chattering with the increasing pain. "You said I needed to get away for a few days. You let me borrow your place. How kind you are." I grimaced. "Get Greg to kill us. Let him think he can blame it on Max since everyone thinks he's done this before."

She was smiling as if proud her student had figured things out so well. "Then you come in, just too late to save us, and spare the State of Texas a trial by plugging the killer in the act. That'd get your name in the papers, wouldn't it? Just in time for the release of *your* brilliant new book."

"Gregory, pick up the damn bat." Her voice was urgent and cold. "I'm not asking you again." She pivoted and motioned toward the bat with the business end of the gun. "Now."

"I can't do it." He sounded regretful, but instead of doing as she demanded, he backed up against the window and held his hands out, palms up. "It's your game. Do what you have to do."

"I always do."

I saw the hole in his chest at the same second I heard the gun fire. Once. Twice. Two star-shaped blotches of red, bright even against his dark sweat suit. The window behind him shattered and he fell, a perfect, silent backward dive out into the waiting fog.

Jo let out a scream to wake the dead, whom I figured we were about to join, and burst into tears. Maybe she'd scare us up a welcoming committee.

"I should have taken the gun class with you and Aggie," she sobbed. "I could have shot him and it would have been over."

"It's all right, honey," I soothed, fighting back an inappropriate urge to laugh. Must be the shock kicking in. I leaned against her body, wanting to go out as close to her as I could be. "It's all right."

Veronica Carey carefully clicked the safety on her gun and slid it in her pocket before reaching down and picking up Gregory's bloody, discarded bat.

CHAPTER FIFTY-THREE

Veronica Carey didn't look like the Angel of Death as she stood over our fallen bodies, but the bat she held would do as much damage as a flaming sword. Even knowing from experience that being dead was sometimes not quite as final as we'd been led to believe, I wasn't ready to go back, but the fog was curling in through the broken window and whispering to me.

Jo was hovering beside me, trembling but not crying. My girl to the end. I looked at her and decided if we were going out, it wouldn't be like this, cowering like animals, cringing and waiting to be slaughtered. If Veronica's plan was going to succeed, she was going to pay for our blood, drop for drop.

"You haven't got the guts to do this, bitch," I said through teeth clenched against the pain. "We aren't going to go without a fight."

Without another word, I pushed Jo hard, sending her sprawling three feet away from me. She was a quick study, scrambling to her feet, poised to move, waiting for an opportunity.

"One of us is going to get away." I nearly blacked out at the streak of fire in my shoulder. "You can't get us both at the same time with that bat."

Veronica Carey wasn't one to panic, I'll give her that. She looked at both of us, assessed her chances and changed her plan on the fly. She let the bat drop and retrieved her pistol in a motion so fluid it seemed practiced.

"True." She took aim at Jo. "And I guess I'll start with her."

"No!" I screamed it, knowing I couldn't reach her in time. "Run, Jo! Get help!"

She was moving before the words were out of my mouth, racing down the staircase as Dr. Carey fired. Once. Twice. As soon as she knew she had missed her chance with Jo, she turned the gun back in my direction and smiled. Not the most friendly smile, but a good effort considering her situation.

"We've ended up partners after all. Two bullets left. One for you. One for me." Her hand wasn't shaking at all. "Bye Cotton. See you in hell."

I tried to stand, but my shattered body had no more reserves. I closed my eyes and waited for the inevitable. I was glad Jo was safe. That was my last thought before I began to fade into oblivion, literally unable to lift a hand to save myself.

But the universe is a mysterious place and sometimes the cavalry does arrive. Just like in the movies, when all was lost, the doors burst open and heroes arrived just in the nick of time. I had a vague recollection of noise and sirens and Sean Himself making a flying tackle on Dr. Carey before she could fire.

There were policemen and I thought for a flash I saw Aggie's ghost. I think I fainted then, but I was laughing because I didn't know ghosts could curse with such enviable alliteration.

"One of you backwoods bozos get that batshit bonkers bitch out of here before I bash her brains out."

As it turns out, I wasn't dreaming—at least most of the time. I neared the edge but I didn't go across the big gulf. However, the next few hours were a blur of reality and something else— sort of like I'd imagine a bad acid trip to be. I remember thinking that Dr. Carey didn't look good in handcuffs, although it seemed as if she should have.

Himself pried Jo off me and handed her off to Aggie, who had a trail of dried blood crusting down the side of her head from her braids to the side of her neck. She seemed to be feeling better than I was at the moment, so I drifted off, letting the pain carry me to unconsciousness. Awareness came and went, fluctuating with the tide of agony.

Sean Greenly carried me down the stairs, whispering reassurances to me. I tried to talk to him, but all I remember are bits and pieces.

"...got the word of your car being run off the road...men following Strickland lost him...found his car at two-bit motel...found Max Sealy's body...SUV missing..."

I didn't really care. I wanted the pain to stop. Himself assured me everything would be all right. Not to worry; he'd take care of everything. I had no doubt about that.

I remember Jo crying and Aggie soothing. I remember more police arriving and all the flashing lights filling the night. I remember the ambulance arriving. Himself promised Aggie and Jo would be in the car with him right behind us.

I recall a lot of pain—a crushed clavicle creates a level of pain that rips reality into confetti and leaves dim and ragged edges because of shock. In fact, the shock was buffering the pain, slowing it to a dull ache for minutes before slamming back like it just happened.

My clearest recollection was before the ambulance arrived— looking out the broken window as Himself lifted me into his arms and seeing Gregory lying dead and twisted on the ground below. The thick white mist swirled around him like a living thing and I thought for a second that I heard a voice saying thank you and something about promises kept, but I wouldn't have sworn on it in a court of law. Best to keep it to myself.

The police were asking questions of all of us, but it was beyond me to be able to answer. Sean handed the lead officer a card and spoke to him for a minute. No one asked me another thing.

Jo, on the other hand, was spilling her guts to anyone who would listen. The fact that she was still wearing a tiny tank top and a pair of pink flannel shorts might have increased the size and attentiveness of her audience. Even in the middle of a crisis, Jo had managed to find her shoes—fluffy hot pink mules, no less. I know policemen and paramedics are a helpful bunch, but still. I smiled until the pain goaded me to groan pitifully again.

On the way to the hospital, I bounced in and out of a red-edged agony. Every time I shut my eyes the fog rolled in around me. I liked it. It was full of buzzing and comfort. Much better than the IV needle, which stung as they put it in my arm. Much better than the pain that yanked me awake every time we hit a bump in the road. I was surprised how fast they seemed to be driving in the pea soup outside, but then I would pass out and forget my worries until the next wave of pain woke me again.

At the hospital, Jo kissed me and stayed with me until they made her leave to get checked out herself. She protested, but I made her go, not wanting her to see me until I was able to at least breathe without wanting to cry. I liked being a tough girl, and this was playing hell with my image.

Aggie wasn't swayed by my half-hearted pleas for her to see a doctor or by the threats of the nursing staff's answer to Nurse Ratchet. She refused treatment until I was in surgery. She insisted she was going to stay at my side until they wheeled me into the operating room.

She was a woman of her word, standing beside me, holding my hand on the uninjured side, turning a funny shade of blackish green when they started giving me my pre-op shots. The grip of the pain lifted by half before the needle was out of my arm, replaced by a peculiar funny-rippling effect.

"Aggie, you're my best friend." My words were slurred like those of a drunken sailor. "My very best friend. I love you."

"Yeah," she muttered, embarrassed by the public declaration in front of the nurses. "I bet you say that to everyone who saves your sorry ass."

"I do." It still hurt when I tried to nod. "Yes, I think I do."

"You got some powerful painkillers on board, babe." She grinned at me and squeezed my hand. "I'll be right here when you wake up."

"Watch out for Jo. She's going to fall apart when it gets quiet." I was starting to feel pretty happy, but my eyes were having some difficulty focusing. "She loves me a lot."

"Right."

"I don't care if she's a gold digger."

"Cotton, babe, I didn't say that—"

"Doesn't matter." I was feeling happier by the moment, but less able to maintain a thought. "I love her, and I love you."

"Yeah. Me too."

She looked at the nurses. No problem—they were smiling. Everyone seemed happy and I was the center of everything. The world was starting to get a little wobbly, kind of like a Jell-O mold, but with people instead of bananas. Know what I mean?

"Aggie?"

"Yeah I'm here."

"How did you get to the lake so fast?"

"Just put the pedal to the metal," she said. "Now shut your eyes."

"I figured you'd have to drive real slow. With all that fog."

"What fog, Cotton? You're getting a little foggy yourself, I think."

"No, the fog was so thick you couldn't see but a few feet. Maybe just at the lake…yes, the fog was at the lake."

"It was clear as a bell tonight, babe. A million stars bright in the sky."

"No fog?" I said. "You sure 'bout that?"

"Clear and not a cloud to be seen." Aggie turned my hand loose as they wheeled me through the double doors into the operating room. "See you in a little while."

"I'm counting on it."

The operating room was blindingly light and freezing cold. The nurses lifted me onto the table. I cried out at the pain. A masked man appeared and held up another syringe. He pumped it into the port in my IV and the universe melted. I smiled my way to sleep.

I like morphine.

* * *

Fog rising like magician's smoke. Filled with comings and goings. Secrets told. Bargains fulfilled. A life returned whole for a job well done. Presto chango! Maybe this would come close to providing the promise of justice I was bound to honor. The thread breaks and I am released. I am free—leaving Jennifer to her plans here; I start my journey back to Jo, back to the world.

On my way out of the fog, I hear a voice that sounds a lot like Gregory. He doesn't sound happy.

Sometimes there are welcoming committees.

Sometimes not.

Bella Books, Inc.

Women. Books. Even Better Together.

P.O. Box 10543
Tallahassee, FL 32302

Phone: 800-729-4992
www.bellabooks.com